The room was dim and swimming, it throbbed with his head, and when he tried to move he found himself weak as a baby. There was a sharp increase in his fear. Fumbling at the sheets, he managed to worm his way to the edge of the bed and roll out. He hardly felt the floor strike him, but the swift movement swirled the air around him and brought him an explanation of his suffocating feeling of fear.

He smelled gas.

YOU'RE ALL ALONE

Fritz Leiber

Carroll & Graf Publishers, Inc.
New York

Copyright © 1972 by Fritz Leiber

All rights reserved

First Carroll & Graf edition 1990

Carroll & Graf Publishers, Inc.
260 Fifth Avenue
New York, NY 10001

ISBN: 0-88184-679-1

Manufactured in the United States of America

CONTENTS

JUST BEFORE Carr Mackay caught sight of the frightened girl, the world went dead on him. You've all had the experience. Suddenly the life drains out of everything. Familiar faces become pink patterns. Commonplace objects look weird. All sounds are loud and unnatural. Of course it lasts only a few moments, but it can be pretty disturbing.

It was pretty disturbing to Carr. Outwardly nothing in the big employment office had changed. The other interviewers were mostly busy with their share of the job-hunters who trickled into the Loop, converged on General Employment, and then went their ways again. There was the usual rat-ta-tat-tat of typing, the click of slides from the curtained cubicle where someone was getting an eye-test, and in the background Chicago's unceasing mutter, rising and falling with the passing elevated trains.

But to Carr Mackay it was all meaningless. The job-hunters seemed like ants trailing into and out of a hole. Big Tom Elvested at the next desk nodded at him, but that didn't break the spell. It was as if an invisible hand had been laid on his shoulder and a cold voice had said "You think it all adds up to something, brother. It doesn't."

It was then that the frightened girl came into the waiting room and sat down in one of the high-backed wooden benches. Carr watched her through the huge glass panel that made everything in the waiting room silent and slightly unreal. Just a slim girl in a cardigan. College type, with dark hair falling untidily to her shoulders. And nervous—in fact, frightened. Still, just another girl. Nothing tremendously striking about her.

And yet . . . the life flooded back into Carr's world as he watched her.

Suddenly she sat very still, looking straight ahead. Another woman had come into the waiting room. A big blonde, handsome in a posterish way, with a stunningly perfect hair-do. Yet her tailored suit gave her a mannish look and there was something queer about her eyes. She stood looking around. She saw the frightened girl. She started toward her.

The phone on Carr's desk buzzed.

As he picked it up, he noticed that the big blonde had

7

stopped in front of the frightened girl and was looking down at her. The frightened girl seemed to be trying to ignore her.

"That you, Carr?" came over the phone.

He felt a rush of pleasure. "Hello, Marcia dear," he said quickly.

The voice over the phone sank to an exciting whisper. "Forgotten our date tonight?"

"Of course not, dear," Carr assured her.

There was a faint laugh and then the phone voice purred, "That's right, darling. If anybody starts forgetting dates, it will be me. I like to agonize my men."

Carr felt his heart go from happy to uneasy. As he tried to figure out how to take Marcia's spur-scratch lightly, his gaze went back to the little drama beyond the glass wall. The big blonde had sat down beside the frightened girl and seemed to be stroking her hand. The frightened girl was still staring straight ahead—desperately, Carr thought.

"Did I hurt your feelings, Carr?" the phone voice inquired innocently.

"Of course not, dear."

"Because there aren't any other men—now—and I'm looking forward to tonight as something very special."

"I'll pick you up at seven," he said.

"That's right. Remember to look nice."

"I will." Then he asked in a lower voice, "Look, do you really mean it about tonight being something special?"

But his question was cut off by a "'Bye now, darling," and a click. Carr prepared to feel agonized as well as bored by the tail end of the afternoon—(If only Marcia weren't so beautiful, or so tormenting!)—when a flurry of footsteps made him look up.

The frightened girl was approaching his desk.

The big blonde had followed her as far as the door in the glass wall and sat watching her from it.

The frightened girl sat down in the applicant's chair, but she didn't look him in the eye. She nervously gathered her wool jacket at the throat.

He twitched her a smile. "I don't believe I have your application folder yet, Miss . . . ?"

The frightened girl did not answer.

To put her at ease, Carr rattled on, "Not that it matters.

We can talk over things while we wait for the clerk to bring it."

Still she didn't look at him.

"I suppose you did fill out a folder and that you were sent to me?"

Then he saw that she was trembling and once again the life seemed to drain out of everything—except her. It was as if the whole office—Chicago—the world—had become mere background for a chalk-faced girl in a sloppy cardigan, arms huddled tight around her, hands gripping her thin elbows, staring at him horror struck.

For some incredible reason, she seemed to be frightened of *him*.

She shrank down in the chair, her white-circled eyes fixed on his. As they followed her movement, another shudder went through her. The tip of her tongue licked her upper lip. Then she said in a small, terrified voice, "All right, you've got me. But don't draw it out. Don't play with me. Get it over with."

Carr checked the impulse to grimace incredulously. He chuckled and said, "I know how you feel. Coming into a big employment office does seem an awful plunge. But we won't chain you to a rivet gun," he went on, with a wild attempt at humor, "or sell you to the white slavers. It's still a free country. You can do as you please."

She did not react. He looked away uneasily. The big blonde was still watching from the doorway, her manner implying that she owned the place. Her eyes looked whiter than they should be and they didn't seem quite to focus.

He looked back at the frightened girl. Her hands still gripped her elbows, but she was leaning forward now and studying his face, as if everything in the world depended on what she saw there.

"You're not one of them?" she asked.

He frowned puzzledly. "Them? Who?"

"You're not?" she repeated, still watching his eyes.

"I don't understand," he said.

"Don't you know what you are?" she asked with sudden fierceness. "Don't you know whether you're one of them or not?"

"I don't know what you're talking about," he assured her, "and I haven't the faintest idea of whom you mean by 'them.'"

Slowly her hands loosened their hold on her elbows and trailed into her lap. "No," she said, "I guess you're not. You haven't their filthy look."

"You'd better explain things from the beginning," Carr told her.

"Please, not now," she begged.

"Who's that woman following you?" he pressed. "Is she one of 'them?'"

The terror returned to her face. "I can't tell you that. Please don't ask me. And please don't look at her. It's terribly important that she doesn't think I've seen her."

"But how could she possibly think otherwise after the way she planked herself down beside you?"

"Please, oh please," She was almost whimpering. "I can't tell you why. It's just terribly important that we act naturally, that we seem to be doing whatever we're supposed to be doing. Can we?"

Carr studied her. She was obviously close to hysteria. "Sure," he said. He leaned back in his chair, smiled at her, and raised his voice a trifle. "Just what sort of a job do you feel would make the best use of your abilities, Miss . . . ?"

"Job? Oh yes, that's why I'd have come here, isn't it?" For a moment she stared at him helplessly. Then, the words tumbling over each other, she began to talk. "Let's see, I can play the piano. I've studied a lot, though. I once wanted to be a concert pianist. And I've done some amateur acting. And I used to play a mediocre game of tennis—" Her grotesquely animated expression froze. "But that isn't the sort of thing you want to know is it?"

Carr shrugged. "Helps give me a picture. Did some amateur acting myself once, in college." He kept his voice casual. "Have you had any regular jobs?"

"Once I worked for a little while in an architect's office."

"Did you learn to read blueprints?" he asked.

"Blueprints?" The girl shivered. "Not much, I'm afraid. I hate patterns. Patterns are traps. If you live according to a pattern, other people know how to get control of you." She leaned forward confidingly, her fingers touching the edge of the desk. "Oh, and I'm a good judge of people. I have to be. I suppose you have to be too." She looked at him strangely. "Don't you really know what you are?" she asked softly. "Haven't you found out yet? Why, you must be almost forty.

Surely in that time . . . Oh, you must know."

"I still haven't the ghost of an idea what you're talking about," Carr said. "What am I?"

The girl hesitated.

"Tell me," she said.

She shook her head. "If you honestly don't know, I don't think I should tell you. As long as you don't know, you're relatively safe."

"From what? Please stop being mysterious," Carr said. "Just what is it about me that's so important?"

"But if I don't tell you," she went on, disregarding his question, "then I'm letting you run a blind risk. Not a big one, but very horrible. And with them so close and perhaps suspecting . . . Oh, it's hard to decide."

A clerk dropped an application folder in the wire basket on Carr's desk. He looked at it. It wasn't for a girl at all. It started, "Jimmie Kozacs. Male. Age 43."

He realized the frightened girl was studying his face again.

"Maybe you weren't what I think you are, until today," she was saying more to herself than him. "Maybe my bursting in here was what did it. Maybe I was the one who awakened you." She clenched her hands, torturing the palms with long, untapering fingers. "To think that I would ever do that to anyone! To think that I would ever cause anyone the agony that *he* caused me!"

The bleak misery in her voice caught at Carr. "What *is* the matter?" He pleaded. "Now we've got a 'he' as well as a 'they.' And what is this business about 'awakening? Please tell me everything."

The girl looked shocked. "Now?" Her glance half-circled the room, strayed toward the glass wall. "No, not here. I can't." Her right hand suddenly dived into the pocket of her cardigan and came out with a stubby, chewed pencil. She ripped a sheet from Carr's scratch pad and began to scribble hurriedly.

Carr started to lean forward, but just then a big area of serge suit swam into view. Big Tom Elvested had ambled over from the next desk. The girl gave him an odd look, then went on scribbling. Tom ignored her.

"Say, Carr," he boomed amiably, "remember the girl Midge and I wanted you to go on a double date with? I've told you about her—Jane Gregg. Well, she's going to be dropping in here a little later and I want you to meet her. Midge had an idea the four of us might be able to go out together tonight."

"Sorry, I've got a date," Carr told him sharply. It annoyed Carr that Tom should discuss private matters so loudly in front of an applicant.

"Okay, okay," Tom retorted a bit huffily. "I'm not asking you to do social service work. This girl's darn good-looking."

"That's swell," Carr told him.

Tom looked at him skeptically. "Anyway," he warned, "I'll be bringing her over when she comes in." And he faded back toward his desk. As he did so, the frightened girl shot him an even odder look, but her pencil kept on scribbling. The scratch of it seemed to Carr the only real sound in the whole office. He glanced guardedly down the aisle. The big blonde with the queer eyes was still at the door, but she had moved ungraciously aside to make way for a dumpy man in blue jeans, who was looking around uncertainly.

The dumpy man veered toward one of the typists. Her head bobbed up and she said something to him. He gave her an "I gotcha pal" nod and headed for Carr's desk.

The frightened girl noticed him coming, shoved aside paper and pencil in a flurry of haste, and stood up.

"Sid down," Carr said. "That fellow can wait. Incidently, do you know Tom Elvested?"

She disregarded the question and quickly moved into the aisle.

Carr followed her. "I really want to talk with you," he said.

"No," she breathed, edging away from him.

"But we haven't got anywhere yet," he objected.

Suddenly she smiled like a toothpaste ad. "Thank you for being so helpful," she said in a loud voice. "I'll think over what you've told me, though I don't think the job is one which would appeal to me." She poked out her hand. Automatically Carr took it. It was icy.

"Don't follow me," she whispered. "And if you care the least bit for me or my safety, don't do anything, whatever happens."

"But I don't even know your name . . ." His voice trailed off. She was striding rapidly down the aisle. The big blonde was standing squarely in her path. The girl did not swerve an inch. Then, just as they were about to collide, the big blonde lifted her hand and gave the girl a stinging slap across the cheek.

Carr started, winced, took a forward step, froze.

The big blonde stepped aside, smiling sardonically.

The girl rocked, wavered for a step or two, then walked on without turning her head.

No one said anything, no one did anything, no one even looked up, at least not obviously, though everyone in the office must have heard the slap if they hadn't seen it. But with the universal middle-class reluctance, Carr thought, to recognize that nasty things happened in the world, they pretended not to notice.

The big blonde flicked into place a shellacked curl, glancing around her as if at so much dirt. Leisurely she turned and stalked out.

CHAPTER II

The most terrible secret in the world? Here's a hint. Think about the people closest to you. What do you know about what's really going on inside their heads? Nothing, brother, nothing at all . . .

Carr walked back to his desk. His face felt hot, his mind turbulent, the office sinister. The dumpy man in blue jeans had already taken the girl's place, but Carr ignored him. He didn't sit down. The scrap of paper on which the girl had scribbled caught his eye. He picked it up.

Watch out for the wall-eyed blonde, the young man without a hand, and the affable-seeming older man. But the small dark man with glasses may be your friend.

Carr frowned grotesquely. ". . . wall-eyed blonde . . ." —that must be the woman who had watched. But as for the other three— ". . . small dark man with glasses may be your friend . . ." —why, it sounded like a charade.

"Carr, if you can spare a moment . . ." Carr recognized Tom Elvested's voice but for the moment he ignored it. He started to turn over the paper to see if the frightened girl had scribbled anything on the other side, when—

". . . I would like to introduce Jane Gregg," Tom finished.

13

Carr looked around at Tom—and forgot everything else.

Big Tom Elvested was smiling fatuously. "Jane," he said, "this is Carr Mackay. Carr, this is Jane." And he moved his hand in the gesture of one who gives a friendly squeeze to the elbow of a person standing beside him.

Only there was no person standing beside him.

Where Tom's gesture had indicated Jane Gregg should be standing, there was only empty air.

Tom's smiling face went from empty air to Carr and back again. He said, "I've been wanting to get you two together for a long time."

Carr almost laughed, there was something so droll about the realism of Tom's actions. He remembered the pantomimes in the acting class at college, when you pretended to eat a dinner or drive an automobile, without any props, just going through the motions. In that class Tom Elvested would have rated an A-plus.

Tom nodded his head and coply asked the empty air, "And does he seem as interesting, now that you've actually met him?"

Suddenly Carr didn't want to laugh at all. If there was anything big Tom Elvested ordinarily wasn't, it was an actor.

"She's a cute little trick, isn't she, Carr?" Tom continued, giving the air another playful pat.

Carr moved forward, incidently running a hand through the air, which was quite as empty as it looked. "Cut the kidding, Tom," he said.

Tom merely rocked on his heels, like an elephant being silly. Once again his hand moved out, this time to flick the air at a point a foot higher. "And such lovely hair. I always go for the page boy style myself."

"Cut it out, Tom, please," Carr said seriously.

"Of course, maybe she's a little young for you," Tom babbled on.

"Cut it out!" Carr snapped. His face was hardly a foot from Tom's but Tom didn't seem to see him at all. Instead he kept looking through Carr toward where Carr had been standing before. And he kept on playfully patting the air.

"Oh yes," he assured the air with a smirk, "Carr's quite a wolf. That's the reason he had those few gray hairs. They're a wolf insignia. You'll have to watch your step with him."

"Cut it out!" Carr repeated angrily and grabbed Tom firmly by the shoulders.

What happened made Carr wish he hadn't. Tom Elvested's face grew strained and red, like an enraged baby's. An intense throbbing was transmitted to Carr's hands. And from Tom's lips came a mounting, meaningless mutter, like a sound tape running backwards at very high speed.

Carr jerked away. He felt craven and weak, as helpless as a child. He edged off until there were three desks between himself and Tom, and he was standing behind Ernie Acosta, who was busy with a client.

He could hardly bring his voice to a whisper.

"Ernie," he repeated, louder, "I need your help."

Ernie continued to talk to his client.

Across the room Carr saw a gray-mustached man walking briskly. He hurried over to him, glancing back apprehensively at Tom, who was still standing there red-faced and softly babbling.

"Dr. Wexler," he blurted, "I'm afraid Tom Elvested's had some sort of attack. Would you—?"

But Dr. Wexler walked on without slackening his pace and disappeared through the black curtains of the eye-testing cubicle.

At that instant, as Carr watched the black curtains swing together, a sudden spasm of extreme terror seized him. As if something huge and hostile were poised behind him, he dared not make a move.

His feelings were like those of a man in a waxworks museum, who speaks to a guide only to find that he has addressed one of the wax figures.

His paralyzed thoughts, suddenly working like lightening, snatched at that idea.

What if the whole world were like a waxworks museum? In motion, of course, like clockworks, but utterly mindless, purposeless, mechanical.

What if a wax figure named Jane Gregg had come alive and moved from her place—or merely been removed, unalive, as a toy is lifted out of a shop window? What if the whole show was going on without her, because the whole show was just a machine and didn't know or care whether a figure named Jane Gregg was there or not?

That would explain Tom Elvested going through the motions of an introduction—one mechanical figure carrying on just as well without its partner.

What if the frightened girl had been a mechanical figure come alive and out of her place in the machine—a—nd desperately trying to pretend that she *was* in her place, because something suspected her? That would fit with the things she'd said.

What if he, Carr Mackay, a mechanical figure like the others, had come alive and stepped out of his place? That would explain why Ernie and Dr. Wexler had disregarded him.

What if it really were true? The whole universe a mindless machine. People just mindless parts of that machine. Only a very few of them really conscious, really alive.

What if the ends of the earth were nearer to you than the mind you thought lay behind the face you spoke to?

What if the things people said, the things that seemed to mean so much to you, were something recorded on a kind of phonograph disk a million million years ago?

What if you were all alone?

Very, very slowly (Carr felt that if he made a quick move, the huge and hostile something poised behind him would grab) he looked around the office. Everything was proceeding normally: murmur-murmur, rat-a-tat-tat, click-click, (and outside rumble-rumble.)

Just like a machine.

What did you do if you found that the whole world was a machine, and that you were out of your proper place in it?"

There was only one thing to do.

Still very, very slowly, Carr edged back to his desk. Tom Elvested had gone back to his own desk and sat down, was leafing through some record cards. He did not look up.

The dumpy man in blue jeans was still sitting in front of Carr's desk. He was talking at Carr's empty chair.

"So you really figure you can get me a job in magnetic at Norcross Aircraft?" he was saying. "That'll be swell."

The mechancial interview had been going on just as well without the interviewer.

Carr cringed down into his chair. With shaking fingers he picked up the last application folder and read again, "Jimmie Kozacs. Age 43." The dumpy man looked about that age. Then, further down, "Magnetic Inspector."

The dumpy man stood up and plucked something invisible from the air, squinted at it, and remarked, "So all I got to do is show them this at the gate?"

"Yes, Mr. Kozacs," Carr heard himself whisper in a cracked voice.

"Swell," said the dumpy man. "Thanks a lot, er . . ." (He glanced at the nameplate on Carr's desk) ". . . Mr. Mackay. Aw, dont' get up. Well, thanks a lot."

The dumpy man thrust out his hand. With a great effort, Carr thrust his own hand into it. He felt his fingers clamped and pumped up and down, as if by rubber-padded machinery.

"Good luck, Mr. Kozacs," he croaked.

The dumpy man nodded and walked off.

Yes, there was only one thing to do.

A creature with a toothbrush mustache and a salesman's smile and eczema scars half-hidden by powder was approaching the chair the dumpy man had vacated. Carr snatched up the next folder—there were two or three in the wire basket now—and braced himself.

. . . one thing. You could go to your place in the machine and pretend to be part of it, so that the huge and hostile something wouldn't notice you were alive.

The creature with the toothbrush mustache seated itself without asking.

"Mr. Weston, I believe," Carr quavered, consulting the folder.

"That's right," the creature replied.

From the next desk Tom Elvested gave Carr a big mechanical grin and a meaningless wink, just like a ventriloquist's giant dummy.

CHAPTER III

Sure, that's the secret—the world's just a big engine. All matter, no mind. You doubt it? Look at a big-city thing. They're just parts of a big engine . . .

By the time five-fifteen came and Carr hurried down the brass-edged steps, taking three at a time, and darted across the lobby and pushed through the squirrel cage of the revolving door, he had mastered his terror—or at least made a good start toward rationalizing his one big fear.

17

Perhaps he had just happened to meet a half dozen psychotics in one day—after all, employment offices have more of a lunatic fringe than most businesses.

Perhaps he had suffered some peculiar hallucinations, including the illusion that he'd been talking loudly when he'd just been whispering.

Perhaps most of it had been an elaborate practical joke—Tom and Ernie were both great kidders.

But when he stepped out of the revolving door into a pandemonium of honking, clanking, whistling, shouting—faces that leaped, elbows that jostled, lights that glared—he found that all his rationalizations rang hollow. There was something terribly like a machine in the swift pound of Chicago's rush-hour rhythm, he thought as he plunged into it.

Perhaps thinking of people solely as clients of General Employment was what was wrong with him, he tried to persuade himself with grim humor. For so long he had been thinking of people as mere human raw material, as window dummies to be put on display or routed back to the storeroom, that now they were having their revenge on him, by acting as if he didn't exist.

He reached Michigan Boulevard. The wall of empty space on the other side, fronting the wall of buildings on this, hinted at the lake byond. The Art Institute traced a classic pattern against the gray sky. The air carried a trace of freshness from the morning's rain.

Carr turned north, stepping out briskly. For the first time in two hours he began to think of Marcia—and that was a good defense against any sort of fear. He pictured her as he'd last seen her, in an exquisitely tailored black suit and stockings that were a faint dark glow on pale flesh.

But just then his attention was diverted to a small man walking a little way ahead of him at an equally fast pace. Carr's legs were considerably longer, but the small man had a peculiar skip to his stride. He was constantly weaving, seeking the open channels in the crowd.

Carr felt a surge of curiosity. He was tempted to increase his pace so that he could get a look at the stranger's face.

At the moment the small man whirled around. Carr stopped. The small man peered at him through horn-rimmed, thick-lensed glasses. Then a look of extreme horror crossed the stranger's swarthy face. For a moment he crouched as if paralyzed. Then he turned and darted away, dancing past people, scurrying from side to side, finally whisking out of sight around the next corner like a puppet jerked offstage.

Carr wanted to laugh wildly. The frightened girl had written, "But the small dark man with glasses may be your friend." He certainly hadn't acted that way!

Someone bumped into Carr from behind and he started forward again. It was as if the governor of a machine, temporarily out of order, had begun to function. He was back in the rush-hour rhythm.

He looked down the next cross street, but the small dark man was nowhere in sight.

Carr smiled. It occurred to him that he really had no good reason to believe that this had been the frightened girl's small dark man. After all, there must be tens of thousands of small dark men with glasses in the world.

But he found he couldn't laugh off the incident quite that easily. Not that it brought back the one big fear, but that it reawakened the earlier mood that the frightened girl had evoked—a mood of frustrated excitement, as if all around him there were a hidden world alive with mystery and wonder, to which he couldn't quite find the door.

His memory fixed on the frightened girl. He pictured her as a college kid, the sort who would cut classes in order to sit on the brink of a fountain and argue with some young man about the meaning of art. With pencil smudges on her cheeks. The picture fitted, all right. Only consider the howling naivete of her wondering whether she had "awakened" him.

And yet even that question might cut a lot deeper than you'd think. Wasn't there a sense in which he actually was unawakened?—a person who'd dodged life, who'd always had that sense of a vastly richer and more vivid existence just out of reach.

For that matter, didn't most people live their lives without really ever awakening—as dull as worms, as mechanical as insects, their thoughts spoonfed to them by newspaper and radio? Couldn't robots perform the much over-rated business of living just as well?

As he asked himself that question, the big fear returned. The life drained out of the bobbing faces around him. The scissoring of the many legs became no less mechanical than the spinning of the wheels beyond the curb. The smoky pattern of light and darkness that was Chicago became the dark metal of a giant machine. And once again there was the feeling of something huge and hostile poised behind him.

Back in the office he had found one thing to do when that feeling struck—go to his place in the machine and pretend to be part of it. But out here what was his place?

He knew in a general way what he had to do. Go home, change, pick up Marcia. But by what route and at what speed?

Each step involved a decision. Should it be fast or slow? Should you glance at shop windows, or keep your eyes fixed ahead? Should you turn at the next corner? If you did, it might change your whole life. Or if you didn't. If you stopped and tried to decide, if you loitered, you might be lost.

But perhaps you were supposed to loiter. Perhaps you were supposed to stop dead, letting the crowd surge past you. Perhaps you were supposed to grin at the robots with twitching lips, gathering your breath for an earsplitting scream, inviting the pounce of that huge and hostile something.

Or perhaps you were only supposed to go on, step after dragging step, toward the bridge.

CHAPTER IV

A big engine—only every now and then one of the parts comes alive, for no more reason than a radio active atom pops. That come-alive part is up against a big problem, brother Don't envy him or her . . .

By the time Carr had crossed the big windy bridge and threaded his way through the dark streets of the Near North Side to the old brownstone house in which he rented a room, he had once more mastered the big fear. The hallway was musty and dim. He hurried up the ornately balustraded stairs, relic of the opulent days of the 1890's. A small stained glass window, mostly patches of dark red and purple, gave the only light.

Just as he reached the turn, he thought he saw himself coming toward himself in the gloom. A moment later he recognized the figure for his reflection in the huge old mirror, its frame still showing glints of gilt, that occupied most of the wall space of the landing.

But still he stood there, staring at the dark-engulfed image of a tall, rather slightly built man with light hair and small, regular features.

There he was—Carr Mackay. And all around him was an unknown universe. And just what, in that universe, did Carr Mackay mean or matter? What was the real significance of the dark rhythm that was rushing him through life at an ever hastening pace toward a grave somewhere? Did it have any significance—especially when any break in the rhythm could make it seem so dead and purposeless, an endless marching and counter-marching of marionettes?

He ran blindly past his reflection up the stairs.

In the hall above it was darker still. A bulb had burned out and not been replaced. He felt his way down the corridor and unlocked the tall door of his room.

It was high-ceilinged and comfortable, with rich old woodwork that ten layers of cheap paint couldn't quite spoil. There was even an ancient gas fixture swinging out from the wall, though it probably hadn't been used for anything for the last thirty years except cooking on the sly. Carr tried to let the place take him and cradle him in its suggestion of the familiar and his life with Marcia and her crowd, make him forget that lost Carr Mackay down there in the mirror. There were his golf clubs in the corner, the box for shirt studs with the theatre program beside it, the sleek military hairbrushes Marcia had given him. But tonight they seemed as arbitrary and poignantly useless an assortment of objects as those placed in an Egyptian tomb, to accompany their owner on his long trek through the underworld.

They were not as alive, even as the long-unopened box of chessmen or the tarnished silver half-pint flask.

He slung his brown suit on a hanger, hung it in the closet, and reached down his blue suit, still in its wrapper from the cleaner's.

There in the gloom he seemed to see the face of the frightened girl. He could make out the hunted eyes, the thin features, the nervous lips.

She knew the doorway to the hidden world, the answer to the question the dark-engulfed Mackay had been asking.

The imagined lips parted, as if she were about to speak.

With an angry exhalation of held breath, Carr jerked back into the room. What could he be thinking? It was only in wistful books that men of thirty-nine fell in love with moody, mysterious, coltish college girls. Or were caught up in the glamorously sinister intrigues that existed solely in such girls' hot-house brains.

He put on his blue suit, then started to transfer to it the stuff in the pockets of the brown one. He came upon the note the frightened girl had scribbled. He must have shoved it there when Tom Elvested had started misbehaving. He turned it over and saw that he hadn't read all of it.

If you want to meet me again in spite of dangers, I'll be by the lion's tail near the five sisters tonight at eight.

His lips twisted in a wry smile. If that didn't prove she'd been suckled on *The Prisoner of Zenda* and weaned on *Graustark*, he'd like to know! She probably carried the Rajah's ruby in a bay around her neck and wrote love letters with a black swan's quill—and she could stop haunting his imagination right now!

No, there was no question but that Marcia was the woman for him—charming, successful, competent at both business and pleasure—even if she did like to be tormenting. What competition could be offered by a mere maladjusted girl?

He hurried into the bathroom, rubbing his chin. Marcia liked him to be well-groomed, and his beard felt pretty conspicuous. He looked into the mirror to confirm his suspicions and once again he saw a different Carr Mackay.

The one on the stairs had seemed lost. This one, framed in surgical white, looked trapped. A neat, wooden Mackay who went trudging through life without inquiring what any of the signposts meant. A stupid Mackay. A dummy.

He really ought to shave, yes, but the way he was feeling, the sooner he and Marcia got started drinking, the better. He'd skip shaving this once.

As he made this decision, he was conscious of a disproportionate feeling of guilt.

He'd probably been reading too many "Five O'Clock Shadow" ads.

Forget it.

He hurried into the rest of his clothes, started toward the door, stopped by the bureau, pulled open the top drawer, looked longingly for a moment at the three flat pints of whiskey nestling inside. Then he shut the drawer quickly and hurried down the stairs, averting his eyes from the mirror. It was a relief to know that he'd be with Marcia in a few minutes.

But eight dark blocks are eight dark blocks, and they have to be walked, and to walk them takes time no matter how rapidly you stride. Time for your sense of purpose and security to dwindle to nothing. Time to get away from the ads and the pink lights and the radio voices and to think a little about the universe—to realize that it's a place of mystification and death, with no more feeling than a sausage grinder for the life oozing through it.

The buildings to either side became the walls of a black runway, and the occasional passersby shadow-swathed automatons. He became conscious of the dark rhythm of existence as a nerve-twisting, insistent thing that tugged at him like a marionette's strings, trying to drag him back to some pattern from which he had departed.

Being with Marcia would fix him up, he told himself, as the dark facades crept slowly by. She at least couldn't ever become a stranger.

But he had forgotten her face.

A trivial thing. A face is as easy to forget as the special place where you've put something for safe-keeping.

Carr tried to remember it. A hundred faces blinked and faded in his mind, some of them so hauntingly suggestive of Marcia that for a moment he would think, "That's her," some of them grotesquely different.

Light from a first story window spilled on the face of a girl in a blue slicker just as she passed him. His heart pounded. He had almost grabbed her and said, "Marcia!" And she hadn't been Marcia's type at all.

He walked faster. The apartment tower where Marcia lived edged into sight, grew threateningly tall.

He hurried up the flagstone walk flanked by shrubbery. The lobby was a long low useless room with lots of carved wood and red leather. He stopped at the desk. The clerk was talking to someone over the phone. Carr waited, but the clerk seemed determined to prolong the conversation. Carr cleared his throat. The clerk yawned and languorously flexed the arm that held the receiver, as if to call attention to the gold seal ring and cuff-linked wrist.

A few steps beyond, the elevator was waiting. Although he knew Marcia always liked him to call up first, Carr delayed no longer. He walked into the cage and said, "Seven, please."

But the tiny gray-haired woman did not move. She seemed to be asleep. She was perched on her stool in front of the panel of buttons like some weary old jungle bird. Carr started to touch her shoulder, but at the last moment reached impulsively beyond to press the seven button.

The door closed with a soft crunch and the cage started upward. The ring of keys at the operator's waist jingled faintly, but she did not wake. Her lips worked and she muttered faintly.

The cage stopped at seven. Again the keys jingled faintly. The door opened. With one last glance at the sleeping woman, Carr stepped softly out. Just before he reached Marcia's door, he heard the operator make a funny little sound between a yawn and a sigh and a laugh, and he heard the door close and the cage start down.

In front of Marcia's door Carr hesitated. She mightn't like him barging in this way. But who could be expected always to await the pleasure of that prissy clerk?

Behind him he heard the cage stop at the ground floor.

He noticed that the door he faced was ajar.

"Marcia," he called. "Marcia?" His voice came out huskily.

He stepped inside. The white-shaded lamp showed dull pearl walls, white bookcase, blue over-stuffed sofa with a coat and yellow silk scarf tossed across it, and a faint curl of cigarette smoke.

The bedroom door was open. He crossed to it, his footsteps soundless on the thick carpet. He stopped.

Marcia was sitting at the dressing table. She was wearing a light gray negligee with a silvery sheen. It touched and fell away from her figure in graceful folds, half revealing her breasts. A squashed cigarette smoldered in a tiny silver ash tray. She was lacquering her nails.

That was all. But to Carr it seemed that he had blundered into one of those elaborately realistic department store window displays. He almost expected to see faces peering in the dark window, seven stories up.

Modern bedroom in rose and smoke. Seated mannequin at vanity table. Perhaps a placard in script: "Point up your Pinks with Gray."

He stood stupidly a step short of the doorway, saying nothing.

In the mirror her eyes seemed to meet his. She went on lacquering her nails.

She might be angry with him for not phoning from downstairs. But it wasn't like Marcia to choose this queer way of showing her displeasure.

Or was it?

He watched her face in the mirror. It was the one he had forgotten, all right. There were the firm lips, the cool forehead framed by reddish hair, the fleeting quirks of expression —definitely hers.

Yet recognition did not bring the sense of absolute certainty it should. Something was lacking—the feeling of a reality behind the face, animating it.

She finished her nails and held them out to dry. The negligee fell open a bit further.

Could this be another of her tricks for tormenting him? Marcia, he knew, thoroughly enjoyed his helpless desire and especially those fits of shyness for which he berated himself afterwards.

But she wouldn't draw it out so long.

A sharp surge of uneasiness went through Carr. This was nonsensical, he told himself. In another moment she must move or speak—or *he* must. But his throat was constricted and his legs felt numb.

And then it came back: the big fear.

What if Marcia weren't really alive at all, not consciously alive, but just a part of a dance of mindless atoms, a clockworks show that included the whole world, except himself? Merely by coming a few minutes ahead of time, merely by omitting to shave, he had broken the clockworks rhythm. That was why the clerk hadn't spoken to him, why the operator had been asleep, why Marcia didn't greet him. It wasn't time yet for those little acts in the clockworks show.

The creamy telephone tinkled. Lifting it gingerly, fingers stiffly spread, the figure at the vanity held it to her ear a moment and said. "Thank you. Tell him to come up."

She inspected her nails, waived them, looked at her reflection in the glass, belted her negligee.

Through the open door Carr could hear the drone of the rising cage.

Marcia started to get up, hesitated, sat down again, smiled.

The cage stopped. There was the soft jolt of its door opening. He heard the operator's voice, but no one else's. He waited for footsteps. They didn't come.

That was *his* elevator, he thought with a shudder, the one *he* was supposed to come up in. The woman had brought it to seven without him, for that was part of the clockworks show.

Suddenly Marcia turned. "Darling," she called, rising quickly, "the door's open." She came toward him.

The hairs on the back of his neck lifted. She wasn't looking straight at him, he felt, but at something behind him. *She was watching him come through the living room.*

She moistened her lips. Her arms went out to him. Just before they touched him, Carr jerked back.

The arms closed on air. Marcia lifted her face. Her back arched as if there were a strong arm around it. There was the sloppy sound of a kiss.

Carr shook as he backed across the living room. "That's enough for you, darling," he heard Marcia murmur sharply to the air. He spun around and darted into the hall—not to the elevator, but to the stairs beyond.

As he plunged down them in strides that were nightmarishly long and slow, a thought popped to the surface of his mind.

The meaning of a phrase he had read uncomprehendingly an hour before: ". . . the lion's tail near the five sisters . . ."

CHAPTER V

If you catch on to the secret, you'd better keep your mouth shut. It never brought anybody anything but grief. If you've got friends, the kindest thing you can do for them is not to let them find out . . .

Few people walk on the east side of Michigan Boulevard after dark. At such times the Art Institute looks very dead. Headlights coming down Adams play on its dark stone like archeologists' flashlights. The two majestic bronze lions might be guarding the portals of some monument of Roman antiquity. The tail of one of the lions, conveniently horizontal and kept polished by the casual elbows of art students and idlers, now served as a backrest for the frightened girl.

She silently watched Carr mount the steps. He might be part of some dream she was having. A forbiddingly cold wind was whipping in from the lake and she had buttoned up her cardigan. Carr stopped a half dozen paces away.

After a moment she smiled and said, "Hello."

Carr smiled jerkily in reply and moved toward her. His first words surprised him.

"I met your small dark man with glasses. He ran away."

"Oh? I'm sorry. He really might be your friend. But he's . . . timid," she added, her lips setting in bitter lines. "He can't always be depended on. He was supposed to meet me here, but . . ." She glanced, shrugging her shoulders, toward the electric numerals glowing high above the north end of Grant Park. "I had some vague idea of introducing the two of you, but now I'm not so sure." The wind blew strands of her shoulder-length hair against her cheek. "I never really thought you'd come, you know. Leaving notes like that is just a way I have of tempting fate. You weren't supposed to guess. How did you know it was one of these lions?"

Carr laughed. "Taft's Great Lakes fountain is a minor obsession of mine. I always try to figure out which of the five sisters is which lake. And of course that's just around the corner." He instantly grew serious again and moved closer to her. "I want to ask you a question," he said.

"Yes?" she asked guardedly.

"Do you think I'm insane?"

Headlights from Adams swept across her gray eyes, enigmatic as those of a sphinx. "That's hardly a question for a stranger to answer." She looked at him a while longer and shook her head. "No, I don't," she said softly.

"All right," he said, "grant I'm sane. Then answer this: Do you think it's reasonably possible for a sane person to meet eight or ten insane ones, some of them people he knows, all in one day? And I don't mean in an asylum."

"I don't know," she whispered. Then, unwillingly, "I suppose not."

"All right,' he said. "Then comes the big question: Do you think . . . (He had trouble getting the words out) ". . . that most people are really alive?"

She seemed to shrink in size. Her face was all in shadow. "I don't understand," she faltered.

"I mean," he said, "do you really believe there's anything behind most people's foreheads but blackness? Do they really think and act, or are they just mindless parts of a mindless pattern?" His voice grew stronger. "Do you think that all that—" (He swept his hand along the boulevard and the towering buildings and the darkness) "—is really alive, or contains life? Or is all Chicago just a big machine, with people for parts?"

She fairly sprang at him from the shadows. The next instant her hands were gripping his together and her strained and apprehensive face was inches from his own.

"Never think that!" she told him rapidly. "Don't even toy with such crazy ideas!"

"Why not?" he demanded, his prisoned hands throbbing as if from an electric shock. "If you'd seen what I've seen today—"

Without warning she laughed gayly, loosed his tingling hands, and spun away from him. "Idiot!" she said in a voice that rippled with laughter, "I know what's happened to you. You've been scared by life. You've magnified a few funny things into a morbid idea."

"A few funny things?" he demanded, confused by her startling change of behavior. "Why, if you'd seen—"

"I don't care!" she interrupted with triumphant gayety. "Whatever it is, its foolishness." Her eyes, dancing with an infectious excitement, fixed on his. "Come with me," she said, "and I'll show you that all that—" (She swept her hand, as he had, at the boulevard) "—is safe and warm and friendly."

"But—" he began.

She danced toward him. "Is it a date?" she asked.

"Well—"

"Is it, Mr. Serious?"

He couldn't stop a big grin. "Yes," he told her.

She held up a finger. "You've got to remember that this is *my* date, that I pick the places we go and that whatever I do, you fall in with it."

"Like follow-the-leader?"

"Exactly like follow-the-leader. Tonight I'm showing you Chicago. That's the agreement."

"All right," he said.

"Then come on."

"What's your name?" he said, catching her elbow.

"Jane," she told him.

"Jane what?"

"You don't need to konw," she replied impishly.

"Wait a minute," he said, pulling them to a stop. "Is it Jane Gregg?"

He couldn't tell from her face whether that question meant anything to her. "I won't tell you," she said, pulling at him. "Do you know Tom Elvested?" he continued.

"I won't answer foolish questions like that," she assured him. "Oh come on, you've got to get in the spirit of the thing, what's-your-name."

"Carr. Two R's," he told her quietly.

"Then we turn north here, Carr," she told him.

"Where to?" he asked.

She looked at him severely. "Follow the leader," she reminded him and laughed and raced ahead. He had to run to keep up with her, and by that time he was laughing too.

They were a block from the Institute when Carr asked, "What about your friend, though—the small dark man with glasses?"

"I don't care," she said. "If he comes now, he can have a date with the five sisters."

"Incidentally," Carr asked, "what's his real name?"

"I honestly don't konw."

"Are they after him too?" Carr persisted, his voice growing somber.

"Who?"

"Those three people you warned me against."

"I don't want to talk about them." Her voice was suddenly flat. "They're obscene and horrible and I don't want to think about them at all."

"But look, Jane, what sort of hold do they have on you? Why did you let that big blonde slap you without doing anything?"

"I tell you I won't talk about them! If you go on like this, there won't be any date." She turned on him, gripping his arm. "Oh, Carr, you're spoiling everything," she told him, close to tears. "Do get in the spirit, like you promised."

"All right," he said gently, "I will, really." He linked his arm through hers and for a while they walked in silence. The wind and the gloom and the wide empty sidewalk seemed strange and lonely so close to the boulevard with its humming cars and its fringe of people and lights on the other side.

Her arm tighened a little on his. "This is fun," she said.

"What?"

"Having a date."

"I shouldn't think you'd have any trouble," he told her.

"Oh? You don't know anything about my troubles—and we're not going to talk about them tonight! Here we turn again."

They were opposite the public library. She led him across the boulevard. It seemed to Carr the loneliness followed them, for they passed only two people as they went by the library.

They sqinted against blown grit. A sheet of newspaper flapped against their faces. Carr ripped it away and it swooped up into the air.

Jane led him down a cobbled alley choked with fire escapes, down some steps and into a little tavern.

The place was dimly lit. None of the booths were occupied. At the bar two men contemplated half empty glasses of beer.

"What'll you have?" Carr asked Jane.

"Let's wait a bit," she said, steering him instead to the last booth. Neither the two drinkers nor the fat and solumn bartender looked up as they went past.

They looked at each other across the splotched table. Color had come into Jane's cheeks. Carr found himself thinking of college days, when there had been hip flasks and roadsters and checks from home and classes to cut.

"It's funny," he said, "I've gone past this alley a hundred times and never noticed this place."

"Cities are like that," she said. "You think you know them when all you know are routes through them."

We're even beginning to talk about life, Carr thought.

One of the beer-drinkers put two nickels in the jukebox. Low strains eddied out.

Carr looked toward the bar. "Maybe they don't serve at the tables now," he said.

"Who cares?" she said. "Let's dance."

"I don't imagine it's allowed,' he said. "Theyd have to have another license.'

"I told you you were scared of life," she said gayly. "Come on."

There wasn't much space, but enough. With what struck Carr as a grave and laudable politeness, the beer drinkers paid no attention to them at all, though one beat time softly with the bottom of his glass against his palm.

Jane danced badly, but after a while she got better. Somewhat solemnly they revolved in a modest circle. She said nothing until almost the end of the first number. Then, in a choked voice—

"It's been so long since I've danced with anyone."

"Not with your man with glasses?" Carr asked.

She shook her head. "He's too scared of life all the time. He can't relax—not even pretend."

The second record started. Her expression cleared. She rested her cheek against his shoulder. "I've got a theory about life," she said dreamily. "I think life has a rhythm. It keeps changing with the time of day and year, but it's always there. People feel it without knowing it and it governs their lives."

"Like the music of the spheres?" Carr suggested.

"Yes, only that makes it sound too nice."

"What do you mean, Jane?"

"Nothing."

Another couple came in, took one of the front booths. The bartender wiped his hands on his apron, pushed up a wicket in the bar, and walked over to them.

The music stopped. Carr dug in his pocket for more nickels, but she shook her head. They slid back into their booth.

"I hope I didn't embarrass you," she said.

"Of course not."

A telephone rang. The fat bartender carefully put down the tray of drinks he had mixed for the other couple and went to answer it.

"Sure you don't want to dance some more?" Carr asked.

"No, let's just let things happen to us."

"A good idea," Carr agreed, "provided you don't push it too far. For instance, we did come here to get a drink, didn't we?"

"Yes, we did," Jane agreed. The impish expression returned to her eyes. She glanced at the two drinks standing on the bar. "Those look good," she said, "Let's have those."

He looked at her. "Seriously?"

"Why not? We were here first. Are you scared of life?"

He grinned at her and got up suddenly. She didn't stop him, rather to his surprise. Much more so, there was no squawk when he boldly clutched the glasses and returned with them.

Jane applauded soundlessly. He bowed and set down the drinks with a flourish. They sipped.

She smiled. "That's another of my theories. You can get away with anything if you aren't scared. Other people can't stop you, because they're more scared than you are."

Carr smiled at her.

"What's that for?" she asked.

"Do you know the first name I gave you?" he asked.

"No."

"The frightened girl. Incidentally, what did startle you so when you sat down at my desk this afternoon. You seemed to sense something in me that terrified you. What could it have been?"

She shrugged her shoulders. "I don't know. You're getting serious again," she warned him.

He grinned. "I guess I am."

More people had begun to drift in. By the time they finished their drinks, all the other booths were filled. Jane was getting uneasy.

"Let's go somewhere else," she said abruptly, standing up.

Carr started to reply, but she had slipped around a couple approaching their booth and was striding toward the door. A fear took hold of him that she would get away like this afternoon and he would never see her again. He jerked a dollar bill from his pocketbook and dropped it on the table. With nettling rudeness the newcomers shoved past him and sat down. But there was no time to be sarcastic. Jane was already mounting the stairs. He ran after her.

She was waiting outside. He took her arm.

"Do people get on your nerves?" he asked, "so you can't stand being with too many of them for too long?"

She did not answer, but in the darkness her hand reached over and touched his.

CHAPTER VI

Don't let on you know the secret, even to yourself. Pretend you don't know that the people around you are

*dead, or as good as dead. That's what you'll do, brother,
if you play it safe . . .*

They emerged from the alley into a street where the air
and an intoxicating glow, as if the lamps puffed out clouds of
luminous dust which rose for three or four stories into the
dark.

They passed a music store. Jane's walk slowed to an inde-
cisive drift. Through the open door Carr glimpsed a mahog-
any expanse of uprights, spinets, baby grands. Jane suddenly
walked in. The sound of their footsteps died as they stepped
onto the thick carpet.

Whoever else was in the store was out of sight somewhere
in the back. Jane sat down at one of the pianos. Her fingers
quested for a while over the keys. Then her back stiffened,
her head lifted, and there came the frantically rippling arpeg-
gios of the third movement of Beethoven's Moonlight Sonata.

She didn't play it any too well, yet she did manage to ex-
tract from it a feeling of wild, desperate wonder. Surely if the
composer had ever meant this to be moonlight, it was moonlight illuminating a white-pinnacled ocean storm or, through
rifts in ragged clouds, the Brocken on *Walpurgis Nacht.*

Suddenly it was over. In the echoing quiet Carr asked, "Is
that more like it? The rhythm of life, I mean?"

She made a little grimace as she got up. "Still too nice,"
she said, "but there's a hint."

They started out. Carr looked back over his shoulder, but
the store was still empty. He felt a twinge of returning fear.

"Do you realize that we haven't spoken with anybody but
each other tonight?" he asked.

She smiled woefully. "I think of pretty dull things to do,
don't I?" she said, and when he started to protest, "No, I'm
afraid you'd have had a lot more fun tonight with some other
girl."

"Listen," he said, "I did have a date with another girl and
. . . oh, I don't want to talk about it."

Her voice was odd, almost close to tears. "You'd even have
had more fun with Midge's girlfriend."

"Say, you do have a memory," he began. Then, turning on
her, "Aren't you really Jane Gregg? Don't you know Tom
Elvested and Midge?"

She shook her head reprovingly and looked up with an uneven smile. "But since you haven't got a date with anybody but me, Mr. Serious, you'll have to make the best of my anti-social habits. Let's see, I could let you look at some other grils undressing on North Clark or West Madison, or we could go to the symphony, or . . ."

They were passing the painfully bright lobby of a movie house, luridly placarded with yellow and purple swirls which seemed to have caught up in their whirlwind folds an unending rout of golden blondes, grim-eyed heroes, money bags, and grasping hands. Jane stopped.

"Or I could take you in here," she said.

He obediently veered toward the box office, but she kept hold of his arm and walked him past it into the outer lobby.

"You mustn't be scared of life," she told him, half gayly, half despairingly, he thought. "You must learn to take risks. You really can get away with anything."

Carr shrugged and held his breath for the inevitable.

They walked straight past the ticket-taker and through the center aisle door.

Carr puffed out his breath and grinned. He thought, maybe she knows someone here. Or else—who knows?—maybe you *could* get away with almost anything if you did it with enough assurance and picked the right moments.

The theater was only half full. They sidled through the blinking darkness into one of the empty rows at the back. Soon the gyrations of the gray shadows on the screen took on a little sense.

There were a man and a woman getting married, or else remarried after a divorce, it was hard to tell which. Then she left him because she thought that he was interested only in business. Then she came back, but he left her because he thought she was interested only in social affairs. Then he came back, but then they both left each other again, simultaneously.

From all around came the soft breathing and somnolent gum-chewing of drugged humanity.

Then the man and woman both raced to the bedside of their dying little boy, who had been tucked away in a military academy. But the boy recovered, and then the woman left both of them, for their own good, and a little while afterwards the man did the same thing. Then the boy left them.

"Do you play chess?" Jane asked suddenly.

Carr nodded gratefully.

"Come on," she said. "I know a place."

They hurried out the bustling theater district into an empty region of silent gray office buildings—for the Loop is a strange place, where loneliness jostles too much companionship. Looking up at the dark and dingy heights, Carr felt his uneasiness begin to return. There was something exceedingly horrible in the thought of miles on miles of darkened offices, empty but for the endless desks, typewriters, filing cabinets, water coolers. What would a stranger from Mars deduce from them? Surely not human beings.

With a great roar a cavalcade of newspaper trucks careened across the next corner, plunging as frantically as if the fate of nations were at stake. Carr took a backward step, his heart pounding.

Jane smiled at him. "We're safe tonight," she said and led him to a massive office building of the last century. Pushing through a side door next to the locked revolving one, she drew him into a dingy lobby floored with tiny white tiles and surrounded by the iron lattice work of ancient elevator shafts. A jerkily revolving hand showed that one cage was still in operation, but Jane headed for the shadow-stifled stairs.

"I hope you don't mind," she said. "It's thirteen stories, but I can't stand elevators."

Remembering the one at Marcia's apartment, Carr was glad.

They emerged panting in a hall where the one frosted door that wasn't dark read CAISSA CHESS CLUB.

Behind the door was a long room. A drab austerity, untidy rows of small tables, and a grimy floor littered with trodden cigarettes, all proclaimed the place to be the headquarters of a somber immovable monomania.

Some oldsters were playing near the door, utterly absorbed in the game. One with a dirty white beard was silently kibitzing, accasionally shaking his head, or pointing out with palsied fingers the move that would have won if it had been made.

Carr and Jane walked quietly beyond them, found a box of men as battered by long use as the half obliterated board, and started to play.

Soon the maddening, years-forgotten excitement gripped Carr tight. He was back in that dreadful little universe where the significance of things is narrowed down to the stratagems whereby turreted rooks establish intangible walls of force, bishops, slip craftily through bristling barricades, and knights spring out in sudden sidewise attacks, as if from crooked medieval passageways.

They played three slow, merciless games. She won the first two. He finally drew the third, his king just managing to nip off her last runaway pawn. It felt very late, getting on toward morning.

She leaned back massaging her face.

"Nothing like chess," she mumbled, "to take your mind off things." Then she dropped her hands.

Two men were still sitting at the first table in their overcoats, napping over the board. They tiptoed past them and out into the hall and went down the stairs. An old woman was wearily scrubbing her way across the lobby, her head bent as if forever.

In the street they paused uncertainly. It had grown quite chilly.

"Where do you live?" Carr asked.

"I'd rather you didn't—" Jane began and stopped. After a moment she said, "All right, you can take me home. But it's a long walk and you must still follow the leader."

The Loop was deserted except for the darkness and the hungry wind. They crossed the black Chicago River on Michigan Boulevard, where the skyscrapers are the thickest. It looked like the Styx. They walked rapidly. They didn't say anything. Carr's arm was tightly linked around hers. He felt sad and tired and yet very much at peace. He knew he was leaving this girl forever and going back to his own world. Any vague notion he'd had of making her a real friend had died in the cold ebb of night.

Yet at the same time he knew that she had helped him. All his worries and fears, including the big one, were gone. The events of the afternoon and early evening seemed merely bizarre, a mixture of hoaxes and trivial illusions. Tomorrow he must begin all over again, with his job and his pleasures. Marcia, he told himself, had only been playing a fantastic prank—he'd patch things up with her.

As if sensing his thoughts, Jane shrank close to his side.

Past the turn-off to his apartment, past the old white water tower, they kept on down the boulevard. It seemed tremendously wide without cars streaming through it.

They turned down a street where big houses hid behind black space and trees.

Jane stopped in front of a tall iron gate. High on one of the stone pillars, supporting it, too high for Jane to see, Carr idly noted a yellow chalk-mark in the shape of a cross with dots between the arms. Wondering if it were a tramps' sign commenting on the stinginess or generosity of the people inside, Carr suddenly got the picture his mind had been fumbling for all night. It fitted Jane, her untidy expensive clothes, her shy yet arrogant manner. She must be a rich man's daughter, overprotected, neurotic, futilely rebellious, tyrannized over by relatives and servants. Everything in her life mixed up, futilely and irremediably, in the way only money can manage.

"It's been so nice," Jane said in a choked voice, not looking at him, "so nice to pretend."

She fumbled in her pocket, but whether for a handkerchief or a key Carr could not tell. Something small and white slipped from her hand and fluttered through the fence. She pushed open the gate enough to get through.

"Please don't come in with me," she whispered. "And please don't stay and watch."

Carr thought he knew why. She didn't want him to watch the lights wink agitatedly on, perhaps hear the beginning of an anxious tirade. It was her last crumb of freedom—to leave him with the illusion she was free.

He took her in his arms. He felt in the darkness the tears on her cold cheek wetting his. Then she had broken away. There were footsteps running up a gravel drive. He turned and walked swiftly away.

In the sky, between the pale streets, was the first paleness of dawn.

CHAPTER VII

Keep looking straight ahead brother. It doesn't do to get too nosy. You may see things going on in the big engine that'll make you wish you'd never come alive . . .

Through slitted, sleep-heavy eyes Carr saw the clock holding up both hands in horror. The room was drenched in sunshine.

But he did not hurl himself out of bed, tear into his clothes, and rush downtown, just because it was half past eleven.

Instead he yawned and closed his eyes, savoring the feeling of self-confidence that filled him. He had a profound sense of being back on the right track.

Odd that a queer neurotic girl could give you so much. But nice.

Grinning, he got up and leisurely bathed and shaved.

He'd have breakfast downtown, he decided. Something a little special. Then amble over to the office about the time his regular lunch hour ended.

He even thought of permitting himself the luxury of taking a cab to the Loop. But as soon as he got outside he changed his mind. The sun and the air, and the blue of lake and sky, and the general feeling of muscle-stretching spring, when even old people crawl out of their holes, were too enticing. He felt fresh. Plenty of time. He'd walk.

The city showed him her best profile. As if he were a god briefly sojourning on earth, he found pleasure in inspecting the shifting scene and the passing people.

They seemed to feel as good as he did. Even the ones hurrying fastest somehow gave the impression of strolling. Carr enjoyed sliding past them like a stick drifting in a slow, whimsical current.

If life has a rhythm, he thought, it has sunk to a lazy summer murmur from the strings.

His mind played idly with last night's events. He wondered if he could find Jane's imposing home again. He decided he probably could, but felt no curiosity. Already she was beginning to seem like a girl in a dream. They'd met, helped each other, parted. A proper episode.

He came to the bridge. Down on the sparkling river deckhands were washing an excursion steamer. The skyscrapers rose up clean and gray. Cities, he thought, could be lovely places at times, so huge and yet so bright and sane and filled with crowds of people among whom you were indistinguishable and therefore secure. Undoubtedly this was the pleasantest half-hour he'd had in months. To crown it, he decided he'd drop into one of the big department stores and make some toally unnecessary purchase. Necktie perhaps. Say a new blue.

Inside the store the crowd was thicker. Pausing to spy out

the proper counter, Carr had the faintest feeling of oppressiveness. For a moment he felt the impulse to hurry outside. But he smiled at it. He located the neckties—they were across the huge room—and started toward them. But before he'd got halfway he stopped again, this time to enjoy a sight as humorously bizarre as a cartoon in *The New Yorker*.

Down the center aisle, their eyes fixed stonily ahead, avoiding the shoppers with a casual adroitness, marched four youngish men carrying a wondow-display mannequin. The four men were wearing identical light-weight black overcoats and black snap-brim hats which looked as if they'd just been purchased this morning. The two in front each held an ankle, the two in back a shoulder. The mannequin was dressed in an ultra-stylish olive green suit, the face and hands were finished in some realistic nude felt, and her arms were rigidly fixed to hold a teacup or an open purse.

There was something so ludicrous about the costume of the four men and their unconcern, both for the shoppers and for the figure they were carrying, that it was all Carr could do not to burst out laughing. As it was, he was relieved that none of the four men happened to look his way and catch his huge grin.

He studied them delightedly, wondering what weird circumstances had caused this bit of behind-the-scenes department-store business to take place in front of everyone.

Oddly, no one else seemed aware of how amusing they looked. It was something for Carr's funny-bone alone.

He watched until they were well past him. Almost regretfully, he turned away toward the tie counter. But just then the rigid arm of the mannequin unfolded and dropped down slackly, and the head fell back and the dark-lashed eyes flickered and fixed on him a sick, doomed stare.

Carr was not quite sure how he got out of the store without screaming or running. There was a blank space of panic in his memory. The next thing, he remembered clearly was pushing his way through the ocean of unseeing faces on State Street. By then he had begun to rationalize the event. Perhaps the mannequin's arm worked on a pivot, and its swinging down had startled him into imagining the rest. Of course the hand had looked soft and limp and helpless as it dragged along the floor, but that could have been imagination too.

After all, a world in which people could "turn off" other

people like clockwork toys and cart them away just wasn't possible—even if it would help to explain some of the hundreds of mysterious disappearances that occur every month.

No, it had all been his damnable imagination. Just the same, his mood of calm self-confidence was shattered and he was tormented by a sudden sense of guilt about his lateness. He must get back to the office as quickly as he could. Behind his desk he'd find security.

The five blocks to General Employment seemed fifty. More than once he looked back uneasily. He found himself searching the crowd for black snap-brim hats.

He hurried furtively through the lobby and up the stairs. After hesitating a moment outside, he gathered his courage and entered the applicants' waiting room.

He looked through the glass panel. The big blonde who had slapped Jane was sitting in his swivel chair, rummaging through the drawers of his desk.

CHAPTER VIII

What's a mean guy do when he finds out other guys and girls are as good as dead? He trots out all the nasty notions he's been keeping warm inside his rotten little heart. Now I can get away with them, he figures . . .

Carr didn't move. His first impulse was to confront the woman, but right on its heels came the realization that she'd hardly be acting this way without some sort of authorization —and hardly obtain an authorization without good cause.

His mind, instinctively preferring realistic fears to worse ones, jumped back to a fleeting suspicion that Jane was mixed up in some sort of crime. This woman might be a detective.

But detectives didn't go around slapping people, at least not before they arrested them. Yet this woman had a distinctly professional look about her, bold as brass as she sat there going through his stuff.

On the other hand, she might have walked into the office without anyone's permission, trusting to bluff to get away with it.

Carr studied her through the glass pane. She was more beautiful than he'd realized yesterday. With that lush figure, faultless blonde hair, and challenging lips, she might be a

40

model for billboard advertisements. Even the slight out-of-focus look of her eyes didn't spoil her attractiveness. And her gray sports outfit looked like five hundred dollars or so.

Yet there was something offkey about even her good looks and get-up. She carried the lush figure with a blank animal assurance. There was a startling and unashamed barbarousness in the two big silver pins piercing her mannish gray sports hat. And she seemed utterly unconcerned with the people around her. Carr felt strangely cowed.

But the situation was impossible, he told himself. You didn't let someone search your desk without objecting. Tom Elvested, apparently busy with some papers at the next desk, must be wondering what the devil the woman was up to. So must the others.

Just then she dropped a folder back, shut a drawer, and stood up, Carr faded back into the men's room. He waited perhaps fifteen seconds, then cautiously stepped out. The woman was no longer in sight. The outside corridor was empty. He ran to the head of the stairs and spotted the gray sports coat going through the revolving door. He hurried down the stairs, hesitated, then darted into the small tobacco and magazine store opening on the lobby. He could probably still catch a glimpse of her through the store's show window. It would be less conspicuous than dashing right out on the sidewalk.

The store was empty except for the proprietor and a rather portly and well-dressed man whose back was turned. The latter instantly attracted Carr's attention by a startlingly nervy action. Without a word or a glance at the proprietor, he leaned across the counter and selected a pack of cigarettes, tore it open from top to bottom with a twisting motion, selected one of the undamaged cigarettes and dropped the rest on the floor.

The proprietor didn't say anything.

Carr's snap-reaction was that at last he'd seen a big-shot racketeer following his true impulses. Then he followed the portly man's gaze to the street door and saw a patch of familiar gray approaching.

The lobby door was too far way. Carr sidled behind a magazine rack just as he heard the street door opening.

The first voice was the woman's. It was as disagreeably

brassy as her manner. "I searched his desk. There wasn't anything suspicious."

"And you did a good job?" The portly man's voice was a jolly one. "Took your time? Didn't miss anything?"

"Of course."

"Hmm." Carr heard the whir of a lighter and the faint crackle of a cigarette igniting. His face was inches away from a line of luridly covered magazines.

"What are you so worried about?" The woman sounded quarrelsome. "Can't you take my word for it? I checked on them both yesterday. She didn't blink when I slapped her."

"Worry pays, Hackman." The portly man sounded even pleasanter. "We have strong reason to suspect the girl. We've seen her—or a very similar girl—with the small dark man with glasses. I respect your intelligence, Hackman, but I'm not completely satisfied. We'll do another check on the girl later tonight."

"Where?"

"But we don't even know if it's the same girl."

"Perhaps we can find out tonight. There may be photographs."

"Pft!" Now the woman was getting really snappish. "I think it's just your desire for her that keeps you doing these things. You hate to realize she's no use to you. You want to keep alive a dream."

The portly man chuckled. "Very often prudence and self-indulgence go hand in hand, Hackman. We'll do another check on her."

"But aren't we supposed to have any time for fun?"

"Fun must be insured, Hackman. Hardly be fun at all, if you felt someone might spoil it. And then if some other crowd should catch on to us through this girl . . . No, we'll do another check."

"Oh, all right!" The woman's voice expressed disgusted resignation. "Though I suppose it'll mean prowling around for hours with the hound."

"Hmm. No, I hardly think the hound will be necessary."

Carr, staring sightlessly at the pulp and astrology magazines and the bosomy paper-bound books, felt his flesh crawl.

"Why not let Dris do it?" he heard the woman suggest. "He's had the easiest end lately."

The portly man laughed dispassionately. "Do you think I'm

going to let Dris work on the girl alone, when I'm the one who's to have her if it turns out she's a live one? And would you trust Dris in that situation?"

"Certainly! Dris wouldn't look at anyone but me!"

"Really?" The portly man's laughter was even colder. "I seem to recall you saying something of the sort about the small dark man with glasses."

The woman's answer was a cat-snarl that made Carr jerk.

"Don't ever mention that filthy traitor to me again, Wilson! I can't sleep nights for thinking of giving him to the hound!"

"I respect your feelings, Hackman," the portly man said placatingly, "and I certainly applaud your plans for the chap, if we ever find him. But look here, facts are facts. I had you —and a very pleasant experience it was, Hackman. You had . . . er . . . the chap and then Dris. So in a sense you're one up on me—"

"I'll say I am!"

"—and so I want to be very sure that I'm the one who gets the next girl. Dris will have to wait a while before he's allowed a conquest."

"Dris will have no one but me! Ever!"

"Of course, Hackman, of course," the portly man buttered.

Just then there was a rush of footsteps outside. Carr heard the street door open fast.

"What the devil is it, Dris?" the portly man managed to say before a new, hard voice blurted, "We've got to get out of here fast. I just saw the four men with black hats!"

There was a scramble of footsteps. The door closed. Carr peered around the rack. Through the window he could see the big blonde and the portly man entering a long black convertible. The driver was a young man with a crew haircut. As he opened the front door for the others, Carr saw that his right arm ended in a hooking contrivance. He felt a thrill of recognition. These were the people Jane had mentioned in her note, all right. ". . . affable-seeming older man . . ." Yes, it fitted.

The driver's hand and hook clamped on the wheel. The blonde, scrambling into the front seat ahead of the portly man, dangled her hand momentarily above the back seat. Something gray flashed up at it. The blonde jerked back her hand and made what might have been a threatening gesture. Carr felt a shiver crawling along his back. Perhaps the blonde had merely flicked up the corner of a gray fur driving robe. But it was almost summer and the gray flash had been very quick.

The convertible began to move swiftly. Carr hurried to the window. He got there in time to see the convertible swinging around the next corner, too fast for sensible downtown driving.

Carr returned. The proprietor was standing behind the counter, head bowed, busy—or pretending to be busy—with some printed forms.

He didn't go back to the window to look for them. He hurried out of the shop and got behind his desk as fast as he could. His mind was occupied by the two things he felt he must do. First, stick out the afternoon at the office. Second, get to Jane and warn her.

Just as he sat down at his desk, his phone rang.

It was Marcia. "Hello, darling," she said, "I'm going to do something I made it a rule never to do to a man."

"What's that?" he asked automatically.

"Thank him. It really was a lovely evening, dear. I've never known the food at the Kungsholm to be better."

"I don't get it," Carr said stupidly, remembering his flight from Marcia's apartment. "We didn't—"

"And then that charming fellow we met," Marcia interrupted. "I mean Kirby Fisher. Darling, he seems to have oodles of money."

"I don't get it at all—" Carr persisted and then stopped, frozen by a vision of Marcia and her invisible man and the three of them talking together, with gaps for the invisible man's remarks. For if yesterday's big fear were true and the world were a machine, and if he'd jumped out of his place in the machine when he ran away from Marcia last night to be with Jane—

"'Bye now, darling," Marcia said. "Be properly grateful."

"Wait a minute, Marcia," he said, speaking rapidly. "Do you actually mean—"

Btu the phone clicked and started to buzz, and Tom Elvested came galumphing over.

"Look," Tom said, "I know it was too short notice when I asked you to go out with me and Midge and Jane Gregg last night. But now you've seen what a charming girl she is, how about the four of us getting together Saturday?"

"Well . . ." Carr said confusedly, hardly knowing what Tom had been saying.

"Swell," Tom told him. "It's a date."

"Wait a minute, Tom," Carr said rapidly. "Is this Jane Gregg a slim girl with long untidy dark hair?"

But Tom had returned to his own desk, and an applicant was approaching Carr's.

Somehow Carr got through the afternoon. His mind kept jumping around in a funny way. He kept seeing the pulp magazines in the rack downstairs. For several minutes he was bothered by something gray poking around the end of one of the benches in the waiting room, until he realized it was a woman's handbag. And there was the constant fear that he'd lost contact with the people he was interviewing, that the questions and answers would stop agreeing.

With a slump of relief he watched the last applicant depart. It was a minute past quitting time and the other interviewers were already hurrying for their hats and wraps. His glance lit on a scrap of pencil by the wire basket on his desk. He rolled it toward him with one finger. It was fiercely chewed, making him think of nails bitten to the quick. He recognized it as Jane's. He rolled it back and forth.

He stood up. The office had emptied itself while he'd been sitting there. The cleaning woman, dry mop over her shoulder, was pushing in a cart for the wastepaper. She ignored him. He grabbed his hat and walked out past her, tramped down the stairs.

Outside the day had stayed sparklingly fair, so that the streets were flooded with a soft white light that imparted a subdued carnival atmosphere to the eager hurry of the rush hour. Carr felt a touch of dancing, adventurous excitement add itself to his tension. Instead of heading over to Michigan Boulevard, he took a more direct route north, crossing the sluggish river by one of the blacker, more nakedly-girdered bridges.

Beyond the river, the street slanted downward into a region of beaneries, secondhand magazine stores, small saloons, drugstores with screaming displays laid out six months ago. This kept up for some eight or ten blocks without much change except an increasing number of cramped nightclubs with tautly smiling photographs of the nearly naked girls who presumably dispensed the "continuous entertainment."

Then in one block, by the stern sorcery of zoning laws, the squalid neighborhood was transformed into a wealthy residential section of heavyset houses with thickly curtained windows and untrod lawns suggesting the cleared areas around forts.

If memory served him right, Jane's house lay just a block and a left turn ahead. He quickened his step. He rounded the corner.

He came to a high iron fence with brick pillars, to a tall iron gate. There was a yellow chalk-mark high on one pillar —a cross with dots between the arms.

He stopped dead, stared, took a backward step.

This couldn't be. He must have made a mistake.

But his memory of the gate—and especially of the chalk-mark—made that impossible.

The sinking sun suddenly sent a spectral yellow aftergolw, illuminating everything clearly.

A gravel drive led up to just the sort of big stone mansion he had imagined—turreted, slate-roofed, heavy-eaved, in the style of the 1890's.

But the gate and the fence were rusty, tall weeds encroached on the drive, lawn and flowerbeds were a wilderness, the upper windows were blank and curtainless, most of them broken, those on the first floor were boarded up, pigeon droppings whitened the somber brown stone, and in the center of the law, half hidden by the weeds, was a weather-bleached sign: FOR SALE.

CHAPTER IX

It doesn't do for too many people to come alive, brother. The big engine gets out of whack. And the mean guys don't want any competition. They get busy and rub it out . . .

Carr pushed doubtfully at the iron gate. It opened a couple of feet, then squidged to a stop against gravel still damp from yesterday morning's rain. He stepped inside, frowning. He was bothered by a vague and dreamlike sense of recognition.

Suddenly he recalled the reason for it. He had seen pictures of this place in popular magazines, even read an article about it. It was the old Beddoes house, home of one of Chicago's most fabulous millionaires of the 1890's. John Claire Beddoes had been a pillar of society, but there were many persistent traditions about his secret vices. He was even supposed to have kept a young mistress in this very house for ten years under the eyes of his wife—though by what trickery or concealment, or sheer brazenness, was never explained.

But the house had been empty for the past twenty-five years. The magazine article had been very definite on that point. Its huge size and the fact that it was owned by an eccentric old maid, last of the Beddoes line, who lived on the Italian Riviera, had combined to make its sale impossible.

All this while Carr's feet were carrying him up the drive, which led back of the house, passing under a porte-cochere. He had almost reached it when he noticed the footprints.

They were a woman's, they were quite fresh, and yet they were sunk more deeply than his own. They must have been made since the ran. There were two sets, one leading toward the porte-cochere, the other back from it.

Looking at the black ruined flowerbeds, inhaling their dank odor, Carr was relieved that there were footprints.

He examined them more closely. Those leading toward the porte-cochere were deeper and more widely spaced. He remembered that Jane had been almost running.

But the most startling discovery was that the footprints apparently didn't enter the house at all. They clustered confusedly under the porte-cochere, then returned toward the gate. Evidently Jane had waited until he was gone, then retraced her steps.

He walked back to the gate. A submerged memory from last night was tugging at his mind. He looked along the iron fence. He noticed a scrap of paper lodged in the low back shoots of some leafless shrub.

He remembered something white fluttering from Jane's handbag in the dark, drifting through the fence.

He worked his way to it, pushing between the fence and the shrubbery. Unpruned shoots caught at his coat.

The paper was twice creased and the edges were yellowed and frayed, as if it had been carried around for a long time. It was not rain-marked. Unfolding it, he found the inside filled with a brown-inked script vividly recalling Jane's scribbled warning. Moving toward the center of the lawn to catch the failing light, he read:

Always keep up appearances.
Always be doing something.
Always be first or last.
Always be alone.
Always have a route of escape.
Never hesitate, or you're lost.
Never do anything odd—it wouldn't be noticed.
Never move things—it makes gaps.
Never touch anyone—DANGER! MACHINERY.
Never run—they're faster.
Never look at a stranger—it might be one of them.
Some animals are really alive.

Carr looked over his shoulder at the boarded-up house. A lean bird skimmed behind the roof. Somewhere down the block footsteps were clicking on concrete.

He considered the shape of the paper. It was about that of an envelope and the edges were torn. At first glance the other side seemed blank. Then he saw a faded postmark and address. He struck a match and, holding it close to the paper, made out the name—Jane Gregg; and the city—Chicago; and noticed that the postmark was at least a year old.

The address, lying in a crease, took him longer to decipher.
1924 Mayberry St.

The footsteps were closer. He looked up. Beyond the fence an elderly couple was passing. He guiltily whipped out the match, but they walked by without turning their heads. After a minute he slipped out and walked west.

The streetlights winked on. The leaves near the lights looked an artificial green. He walked faster.

The houses shouldered closer together, grew smaller, crept toward the street. The trees straggled, gave out, the grass sickened. Suddenly the houses coalesced, reached the sidewalk with a rush, shot up in towering brick combers, became the barracks of the middle classes.

His mind kept repeating a name. Jane Gregg. He'd half believed all along she was the girl loony Tom Elvested had talked about—the girl he'd made a date with, through Tom, this very afternoon.

"A bent yellow street sign said, "Mayberry." He looked at

the spotty gold numerals on the glass door of the first apartment. They were 1954-58. As he went down the street he had the feeling that he was walking across the years.

The first floor of 1922-24 was lighted on the 24 side, except for a small dark sunporch. Behind one window he saw the edge of a red davenport and the head and shoulder of a gray-haired man in shirt-sleeves reading a newspaper. Inside the low-ceilinged vestibule he turned to the brass letter boxes on the 24 side. The first one read: "Mr. and Mrs. Herbert Gregg." After a moment he pushed the button, waited a moment, pushed it again.

He could hear the bell clearly, but there was no response, neither a mumble from the speaking tube, nor a buzz from the lock of the door to the stairs.

Yet the Gregg apartment ought to be the one in which he had seen the old man sitting.

He went outside. He craned his neck. The old man was still sitting there. An old man—perhaps deaf?

Then, as Carr watched, the old man put down his paper, settled back, looked across the room, and from the window came the opening triplets of the first movement of the Moonlight Sonata.

Carr felt the wire that fenced the tiny, nearly grassless plot press his calf, and realized that he had taken a backward step. He reminded himself that he'd heard Jane play only the third movement. He couldn't know she'd play the first just this way.

He went back into the vestibule, again pushed the button, heard the bell. The piano notes did not falter.

He peered once more through the inner door. A little light trickled down from the second floor landing above. He tried the door. Someone must have left it off the buzzer, for it opened.

He hurried past the blackness of the bottom of the stair well. Five steps, a turn, five steps more. Then, just as he reached the first landing, he felt something small and silent come brushing up against his ankle from behind.

The next moment his back and hands were pressed to the plaster wall across the landing, where it was recessed about a foot.

Then he relaxed. Just a cat. A black cat. A black cat with a white throat and chest, like evening clothes.

And a very cool cat too, for his jump hadn't even fazed it. It walked suavely toward the door of the Gregg apartment.

But about two feet away it stopped. For several seconds it stood there, head upraised, making no movement except that its fur seemed to thicken a trifle. Then, very slowly, it looked around.

It stared at Carr.

Beyond the door, the piano started the sprightly second movement.

Carr edged out his hand. His throat felt dry and constricted. "Kitty," he croaked.

The cat arched its back, spat, made a twisting leap that carried it halfway up the next semi-flight of stairs. It crouched on the top step, its bugged green eyes peering down at him luminously.

One of the notes came back to Carr's mind: "Some animals are really alive."

There were footsteps. Carr shrank back into the recess. The door opened, the music suddenly swelled, and a gray-haired lady in a blue and white dress looked out and called, "Gigolo! Here, Gigolo!"

She had Jane's small chin and short straight nose, behind veils of plumpness. She was rather dumpy. Her face had a foolish look.

And she must be short-sighted, for although she looked up the stairs, she didn't see the cat, nor did she notice Carr. Feeling uncomfortably like a prowler, he started to step forward, then realized that she was so close he would give her a fright.

"Gigolo!" she called again. Then, to herself, "That cat!" A glance toward the dead bulb in the ceiling and a distracted headshake. "Gigolo!"

She backed inside. "I'm leaving it open, Gigolo," she called. "Come in when you want to."

Carr stepped out of the recess with a husky, "Excuse me," but the opening notes of the fast third movement drowned him out.

He crossed to the door. The greens eyes at the top of the stairs followed him. He raised his hand to knock. But at the same time he looked through the half-open door, across a tiny hall, into the living room.

It was small, with too much furniture and too many lace runners and antimacassars. He could see the other end of the red davenport and the slippered feet of the old man sitting in it. The woman had returned to the straight-backed chair across the room and was sitting with her hands folded, her lips worriedly pursed.

Between them was the piano, an upright.

There was no one sitting at it.

To Carr, the rest of the room seemed to darken and curdle as he stared at the rippling keys.

Then he puffed out his breath. Of course, it must be some kind of electric player.

Again he started to knock, hesitated because they were listening to the music.

The woman moved uneasily on her chair. Her lips anxiously puckered and relaxed, like those of a fish behind aquarium glass. Finally she said, "Aren't you tiring yourself, dear? You've been at it for hours."

Carr looked toward the man, but he could see only the slippered feet. There was no reply.

The piano stopped. Carr took a step forward. But just then the woman got up. He expected her to do something to the mechanism, but instead she began to stroke the air a couple of feet above the piano bench.

Carr felt himself shivering.

"There, there, dear," she said, "that was very pretty, I know, but you're really spending too much time on your music. At your age a girl ought to be with other young people." She bent her head as if she were looking around the shoulder of someone seated at the piano, wagged her finger, and said, "Look at the circles under those eyes."

For Carr, time stopped, as if a clockworks universe hesitated before the next tick. In that frozen pause only his thoughts moved. It was true, then. Tom Elvested . . . The dumpy man . . . The room clerk . . . The Negress . . . Marcia in her bedroom . . . Last night with Jane—the bar, the music shop, the movie house, the chess players . . . The horizontal mannequin . . . The tobacconist . . . And now this old woman . . . All, all automatons, machines!

Or else (time moved again) this old woman was crazy.

Yes, that was it. Crazy. Behaving in her insanity as if her absent daughter were actually there. Believing it.

He clung to that thought.

"Really, Jane," the old woman was saying rapidly, "you must rest."

The slippered feet protruding from the davenport twisted. A weary voice said, "Now don't worry yourself over Jane, Mother."

The woman straightened. "Too much practicing is bad for anyone. It's undermining her health."

The davenport creaked. The man came into sight, not quite as old as Carr had guessed, but tired-looking. "Now, Mother, don't get excited," he said soothingly. "Everything's all right."

The father insane too, Carr thought. No, humoring her. Pretending to believe her hallucinations. That must be it.

"Everything isn't all right," she contradicted tearfully. "I won't have Jane practicing so much and taking those wild long walks by herself. Jane, you mustn't—" Suddenly a look of fear came over her. "Oh don't go. Please don't go, Jane." She stretched out her hand toward the hall as if to restrain someone. Carr shrank back. He felt sick. It was horrible that this mad old woman should resemble Jane.

She dropped her hand. "She's gone," she said and began to sob.

The old man put his arm around her shoulders. "You've scared her off," he said softly. "But don't cry, Mother. Tell you what, let's go sit in the dark for a while. It'll rest you." He urged her toward the sunporch. "Jane'll be back in a moment. I'm sure."

Just then, behind Carr, the cat hissed and retreated a few steps higher, the vestibule door downstairs was banged open, there were loud footsteps and voices raised in argument.

"I tell you, Hackman, I don't like it that Dris excused himself tonight."

"Show some sense, Wilson! This afternoon you didn't want him to come here at all."

"Not by himself, no. With us would be different."

"Pft! Do you always have to have the two of us in the audience when you chase girls?"

The first voice was cool and jolly, the second brassy. They were those Carr had overhead in the cigarette shop.

Before he had time to weigh his fears or form a plan, Carr had slipped through the door in front of him—Jane's parents were out of sight—tiptoed down the hallway leading to the back of the apartment, turned into the first room he came to, and was standing with his cheek to the wall, squinting back the way he had come.

He couldn't quite see the front door. But in a little while long shadows darkened the calcimine of the hallway.

"I came to check on her first, to chase her second," he heard Wilson say. "She doesn't seem to be around."

"But we just heard the piano and we know she's a music student. Practices constantly."

"Use your head, Hackman! You know the piano would play whether she was here or not. If it plays when she's not here, that's the sort of proof we're looking for."

Carr waited for the footsteps or voices of Jane's parents. Surely they must be aware of intruders. The sunporch wasn't that isolated.

Perhaps they were as terrified as he.

"She's probably wandered off to the back of the flat," Hackman suggested.

"Or hiding there," Wilson amended. "And there may be photographs. Let's look"

Carr was already retreating noiselessly across the fussy, old-fashioned bedroom toward where light poured into it from a white-tiled bathroom a short distance away.

"Stop! Listen!" Wilson called. "The sunporch!"

Footsteps receded down the hall, crossed the living room.

"It's the parents," he heard Hackman say in the distance. "I don't see the girl."

"Yet—listen to that!—they're talking as if she might be here."

The footsteps and voices started to come back.

"I told you I didn't like it when Dris bowed out, Hackman. This makes me more suspicious." For once the jolliness was absent from Wilson's voice. "I wouldn't be surprised if he's got in ahead of me and taken the girl somewhere."

"Dris wouldn't dare do a thing like that!"

"No?" The jolliness came back into Wilson's voice, nastily. "Well, if he's not with her, he's fooling around with dead girls, you can bet."

"That's a dirty lie!" Hackman snarled. "Dris might fool around with dead girls when we're all having fun together. Naturally. But not by himself, not alone!"

"You think you're the whole show with him?"

"Yes! You're just jealous because I dropped you."

"Ha! I dont care what Dris—or you—do in your private lives. But if he's taking chances to cheat with this girl, when he knows that the four men in black hats are hunting for us, he's endangering us all. And if that's the case I'll erase him so fast that—*What's that?*"

Carr stiffened. Looking down he saw that he had knocked over a stupid little porcelain pekinese doorstop. He started for the bathroom door, but he had hardly taken the first painfully cautious step when he heard, from that direction, the faint sound of movement. He froze, then turned toward the hallway. He heard the stamp of high heels, a throaty exclamation of surprise from Wilson, a softly pattering rush, the paralyzing fighting-squall of a cat, a smash as if a cane or umbrella had been brought down on a table, and Wilson's, "Damn!"

Next Carr caught a glimpse of Hackman. She had on a pearl gray evening dress, off the shoulders, and a mink wrap over her arm. She was coming down the hall, but she didn't see him.

At the same moment the cat Gigolo landed in the faultless hair, claws raking. Hackman screamed.

The ensuing battle was too quick for Carr to follow it clearly. Most of it was out of his sight, except for the shadows.

Twice more the cane or umbrella smashed down, Wilson and Hackman yelled at each other, the cat squalled. Then Wilson shouted, "The door!" There was a final whanging blow, followed by, "Damn!"

For the next few moments, only heavy breathing from the hallway, then Hackman's voice, rising to a vindictive wail, "Bitch! Look what it did to my cheek. Oh, why must there be cats!"

Then Wilson, grimly businesslike: "It's trapped on the stairs. We can get it."

Hackman: "This wouldn't have happened if we'd brought the hound."

Wilson: "The hound! This afternoon you thought differently. Do you remember what happened the first time you brought the hound here? And do you remember what happened to Dris?"

Hackman: "It was his own fault that he got his hand snapped off. He shouldn't have teased it. Besides, the hound likes me."

Wilson: "Yes, I've seen him look at you and lick his chops. You'll have a lot more than a scratched cheek—or a snapped-off hand—to snivel about if we don't clear up this mess right away. Come on. To begin with, we've got to kill that cat."

Carr heard footsteps, then the sound of Wilson's voice growing fainter as he ascended the stairs, calling wheedlingly, "Here, kitty," and a few moment later Hackman's joined in with a sugariness that made Carr shake: "Here, kitty, kitty."

Carr tiptoed across the room and peered through the bathroom door. The white-tiled cubicle was empty, but beyond it he could see another bedroom that was smaller but friendlier. There was a littered dressing table with lamps whose little pink shades were awry. Beside that was a small bookcase overflowing with sheet music piled helter-skelter.

His heart began to pound as he crossed the bathroom's white tiles.

But there was something strange about the bedroom he was approaching. Despite the lively adolescent order, there was a museum feel to it, like some historic room kept just as its illustrious occupant had left it. The novel open face down on the dressing table was last year's best-seller.

He poked his head through the door. Something moved beside him and he quickly turned his head.

He had only a moment to look before the blackjack struck. But in that instant, before the cap of pain was pulled down over his eyes and ears, blacking out everything, he recognized his assailant.

The cords in the neck stood out, the cheeks were drawn back, exposing the big front teeth like those of a rat. Indeed the whole aspect—watery magnified eyes, low forehead, taut and spindle-limbed figure—was that of a cornered rat.

It was the small dark man with glasses.

CHAPTER X

I've told you to forget the secret, but I've got to admit that's a hard thing to do. Once a mind wakes up, it's got an itch to know the whole truth . . .

A black sea was churning in front of Carr, but he couldn't look out into it because there was a row of lights just a little way beyond his feet, so bright that they made his head ache violently. He danced about in pain, flapping his arms. It seemed a degrading thing to be doing, even if he were in pain so he tried to stop, but he couldn't.

Eventually his agonized prancing turned him around and he saw behind him a forest of dark shabby trees and between them glimpses of an unconvincing dingy gray sky. Then he whirled a little way farther and saw that Jane was beside him, dancing as madly as he. She still wore her sweater, but her skirt had become short and tight, like a flapper's, and there were bright pats of rouge on her cheeks. She looked floppy as a French doll.

The pain in his head lessened and he made a violent effort to stop his frantic dancing so he could go over and stop hers, but it was no use. Then for the first time he noticed thin black cords going up from his wrists and knees. He rolled his eyes and saw that there were others going up from his shoulders and head and the small of his back. He followed them up with his eyes and saw that they were attached to a huge wooden cross way up. A giant hand gripped the cross, making it waggle. Above it, filling the roof of the sky, was the ruddy face of Wilson.

Carr looked down quickly. He was thankful the footlights were so bright that he couldn't see anything of the silent audience.

Then a thin, high screaming started and the cords stopped tugging at him, so that at least he didn't have to dance. A steady pull on his ear turned his head slowly around, so that he was looking into the forest. The same thing was happening to Jane. The screaming grew and there bounded fantastically from the forest, the cords jerking him higher than his head, the puppet of the small dark man with glasses. His face was carved in an expression of rat-like fear. He fell in a disjointed heap at Carr's feet and pawed at Carr with his stiff hands. He kept gibbering something Carr couldn't understand. Every once in a while he would turn and point the way he had come and gibber the louder and scrabble the more frantically at Carr's chest.

Finally his backward looks became a comically terrified head-wagging and he resumed his flight, bounding off the stage in a single leap.

Carr and Jane continued to stare at the forest.

Then she said, in a high squeaking voice, "Oh save me!"

and came tripping over to him and flung her corded arms loosely around his neck and he felt his jaw move on a string through his head and heard a falsetto voice that came from above reply, "I certainly will, my princess."

Then he pawed around on the ground as if he were hunting for something and she clung to him in a silly way, impeding his efforts. Finally a cord that went up his sleeve pulled a little sword into his hand. Then he saw something coming out of the forest, something that wasn't nice.

It was a very large hound, colored a little darker slate gray than the sky, with red eyes and a huge tusky jaw. But what was nasty about it as it came nosing through the trees was that, although there were cords attached to it at the proper points, they were all slack. It reached the edge of the forest and lifted its head and fixed its red eyes on them.

There followed a ridiculous battle in which the hound pretended to attack Carr and Jane, and he flailed about him with his sword. At one point the hound grabbed Jane's arm in its teeth and he poked at it, but it was all make-believe. Then he made a wilder lunge and the hound turned over on its back and pretended to die, but all the while its red eyes looked at him knowingly.

Then, as he and Jane embraced woodenly, the curtain swished down without the least applause from the silent audience, and he and Jane were twitched high into the air. A hand with red-lacquered nails as big as coal-shovels grabbed him and Hackman peered at him so closely that the pores of her skin were like smallpox pits.

"This little one looks as if it might be coming alive," she rumbled. The nails pinched his arm so cruelly that it was all he could do not to cry out.

"You're imagining things," came Wilson's voice like distant thunder. "Just like those black hats you thought you saw in the audience. What bothers me is that I can't find the little sword."

"Never mind," Hackman replied, and her breath was like a wind from rotting flowerbeds. "Dris will check on it."

"Dris!" Wilson boomed contemptuously. "Come on, put the puppet away."

"Very well," Hackman said, hanging Carr by his cords to a high hook. "But listen to me, little one," and she shook Carr until his teeth rattled. "If you ever come alive, I will give you to the hound!" She let him go. He swung and hit the wall so hard it knocked the breath out of him and he had to fight not to writhe.

With earthquake treadings and creakings, Wilson and Hackman went away. Carr looked cautiously to either side. To his left, a wooden shelf projected from the wall at about the level of his head. To his right Jane hung. Other dangling puppets were dark blobs beyond her.

Then Carr withdrew from his jacket the sword he had hidden there just before the curtain came down, and with it he cut the black cords attached to his knees, then all the others but those fixed to his wrists. He saw that Jane was watching him.

He tucked his sword in his belt and, gripping his wrist cords, pumped with his arms so that he was swinging back and forth along the wall. Soon the swings became so long that his feet were just missing the edge of the wooden shelf and he was soaring well above it. On the next swing he managed to catch hold of one of Jane's cords. It burned his hand as they careened wildly, but he held on until they came to rest.

Then came ticklish work. Supporting himself on Jane's cords, he cut his own last two, keeping hold of one of them and making a little loop at the bottom. Setting his foot in this stirrup, he took Jane around the waist. He hooked his other arm around the stirrup-string, drew his sword with that arm, and cut all of Jane's cords. As the last one parted, he felt she was no longer a limp puppet slung over his arm, but a tiny living woman.

Next moment they were swinging through space. He let the sword fall and clung to the string with that hand. And now he realized that the shortened string was carrying them too high. He let go his hand, kicking loose with his foot, and dropped with Jane. They landed on the edge of the shelf with a breath-taking jar, just managed to wriggle to safety with stomach and knee.

Then they were running along the shelf. From that they dropped to the top of a book-case, to a table, to a chair and so to the floor. Ahead of them was a huge door, slightly ajar. Carr knew it led to safety.

But at that moment there began a high thin screaming. Looking back, Carr saw that it came from the puppet of the small dark man with glasses, who had been hanging beyond Jane.

"You wouldn't take me," he screamed.

And now other sounds could be heard—giant footsteps.

Grabbing Jane's wrist, Carr sprinted toward the door, but to his dismay he found that his legs were becoming wobbly. He prayed for strings to make them move. Furthermore, the floor was acquiring an oddly yielding texture. It was as if he and Jane, rubber-jointed, were trying to run through piled hay.

The screaming became earsplitting.

Throwing back a quick glance over his shoulder, Carr saw the angry faces of Wilson and Hackman careening toward him like huge red balloons.

But much nearer, in fact just at his heels, bounded the hound. Tucked back between its slavering jaws was a bitten-off hand.

Carr made one last effort to increase his speed. He sprawled headlong on the billowy floor.

He felt stiff paws on his back, pinning him down. He squirmed around and grappled feebly. The screaming continued.

But then the hound seemed to collapse, to crumple under his fingers. Hitching himself up, he realized that he was in his own room, in his own bed, fighting the bedclothes, and that the screaming in his ears was the siren of a passing fire engine.

He shakily thrust his feet out of bed and sat on the edge of it, waiting for the echoes of his nightmare to stop swirling through his senses.

His head ached miserably. Lifting his hand, he felt a large sensitive lump. He recalled the small dark man hitting him, though the memory was still mixed up with the dream-betrayal.

Pale light was sifting through the window. He went over to the bureau, opened the top drawer. He looked at the three pint bottles of whisky. He chose the quarter full one, poured himself a drink, downed it, poured himself another, looked around.

The clothes he had been wearing were uncharacteristically laid out on a chair.

His head began to feel less like a whirlpool. He went over

and looked out the window. The pale light was not that of dawn, but gathering evening. Unwillingly he decided that he had been unconscious not only last night, but also all of today.

A coolness on his fingers told him that whisky was dribbling out of the shot glass. He drank it and turned around. A gust of anger at the small dark man (may be your friend!) went through him.

Just then he noticed a blank envelope propped on the mantlepiece. He took it down, snapped on a light, opened it, unfolded the closely scribbled note it contained. It was from Jane.

You're in danger, Carr, terrible danger. Don't stir out of your room today. Stay away from the window. Don't answer if anyone knocks.

I'm terribly sorry about last night. My friend is sorry too, now that he knows who you are. He thought you were with Wilson and Hackman, so his attack on you was excusable. We would stay with you longer, but our mere presence would mean too much danger for you. My friend says you'll come out of it okay.

I'm sorry that I can't explain things more. But it's better for you not to know too much.

Don't try to find me, Carr. It isn't only that you'd risk your own life. You'd endanger mine. My friend and I are up against an organization that can't be beaten, only hidden from. If you try to find me, you'll only spoil my chances.

You want a long happy life, don't you?—not just a few wretched months or hours before you're hunted down. Then your only chance is to do what I tell you.

Stay in your room all day. Then arrange your things just as you usually do before going to work in the morning. Set your alarm for the usual time. You must be very exact—a lot depends on it. Above all, burn this letter—on your honor do that. Then dissolve in a glass of water the powders you'll find on the table beside your bed, and drink it. In a little while you'll go to sleep and when you wake up, everything will be all right.

You may not believe me, but what reason would I have to lie? Honestly, Carr, your only chance to get clear of the danger you're in, and to help me, is to do exactly what I've told you. And forget me forever.

Carr walked over to the bed. On the little table, leaning against an empty tumbler, were two slim paper packets. He felt one between finger and thumb. It gritted.

He glanced again at the letter. His head had begun to ache stabbingly. Phrases that were anger-igniting sparks jumped at him: ". . . is sorry too . . . excusable . . ." What sort of a nincompoop did they think he was. Next she'd be saying, "So sorry we had to poison you." She was a nice girl, all right—of the sort who throws her arms around you so her boyfriend can stick a gun in your ribs.

He'd blundered into a nasty affair, and maybe he'd picked the wrong side.

And she did have a reason to lie. She might want to scare him off, keep him from discovering what she and her precious friend were up to, maybe gain time for some sort of getaway.

He hurried into his clothes, wincing at the jabs of pain. After pulling on his topcoat, he drained the last shot from the whisky bottle, tossed it back in the drawer, looked at the full bottles a moment, stuck one in his pocket, and went out, glaring savagely at the mirror-imprisoned Carr on the stairs.

He walked a block to the nearest hotel and waited for a cab. Two cruised by with their flags up, but the drivers ignored his arm-wavings and calls. He ground his teeth. Then one drew in to the curb, but just as he was getting ready to board it, two cold-eyed show-girls from the hotel swept by him and piled in. He swore out loud, turned on his heel and started walking deliberately.

It was a nice evening and he detested it. He felt a senseless rage at the people he passed. How nice it would be to smash all the neon signs, rip down the posters, break into the houses and toss out of the windows the crooning, moaning, brightly-blatting radios. Come the atom bomb!

But for all that, the fresh air was helping his head. As he neared Mayberry Street he began to calm down, or at least focus his anger.

Halfway down the last block a car was parked with its motor softly chugging—a roadster with its top down. Just as he passed it, Carr saw a heavily-built man come out of the entry to the Gregg apartment. He strolled off in the opposite direction but Carr had already recognized him. It was Wilson.

Repressing the fear that surged through him, Carr made a snap decision and hurried after him.

But just then a voice behind him said, "If you value your life or your reason, keep away from that man." At the same time a hand gripped his elbow and spun him around.

This time the small dark man with glasses was wearing a black snap-brim hat and a tightly buttoned trenchcoat. And this time he didn't look terrified. Instead he was sardonically smiling. He rocked back and forth on his heels teetering precariously.

"I knew you wouldn't stay in your room," he said. "I told Jane her letter would have just the opposite effect."

Carr doubled his fist, swung back his arm, hesitated. Damn it, he *did* wear glasses—pitifully thick-lensed ones.

"Go ahead," said the small dark man, "make a scene. Bring them down on us. I don't care."

Carr stared at the glasses bright with reflected street light. He caught a whiff of liquor.

"You wouldn't think, would you," the small dark man mused, "that as we stand here, conversing idly, we are both in deadly peril." He smiled. "No, I'm sure you wouldn't think that..And as for me, I'm not afraid of anything."

"Listen," Carr said, advancing with balled fist, "you slugged me last night. I didn't like that."

"So I did," said the small dark man, again rocking on his heels.

"Well, in that case—" Carr began, and then remembered Wilson. He whirled around. The portly man was nowhere in sight. He took a few steps then looked back. The small dark man was walking rapidly toward the purring roadster. Carr darted after him and sprang on the running board just as the other slipped behind the wheel.

"You wanted to distract me until he was gone," Carr accused. "You didn't want me to talk to him."

"That's right," the small dark man said carelessly. "Jump in."

Angrily Carr complied, as the small dark man pushed down on the clutch, shifted into first and stretched out in that position, put his face close to Carr's and began to talk. His words rode on a wind of whisky, but the voice was bitter and confessional.

"In the first place," he said, "I hate you—otherwise I'd be doing my best to get you out of this instead of leading you straight toward the center. I don't care what happens to you and tonight I don't give a damn what happens to me. But I still have a certain quixotic concern for Jane's feelings—her li'l romantic dreams. It's for her sake that I'm going to do what I'm going to do."

"And what are you going to do?" snapped Carr.

The roadster bucked, leaped forward with a roar.

CHAPTER XI

When you know the world's a big engine, it may go to your head. You'll think you can take crazy chances. But the big engine can chew you up just as quick as an ordinary engine chews up a smart-alecky factory hand. . .

Carr's gaze swung up as the grimy bed wall of a truck loomed higher, higher. "World Movers," the sign said. He closed his eyes. He felt a blood-checking swerve and a chalk-on-slate caress along their fender. When he opened his eyes again, it was to see a woman and child flash by not a foot from the running board. He lurched side-ways as they screamed around a corner, let go his hat to cling to the car, watched a coupe and streetcar converge ahead of them, closed his eyes again as they grazed through the gap.

"Stop, you idiot!" he commanded. "You're drunk!"

The small dark man leered at him. "That's right," he said triumphantly and turned back to the wheel just in time to miss taking the side off a parked sedan.

To either side small indistinguishable stores and dusty white street globes shot by, while blocks of brick and gleaming streetcar tracks vanished under the hood.

"Tell me what its all about before you kill us," Carr yelled.

The small man snickered through his teeth. His hat blew off. Watching it go, Carr demanded, "Are you one of the men with black hats?"

The roadster went into a screaming skid. Carr cringed as a hot-dog vender's white stand ballooned in size. But the small dark man managed to straighten the roadster out in time, though Carr got a whiff of hot dogs.

"Don't ask questions like that," the small dark man warned. "I'm not brave." Then he goggled at Carr, drove with his left hand for a moment while he tapped his bare head with his right and said wisely, "Protective coloration."

Ahead cars skittered to the curb like disturbed ants. Over the motor's roar Carr became aware of a wailing that grew in volume. A wild white light mixed with red began to flood the street from behind them, its beam swinging back and forth like a giant pendulum. Then from the corner of his eye Carr noticed a seated man in a big black slicker heave into view several feet above him, creep abreast. Below the man was a vermilion hood. Behind him were dim ladders and coils, other slickered figures.

Ahead the street took a jog. It was impossible for both the roadster and the fire engine to get through.

Grinning, the small dark man nursed the throttle. The fire engine dropped back just enough for them to careen through the gap ahead of it, under a maze of trolley wires, while frozen pedestrians gaped.

Carr's fear left him. There was no use to it.

The street narrowed, its sides grew dark. Behind them the fire engine braked, took a turn.

"You're mixed up with Wilson and Hackman and Dris, aren't you?" Carr asserted loudly.

This time the roadster swerved to the left, and for a few moments roared along only inches from the curb, kicking up mud.

"Not that brave," the small dark man told him reprovingly as the roadster came back into the middle.

Carr caught a cold whiff of water and oil. Skyscrapers twinkled against the sky ahead, but just this side of them a gap in the buildings was widening and a black skeletal structure loomed.

A rapid clanging started. Towers flanking the black structure began to blink red. Carr grabbed for the wheel, stamped at the brake. "They're opening the bridge!" he yelled.

The small man kicked him in the ankle, clubbed his hands aside, and accelerated. Ahead were stopped autos and a black and white barrier. Swinging far to the left, they struck its flexible end. It rasped along the roadster's side, tore free with a great twang. They shot forward onto the dark span. To either side solidity dropped away. Far below, yellow windows of skyscrapers flowed in uneven patterns on the water.

They were three-quarters of the way across when, through their hurtling speed, Carr felt the feather touch of a titan. Under them the span had begun to rise. Ahead of them a thread of blackness appeared at the break in the jack-knife of the span.

The small dark man clamped the throttle to the floor. There was a spine-compressing jar and jounce, the skyscrapers reeled, then another jar as the roadster came down—on its wheels. The tip of the second barrier broke off with a giant snap.

The open bridge had cleared the street ahead of traffic going their way. The small dark man breezed along it for four blocks like the winner of a race, then suddenly braked and skidded around the corner and across to the wrong side of the street. The two wheels on his side hit the curb and the roadster rocked to a stop.

. Carr loosened his death-grip on dashboard and door handle, balled a fist and turned, this time without any compunction about glasses.

But the small dark man had vaulted out of the roadster and was lightly running up the steps of a building that Carr now realized was the public library. As he hit the sidewalk in pursuit, he saw the small dark man briefly silhouetted against the yellow rectangle of a swinging door. When Carr stiff-armed through it, the man was vanishing at the top of a flight of marble stairs.

Reaching the top, Carr felt a spurt of savage pleasure. He was gaining. Before him was a large, domed room, open shelves to one side, counters and booths to the other, unoccupied except for a couple of girls behind a window and a baldheaded man burdened with a stack of books and a briefcase.

The small dark man, with Carr almost at his heels, was racing toward a wall decorated with twinkling gold mosaic. He ducked down a narrow corridor and to his shock Carr realized they were both running on glass.

For a moment Carr thought that the small dark man had led him this long chase solely to get him to step through a skylight. Then he realized that he was on one of the many translucent cat-walks that served as aisles in the stacks of the library. He sprinted forward again, guided by the sonorous pit-pat of receding footsteps.

He found himself in a silent world within a world. A world several stories high and covering a good part of a block. An oddly insubstantial world of metal beams, narrow stairs, translucent runways, and innumerable books.

Like some animal that had reached its native element, the small dark man now held his lead, craftily doubling and redoubling his course. Carr caught glimpses of a cream-colored raincoat, he shook his fist at teeth and a grin spied through gaps in successive tiers of books, he clutched futilely at a small, expensive-looking shoe disappearing up a metal-treaded stair in a tantalizingly leisurely way.

He was panting and his side had begun to hurt, something in his topcoat was growing heavier. It began to seem to him that the chase would never end, that the two of them would go skipping and staggering on indefinitely, always the same distance apart.

The whole experience had acquired nightmarish overtones. It pleased Carr to remember that the Dewey Decimal System of book classification has an end. "If I don't catch him in the four hundreds, I'll get him in the fives. If not in the useful arts, then in the fine. He shan't double back to Mysticism and Witchcraft!"

He lurched around a corner and there, not ten feet away, back turned, standing beside an old brass-fitted drinking fountain that gurgled merrily, was his quarry.

Carr hiccuped a laugh between his gasps for air. This was no sinister metaphysical pursuit after all. It was just a chase in a Chaplin film. They would both refresh themselves at the fountain, commenting on the excellence of the water. Then the small dark man would nod politely and walk off. Carr would realize with whom he'd been drinking, and the whole chase would start over again.

But first, Carr decided, he'd slug the guy.

As he moved forward, however, it was inevitable that he should look at the thing at which the small dark man was looking.

Or rather, at the person.

For just inside the next aisle, gilt-buttoned brown suit almost exactly the same shade as the buckram bindings that made a background, lips formed in an ellipse of dismay that couldn't quite avoid being a smile, was Jane.

Carr drifted past the small dark man as if the latter were part of a dissolving dream. With every step forward the floor seemed to get solider under his feet.

Jane's lips held the same shape, she just tilted her head, as he put his arms around her and kissed her. He felt as if he had grasped the one real figure out of thousands in a room of mirrors.

She pushed away, looking up at him incredulously. His nerves reawoke with a jerk. "Where's he gone?" he asked, looking around him.

"Who?"

"The small dark madman with glasses."

"I don't know," she said. "He has a way of fading."

"I'll say he has!" He turned on her. "Though generally he tries to murder you first." His hands were beginning to tremble from delayed reaction to his ride.

"What?"

"Yes. I thought you said he was retiring. Even timid."

"He is. Terribly."

"Then you should have seen him tonight." And he told her about the ride. "I guess he got his courage out of a bottle," he finished, really shaking now.

"Oh, the coward," she breathed. "Pretending to sacrifice his own feelings, even to the point of bringing you to me— but really just doing it to hurt me, because he knew I wanted to keep you out of this. And then on top of it all, taking chances with your life, hoping that you both would die while he was being noble." Her lips curled.

"All right, all right!" Carr said, "But what's it all about?"

"What do you mean?"

"You know what I mean. Your friend and Hackman and Wilson and Dris and the four men with black hats and you being Tom Elvested's Jane Gregg, who wasn't there, and Jane Gregg of Mayberry Street."

She backed away from him, shaking her head.

He followed her. His voice was harsh. "Look, Jane," he said, "day before yesterday your friend ran away from me. Last night he knocked me out. Tonight he took crazy chances with my life. Why?"

The fear in her eyes brought his exasperation to the boil. "What have you and he done? Why are the others after you? What's wrong with your father and mother? What are you doing here? You've got to tell me!"

He had her backed against the shelves and was shouting in her face. But she would only goggle up at him and shake her head. His control snapped. He grabbed her by the shoulders and shook her hard.

But no matter how violently her head snapped back and forth, her lips stayed pressed tightly together. He suddenly loosed her and turned away, burying his head in his hands, breathing heavily.

When he looked up she was smoothing her suit. She bit her lip when her hand touched her shoulder. "Do I shake well?"

He winced. "Sorry," he said dully. "But I've just got to know."

"It would be the worst thing that could happen to you," she told him simply.

"I don't care."

"It would be like signing your death warrant."

"I tell you I don't care." He looked at her in a misery of exasperation. "Jane!"

"All right," she said quietly, "I'll tell you everything."

He looked at her incredulously. Then his eyes widened. For the first time he actually realized where he was.

"We've got to get out of here!" he said, jumping away from the shelves against which he'd been leaning.

"Why?" She was as cool as ever.

"We're in the stacks." His voice automatically hushed itself. "No one can come here without a pass. We made enough racket to wake the dead. They're bound to come looking for us."

"Are they?" She smiled. "They haven't yet."

"And then—oh Good Lord—the traffic cops and who knows who else . . . they're bound to!" He looked down the long aisles apprehensively.

She smiled again. "But they haven't."

Carr turned wondering eyes on her. Something of the charming willfulness of the night before last seemed to have returned to her. He felt an answering spirit rising in himself.

And it did seem the height of silliness to worry about breaking library regulations just after you'd escaped a messy death a dozen times—and were about to hear the most important story in the world.

"All right," he said, "in that case let's have a drink." And he fished out of his pocket the unopened pint of whisky.

"Swell," she said, her eyes brightening. "The fountain's right there. I'll get paper cups."

CHAPTER XII

Of course if there's someone you really love, you've got to tell them the secret. For love means sharing everything, even the horrors . . .

Carr lowered his cup, half emptied.

"Listen," he said, "there's someone coming."

Jane seemed unconcerned. "Just a page."

"How do you know? Besides, he's coming this way."

He hustled Jane to the next aisle, where there was less light. The footsteps grew louder, ringing on the glass.

"Let's go farther back," Carr whispered. "He might see us here."

But Jane refused to budge. He peered over her shoulder. "Damn!" he breathed, "I forgot the bottle. He's bound to spot it."

Jane's shoulders twitched.

The he turned out to be a she, Carr saw by patches through the gaps between the shelves. A she with sleek black hair cut in bangs across the forehead, and a tight, dark red dress. She walked past their aisle, stopped at the second one beyond. She looked up.

"Here we are, boys and girls," they heard her say to herself in a loud bitter voice. "Oh, in six volumes, is it? Is that all he expects at closing time?" She scribbled briefly on a slip of paper she was carrying. "Sorry, Baldy, but—out! You'll have to learn about the secrets of sex some other day."

And she returned the way she had come, humming "St. Louis Woman."

Carr recovered the bottle. "Quite a character," he said with a smile. "I'm not sure but what she didn't see us."

Jane gave him a look. Then she went to the next aisle and returned with a couple of stools. Carr pushed his topcoat back over some books. His face grew serious. For a moment they were silent. Then he said, "Well, I'm waiting."

Jane moved nervously. "Let's have another drink."

Carr refilled their cups. Jane just held hers. It was shadowy where they were. She reached up and tugged a cord. Extra light spilled around them. There was another pause. Jane looked at him.

"You must think of my childhood," she began, "as an empty, middle-class upbringing in a city apartment. You must think of me as miserable and lonely, with a few girlfriends whom I thought silly and at the same time more knowing than I. And then my parents—familiar creatures I was terribly tied to, but with whom I had no real contact. They seemed to go unhappily through a daily routine as sterile as death.

"The whole world was an ugly mystery to me. I didn't know what people were after, why they did the things they did, what secret rules they were obeying. I used to take long walks alone in the park, trying to figure it out." She paused. "It was in the park that I first met the small dark man with glasses.

"No," she corrected herself, frowning, "I didn't exactly meet him. I just noticed him watching me. Usually from a distance—from another path, or across the lagoon, or through a crowd of people. He'd watch me and follow me for a way and then drift out of sight and maybe turn up again farther on.

"I pretended not to notice him. I knew that strange men who followed girls were not to be trusted. Though I don't think I was ever frightened of him that way. He looked so small and·respectful. Actually I suppose I was beginning to feel romantic about him." She took a swallow of her drink.

Carr had finished his. "Well?"

"Oh, he kept coming closer and then one day he spoke to me. 'Would you mind if I walked with you for a while?' he asked. I gulped and managed to say, 'No.' That's all. He just walked beside me. It was days before he even touched my arm. But that didn't. matter. It was what he said that was important. He talked hesitatingly, but he knew the thoughts inside me I'd never told anyone—how puzzling life was, how alone you felt, how other people sometimes seemed just like animals, how they could hurt you with their eyes. And he knew the little pictures in my mind too—how the piano keys looked like champing teeth, how written words were just meaningless twists of ribbon, how snores sounded like faraway railway trains and railway trains like snores.

"After we'd walked for a while that first day, I saw two of

my girlfriends ahead. He said, 'I'll leave you now,' and went off. I was glad, for I wouldn't have known how to introduce him.

"That first walk set a pattern, almost as if we'd learned a list of magic rules. We must always meet as if by accident and part without warning. We must never go any special place. We must never tell our names. We must never talk of tomorrow or plan anything, just yield to a fatalistic enchantment. Of course I never mentioned my friend to a soul. Away from the park I'd say, 'You dreamed him, Jane,' almost believing it. But the next afternoon I'd go back and he'd appear and I'd walk with him and have the feeling of a friend seeing into my mind. It went on that way for quite a while." She emptied her cup.

"And then things changed?" Carr asked as he poured her more.

"In a way."

"Did he start to make love to you? It would seem he . . ."

"No. Perhaps that was what was wrong. Perhaps if he'd made love to me, everything would have been all right. But he never did any more than take my arm. He was like a man who walks with a gun at his back. I sensed a terrible, mute tension inside him, born of timidity or twisted pride, a seething flood of frustrated energy. Eventually it began to seep over into me. For no good reason my heart would start to pound, I could hardly breathe, and little spasms would race up and down me. And all the while he'd be talking calmly. It was awful. I think I would have done something to break that tension between us, except for the magic rules and the feeling that everything would be spoiled if we once disobeyed them. So I did nothing. And then things began to get much worse."

"How do you mean?" Carr asked.

Jane looked up at him. Now that she was lost in her story, she looked younger than ever.

"We were stuck, that's what it amounted to, and we began to rot. All that knowledge he had of my queer thoughts began to terrify me. Because, you see, I'd always believed that they were just quirks of my mind, and that by sharing them I'd get rid of them. I kept waiting for him to tell me how silly they were. But he never did. Instead, I began to see from the way he talked that my queer thoughts weren't illusions at all, but the truth. Nothing did mean anything.

Snores actually were a kind of engine-puffing, and printed words had no more real meaning than wind-tracings in sand. Other people weren't alive, really alive, like you were. You were all alone."

A bell clanged. They both started.

Jane relaxed. "Closing time," she explained.

Carr shrugged. That they were in the stacks of the library had become inconsequential to him. "Go on," he said.

"Now the walks did begin to affect the rest of my life. All day long I'd be plunged in gloom. My father and mother seemed a million miles away, my classes at the music academy the stupidest things in the world. And yet I didn't show anything outwardly. No one noticed any change, except Gigolo my cat, who sometimes acted afraid and spat at me, yet sometimes came purring to me in a most affectionate way—and sometimes watched at the windows and doors for hours, as if he were on guard. I was lost and not one soul tried to save me, not even my man in the park."

She took a drink and leaned back. "And then one autumn day when the clouds were low and the fallen leaves crackled under our feet, and we'd walked farther together than ever before, in fact a little way out of the park, I happened to look across the street and I noticed a spruce young man looking at us. I called my friend's attention to him. He peered around through his thick glasses.

"The next instant he had grabbed me tight above the elbow and was marching me ahead. He didn't speak until we got around the corner. Then he said, in a voice I'd never heard him use before, 'They have seen us. Get home.'

"I started to ask questions, but he only said, 'Don't talk. Don't look back.' I was frightened and obeyed him.

"In the hours afterwards my fear grew. I pictured 'them' in a hundred horrible ways. I went to sleep praying never to see the small dark man again and just be allowed to live my old stupid life.

"Some time after midnight I awoke with my heart jumping, and there was Gigolo standing on the bedclothes spitting at the window. I made myself get up and tiptoe to it. Two dark things rose above the outside sill. They were the top of a ladder resting against it. I looked down. Light from the alley showed me the smiling face of the young man I'd seen across the street that afternoon. You know him, Carr. The one they call Dris—Driscoll Ames. He had two hands then. He reached them up to open the bedroom window.

"I ran to my father's and mother's room. I called to them to wake up. I shook them, And then came the most terrible shock of my life. They wouldn't wake, no matter what I did. Except that they breathed, they might have been dead. I remember pounding my father's chest and digging my nails into his arms.

"I think that even without Gigolo's warning snarl and the sound of footsteps coming swiftly through the bathroom, I would have rushed out of the apartment, rather than stay a moment longer with those two living corpses who had brought me into the world."

Her voice was getting high. Carr looked uneasily down the empty, booklined aisles.

"I darted down the front stairs and there, peering at our mailbox, I saw an older man. You know him too, Carr. Wilson. He looked at me through the glass panel of the inner door and then he looked at my nightdress, and then he smiled like the young man on the ladder.

"With steps pounding down the stairs there was only one way for me to go. I ran down through the basement, past the stone wash tubs and the padlocked storage rooms, and out into the dirty cement area-way. And there, standing in the alley, in the light of one high naked bulb, I saw my handsome fairy godmother."

Carr blinked. She smiled thinly and said, "Oh yes, my fairy godmother, just like Cinderella's, come to rescue me. A tall beautiful golden haired woman in a golden evening dress. There was a black band around her wrist, like the strap of a handbag.

"Then I saw that the black band was a leash, and at the other end of the leash was a huge hound that stood high as her waist and was dirty gray like the fence behind them. It was snuffing at the rubbish.

"Then Hackman—for of course it was she—saw me crouching under the back porches and her lips formed in a smile, but it was different from the men's smiles, because it was at the thought that the hound would get me before the men.

"Just at that moment Gigolo shot past my legs with squalling cry and hurtled off down the alley. With a great bound the hound was after him, dragging my fairy godmother after him stumbling and slipping, ignoring her curses and frantic commands, dirtying her lovely golden gown. And I was racing off in the opposite direction, the hound's baying filling my ears.

"I ran for blocks, turning corners, cutting across lawns, before I stopped—and then only because I couldn't run any farther. But it was enough. I seemed to have gotten away to safety.

"But what was I to do? I was cold. The windows peered. The street lights whispered. The shadows pawed. There was always someone crossing a corner two blocks away. I thought of a girlfriend who was at least a little closer to me than the others, a girl named Midge who was studying at the music academy.

"She lived in a duplex just a few blocks away. Keeping out of the light as much as I could, I hurried over to it. Her bedroom window was open a little. I threw some pebbles at it, but nothing happened. I didn't like to ring. Finally I managed to step from the porch to her window and crawl inside. She was asleep, breathing easily. But this time I was telling myself that my father and mother had been drugged as part of a plan to kidnap me. But not for long.

"For you see, I was no more able to rouse Midge than my parents.

"I dressed in some of her clothes and climbed out the window and walked the streets until morning. Then I tried to go home, but I went cautiously, spying out the way, and that was lucky, for in a parked automobile across from our apartment sat Wilson. I went to the academy and saw Hackman standing at the head of the steps. I went to the park and there, where my small dark man used to wait for me, was Dris. And then I knew for sure."

"Knew what?" Carr asked after a pause.

She looked at him. "You know," she said. "You told me yourself in front of the Art Institute."

"What?" Carr repeated uneasily.

Her face seemed incredibly tiny as she sat hunched on her stool, her brown suit shading into the background. The stacks were silent, the mutter of the city was inaudible, a scampering mouse at the other end of the building might have been heard. In all directions the narrowing aisles stretched off. All around them was the pressure of the hundreds of thousands of books. But always the tunneling gaps, the peepholes, the gaps between the books.

And then, one by one, moving in on them, the lights in the stacks began to wink out.

"Just that everything's dead," Jane whispered. "Just that people are corpses. You don't have to have the psychologists tell you that consciousness is unnecessary. You don't have to listen to the scientists who say that everything's atoms. All you have to do is read the schoolbooks, the schoolbooks written by dead minds the same way a newspaper is printed by dead metal. They all tell you the same thing—that the universe is just a big machine."

CHAPTER XIII

If you can't get back to your place in the machine, your chances are slim, brother. By being smart and never making a mistake, you may be able to stay alive. But it's lonely work, even if you've got a buddy. . . .

"No," Carr breathed. All the lights had gone out except the one above their heads, which seemed to glow like some limpid eye.

Jane smiled at his crookedly. "But you told me that yourself," she repeated, "not knowing half of what you know now. Just a big machine, that's all it is. Except every now and then a mind awakens, or is awakened by another mind. One in a million. If the wakened mind keeps to its place in the machine, it may be safe. But if it leaves its place, God help it!"

"Why?" Carr asked unwillingly.

"Because the pattern won't change for it—and the minds that have weakened first will hunt it down and destroy it. Or else they'll corrupt it."

"Why should that be?" Carr demanded. "Why wouldn't the wakened minds want to waken other minds, more and more of them, until the whole machine's awake?"

Jane's lips shaped themselves in a sneer. "Because that isn't the way wakened minds operate—and besides, they can't waken other minds, except in a few lucky cases by a tremendous and uncontrollable effort of will. But they don't want to waken other minds, except to torture them. They're selfish and frightened and mad with desire. They glory in being able to do whatever they want, no matter how cruel or obscene, in a dead world that can't stop them." (There sprang into Carr's mind the memory of the four men with black hats and the dead-alive mannequin.) "They're deathly afraid of rivals stealing their privileged position—and every wakened mind is a rival, to be corrupted and joined with them in their selfishness, or else destroyed. All they can see is the prey and the loot."

"No," Carr breathed, "I can't believe it."

"Can't believe it!" Again Jane smiled crookedly. "If you'd seen and known what I've seen and known this past year—"

"Year?" Carr said incredulously.

"Yes, it's that long since I ran away from my fairy godmother. Give me another drink. No, more. And take some yourself. Yes, a whole year."

She drank greedily and looked at him for a while. "Do you know Chicago, Carr? I do. I know it like a big museum, with all sorts of interesting dead things in the showcases and the animated exhibits. At times it's almost restful. And at times it's almost beautiful, like an elaborate automaton set before a European king. Only every once in a great while you see someone else in the museum, perhaps at the end of a long corridor. You might call them the museum guards, for they don't want you to be there. And you can't go home from the museum, you have to live there forever. Is there anything left in the bottle?"

"A little," he said. "No, enough for two."

"I've lived a year in the museum," she continued, receiving the paper cup from him. "I've slept in parks, in empty furnished flats, in department store display rooms, in that boarded-up old Beddoes mansion, on leather couches in clubs and waiting rooms that are closed at night, on stolen campbeds in offices and warehouses—but not in empty hotel rooms, for you can't tell when they'll be occupied. I've stolen food from delicatessens, snatched it from the plates of people who couldn't see me or anything, gone straight into the kitchens of the most expensive restaurants—and hooked candy bars from drugstore stands. Shall I tell you about the blind crowds I've threaded through, the unseeing trucks I've dodged, the time I got blood-poisoning and cured it myself behind a prescription counter, the theaters I've haunted, the churches I've crept into, the els I've ridden back and forth for hours, the books I've read down here—and all of it alone."

"Still you had one person," Carr said slowly. "The small dark man with glasses."

"That's right," she said bitterly, "we did meet again."

"I suppose you lived together?" Carr asked simply.

She looked at him. "No, we didn't. We'd meet here and there, and he taught me how to play chess—we played for days and days—but I never lived with him."

Carr hesitated. "But surely he must have tried to make love to you," he said. "And when you realized there was no one in the whole world but the two of you . . ."

"You're right," she said uncomfortably. "He did try to make love to me."

"And you didn't reciprocate?"

"No."

"Don't be angry with me, Jane, but that seems strange. After all, you had only each other."

She laughed unhappily. "Oh, I would have reciprocated, except for something I found out about him. I don't like to talk about it, but I suppose I'd better. A few weeks after I ran away, I met him in another park. I came on him unawares and found him holding a little girl. She was standing there, flushed from running, looking very alive, her bright eyes on her playmates, about to rush off and join them. He was sitting on the bench behind her and he had his arm lightly around her and he was stroking her body very tenderly, but with a look in his eyes as if she were so much wood. Sacred wood, perhaps, but wood." Jane sucked in her breath. "After that I couldn't bear to have him touch me. In spite of all his gentleness and understanding, there was a part of him that wanted to take advantage of the big machine for his cold private satisfactions—take advantage of poor dead mechanisms because he was aware and they weren't. You've seen the same thing, Carr, in the eyes of Wilson and Hackman and Dris—that desire to degrade, to play like gods earthly puppets? Well, something's corrupting my friend in the same way. He's never told me. But I know."

Carr said, "I heard Wilson tell Hackman that your friend had once been hers. It made her very angry."

"I might have guessed," Jane said softly. "That's where the nasty streak in him comes from. And that's why they're hunting him—because they're afraid he'll betray them to . . . still others."

"To the four men with black hats?" Carr asked.

She looked at him with a new fear in her eyes. "I never heard of them," she said.

"Go on," Carr urged.

"He must have run away from Hackman and Wilson and Dris," she said, her eyes seeing things distant. "And then, because he was lonely, he was drawn to me, one girl picked from a million. He didn't want to wake me, because he lacked the courage to love me or corrupt me, either. So he half wakened me, wanting to keep me in a dream world forever."

She looked at Carr unsmilingly. "I never wanted to do anything like that to you," she said. "I came to you in desperation, when I was followed by Hackman. I ran into the office because I knew the place from Midge's boyfriend working there. The applicant's chair at your desk was empty. I thought you were just another puppet, but I hoped to fool Hackman by pretending to be part of the pattern around you.

"For you see, Carr, they'd never seen me clearly. Hackman couldn't be sure I was the girl in the alley, though I must have looked enough like her to make Hackman suspicious. And they don't want to disturb the world too much and they're afraid of attracting the attention of . . . still others. Though in the end she took the risk of slapping my face—and of course I had to walk on without noticing, like a machine.

"But as soon as I realized you were awake, Carr, I did my best to keep you out of it. I knew the only safe thing for you would be to stay in your pattern."

"How can a wakened person stay in his pattern?" Carr demanded.

"It can be done," Jane assured him. "Haven't you managed to stay in your pattern most of the time, even since you've known or at least suspected? Haven't you been able to do and say the right things at your office, even when you were terribly afraid that you couldn't?"

He had to admit that was so.

"Why, even I could go back to my pattern tomorrow," Jane continued, "go back to my parents and Mayberry Street and the academy, except—another drink, please—" (There were only drops, but they shared them) "—except that *they* know about me now, they know my pattern and so they'd be able to get me if I should go back.

"So I did my best to keep you out of it," she hurried on. "The first time I warned you and went away from you. Then that night, when you came to me with all your suspicions of the truth, I laughed at them and I did everything I could to convince you they were unreal . . . and I left you again."

"But even the first time," Carr said gently, "you left me that note, telling me where I could meet you."

She looked away from him. "I wasn't strong enough to make a complete break. I pretended to myself you'd find that first note too silly to bother about. There's an unscrupulous part of my mind that does things I really don't want to . . . or perhaps that I really want to. The second time it made me drop that envelope with my address in front of the Beddoes house, where you'd remember it and find it the next evening."

"Because I was watching you," she admitted, dropping her gaze.

"Watching me?"

"Yes through a crack in one of the boarded-up windows."

"But why didn't you come out when you saw me?" Carr asked.

"I didn't want you to find me again. But I was worried about you and when I saw you pick up that envelope I knew what you were going to do. So I followed you."

"To Mayberry?"

She nodded. "When you went in I waited outside, hiding in the shadows across the street, until Hackman and Wilson came. Then I ran around through the alley—"

"Remembering what had been there the last time?" Carr interrupted.

She grinned nervously. "—and went up the back stairs. I found you and my friend in the bedroom. He'd just hit you. Hackman and Wilson were killing Gigolo in the front hall—"

"Your cat?"

She shut her eyes. "Yes, Gigolo's dead."

She went on after a moment, "While they were doing that I told my friend who you were and we carried you down the back way to his car and . . . "

"How did your friend happen to be there in the first place?" he asked.

"He has queer habits," she said uncomfortably, "a sort of morbid sentimentality about objects connected with me. He often goes to my room though I'm never there."

"All right, so you carried me down to his roadster," Carr said.

"And then we found your address in your pocket book and drove you back to your room and put you to bed. I wanted to stay though I knew it wouldn't be safe for you, but my friend said you'd be all right, so—"

"—you departed," he finished for her, "after writing me that letter and leaving me those powders. What were they, by the way? Medicine of some sort?"

"Just two sleeping tablets crushed up," she told him. "I hoped they'd get you started right the day after, help you get back into the pattern. Sleeping tablets are very useful there."

He shook his head. "I can't get back into the pattern, Jane."

She leaned toward him. "But you can, Carr. They don't know anything about you. They may suspect, but they can't be sure. If you stay in the pattern—your old job, your old girl—they'll forget their suspicions."

"I don't think I could manage it. I'd crack up," he said, adding in lower tones, "besides, I wouldn't leave you."

"But I'm lost forever," she protested. "You aren't. You still have a safe path through life. You don't have to stay in the dark museum."

He looked around at the actual darkness of the stacks and for the first time it all really hit him. Chicago a dead city, empty as the aisles around them, but here and there at great intervals the faintest of evil rustlings. Hundreds of blocks of death, or nonlife, and here two motes of awareness.

"No," he said slowly, "I won't go back."

"But you can't help me," she told him. "You'll only make it harder." She looked down. "It isn't because I think you can help me that the unscrupulous part of my mind keeps drawing you back."

"We could go far away," Carr said.

"We'd still be out of the pattern. More conspicuously than ever. And there would be other gangs."

"But at the worst these awakened ones are only people, Jane."

"You think so?" she said scornfully. "You don't think their

minds are strong with the evil wisdom of the wakened, passed down from wakened mind to mind for centuries?"

"But there must be some decent wakened people."

She shook her head. "I've never heard of any, only the cruel little gangs."

"And the little man?"

"After tonight? He's my friend no longer. Besides, fear will make him do anything. He can't be trusted."

"But I can help you," Carr insisted stubbornly. "I had a sign in a dream last night."

"What was that?"

"It's fuzzy now, but you and I were prisoners somewhere, all tied up, and I cut your bonds and we escaped."

"Was that the finish?"

He frowned. "I'm not sure. Maybe something got us in the end."

"You see?"

"But that was only a dream," he protested with a smile.

"And a sign, you said."

"Jane, don't you understand? I have to help you." He started to put his arms around her, but she quickly got up and turned away.

"What's the matter?" he asked, following her.

She held her shoulders stiffly, but she had trouble speaking. "Go away, Carr. Go away right now."

"I can't, Jane."

"Now, Carr. Please."

"No, Jane, I won't."

She stood there a moment longer. Then her shoulders sagged. Carr felt the tension go out of him too. He rubbed his eyes.

"Lord," he exclaimed, "I wish I had another drink."

She turned around and her face was radiant. Carr looked at her in amazement. She seemed to have dropped her cloak of fear and thrown around her shoulders a garment that glittered.

"Come on," she said.

He followed her as if she were some fairy-tale princess— and she did seem to have grown taller—as she went three aisles over, pulled on a light, took down from an upper shelf three copies of *Marius the Epicurean,* stuck her hand into the gap and brought out a fifth of scotch.

His eyes widened. "You certainly do yourself proud."

She laughed. "Would you really like to see?" And recklessly tumbling down other clutches of books, she showed him a packrat accumulation of handkerchiefs, peanuts and candy, jewelry, cosmetics, even a long golden wig (she held that to her cheek a moment, asking him if he liked blondes), shoes, stockings, dresses, scarves, and all sorts of little boxes and bottles, cups, plates, and glasses.

Taking two of the latter, crystal-bright and long stemmed, she said, "And now will you have a drink with me, prince, in my castle?"

CHAPTER XIV

There's one nice thing about the world being an engine. It gives you something exciting to watch. You can even have some fun with it, kid it a little. But don't hurt the poor puppets . . .

Like two drunken pirate stowaways from the hold of a Spanish galleon, tipsily swaying and constantly shushing each other, Carr and Jane went up a narrow stair, groped through the foreign language section, and crossed the library's unlighted rotunda. Carr's heart went out to the shadows festooning the vast place. He felt he could fly up to them if he willed, wrap them around him fold on fold. They looked as warm and friendly as the scotch felt inside him.

Then, weaving behind Jane down a broad white stairway, it occurred to him that they might be prince and princess stealing from a marble castle, bound on some dangerous escapade. Here within, all gloom and silent grandeur, save where an unseen guard rattled his pike—say over there, by the elevator, or behind that high glass case. Outside, the city, restless and turbulent, holding wild carnival, but full of rebellious mutterings, ". . . in a nasty mood," the old Archduke had said, tugging his silvered sideburns. "'Twere well your majesties not show yourselves. I have given order to double the palace guard. If only we could set hand on those two young firebrands who raise this malcontent!" Here he knotted his veiny white fist. "The Flame, the girl is called. 'Tis said she bears a likeness to your majesty. Our spies are everywhere, we have set traps at every likely gathering place, but still the two elude us!"

Then, just as the Archduke was launching into his baritone solo, "The awful grandeur of the state strikes terror in men's souls," Carr realized that Jane had got through the door to the street. He followed her outside and halted, entranced. For there, beyond the wide sidewalk, was a most fitting continuation of his fantasy—a long low limousine with silvery fittings and softly glowing interior.

Then he saw that it was no pumpkin coach, at least not for himself and Jane, for approaching it at a stately waddle came two well-fed elderly couples, the men in top hats. Under the street lights, the features of all four were screwed up into an expression of germicidal haughtiness. While they were still some yards away, a Negro chauffeur opened the door and touched his visored cap.

Jane suddenly scampered straight at the sedate waddlers. Carr watched in growing amazement and delight as she veered off at the last moment, but in passing reached out and knocked off the nearest top hat. And the old fool wearing it marched on without even turning his head.

It hit Carr with all the instant impact of that crucial drink which opens the door to wonderland. There at his feet and Jane's lay the city—a playground, a nursery, a zoo, a congregation of lock-stepping robots, of mindless machines. You could do anything! No one could stop you!

With a whoop he raised his arms and ran lurchingly across the sidewalk at a wide angle that caught him up with Jane so that they raced around the corner hand in hand.

And now they were prince and princess no longer, but wizard's children with stolen cloaks of invisibility. Under their winged feet the pavement fled. Horns and street car bells struck up a dulcet, nerve-quickening music, as if for acrobats preparing for their star turn.

Across their path a theater lobby spilled a gabbling, cigarette-puffing, taxi-hailing horde. Oh, the beautiful joy of rushing through them, of jostling powdered shoulders, of hopelessly tangling half-donned overcoats, of plucking at ties and shawls under the glare of yellow lights, of bobbing up and gibbering like apes into stuffy, unseeing faces.

Next, in an exhibition of hair-raising daring and split-second dexterity, to spring from the sidewalk and dart between speeding cab and green sedan, to jeer at the blind drivers, almost to slip and sprawl on gleaming tracks in front of a vast rhinoceros of a streetcar, to regain balance deftly and glide between moving chromium bumpers just beyond, finally to gain the opposite sidewalk, your ears ringing with a great shout of applause—and to realize you had uttered that shout yourself!

Oh, to hiss into the ear of a fat woman with smug suburban face, "The supreme court has just declared soap-operas unconstitutional," to scream at a solemn man with eleven-dollar shirt, "The Communists have set up a guillotine in Grant Park!" to say to a mincing, dopey-eyed sweater-girl, "I'm a talent scout. Follow me," to a well-dressed person with an aura of superiority, "Gallup Poll. Do you approve of Charlemagne's policies toward the Saxons?" to a slinking clerk, "Burlesque is back," to a dull, beefy jerk in overalls, "Free beer behind the booths, ask for Clancy," to a fish-faced bookie, "Here, hold my pocketbook," to a youth, "Follow that man," to a slim intellectual with briefcase, at court-stenographer speed, "Watch the sky. A wall of atomic catastrophe, ignited by injudicious Swedish experiments, is advancing across Labrador, great circle route, at the rate of seventeen hundred and ninety-seven miles an hour."

And finally, panting, sides needled by delicious breathlessness, to sink to a curb and sit with back resting against metal trash box and laugh gaspingly in each other's faces, doubling up after each new glimpse of the blind, grotesque faces on the conveyor-belt called a sidewalk.

Just then a police siren sounded and a large gray truck grumbled to a stop in front of them. Without hesitation, Carr scooped up Jane and sat her on the projecting backboard, then scrambled up beside her.

The light changed and the truck started. The siren's wail rose in volume and pitch as a paddy wagon turned into their street a block behind them. It swung far to the left around a whole string of traffic and careened into a pocket just behind them. They looked into the eyes of the red-jowled coppers. Jane thumbed her nose at them.

The paddy wagon braked to a stop and several policemen poured out of it and into a dingy hotel.

"Won't find us there," Carr smirked. "We're gentlefolk."
Jane squeezed his hand.

The truck passed under the dark steel canopy of the
elevated. Its motor growled as it labored up the approach to
the bridge.

Carr pointed at the splintered end of a barrier. "Your
friend did that on the way down," he informed her amiably.
"I wish he were along with us." He looked at Jane. "No, I
don't," he added. "Neither do I," she told him.

His face was close to hers and he started to put his arms
around her, but a sudden rush of animal spirits caused him
instead to plant his palms on the backboard and lift himself
up and kick his feet in the air.

He fell backwards into the truck as Jane yanked at him.
"You're still quite breakable, you know," she told him and
kissed him and sat up quickly.

As he struggled up beside her, the truck hustled down the
worn brick incline at the opposite end of the bridge and
grated to a stop at a red light. A blue awning stretched to
the edge of the sidewalk. Above the awning, backed by
ancient windows painted black, a bold blue neon script proclaimed "Goldie's Casablanca."

"That's for us," Carr said. He hopped down and lifted Jane
off the truck as it started up again.

Inside the solid glass door beneath the awning, a tall,
tuxedo-splitting individual with the vacant smile of a one-
time sparring partner, was wagging a remonstrating hand at
a fist-swinging fat man he held safely pinned against the wall
with the other. Carr and Jane swept past them. Carr whipped
out several dollar bills importantly, then remembered that
the world is a machine and dropped them on the floor. They
descended a short flight of stairs and found themselves in the
most crowded nightclub in the world.

The bar, which ran along the wall to their left, was jammed
three deep. Behind it towered two horse-faced men in white
coats. One was violently shaking a silver cylinder above his
head, but its rattle was lost in the general din.

Packed tables extended from the foot of the stairs to a
small, slightly raised dance floor, upon which, like some thick
vegetable stew being stirred by the laziest cook in creation,
a solid mass of hunchedly embracing couples was slowly revolving. The tinkly and near-drowned musical accompaniment

for this elephantine exercise came from behind a mob of people at the far end of the wall to the right, which was lined with shallow booths.

Like tiny volcanos in the midst of a general earthquake, all the figures were spewing words and cigarette smoke.

Two couples marched straight at Carr. He swung aside, lightly bumping a waiter who was coming around the end of the bar, with a tray of cocktails. The waiter checked himself while the couples passed and Carr deftly grabbed two of the cocktails just as another couple came between them. He turned to present one of the cocktails to Jane. But she had already left him and was edging through the press along the booths. Carr downed one of the cocktails, put the empty glass in his pocket and followed her, sipping at the other. But as soon as he reached the first booth, he stopped to stare.

Marcia was sitting opposite a handsome young man with stupid eyes and not much of a chin. He sported white tie and tails. Marcia was wearing her silver lame, a dress with two fantastic flounces and a plunging neckline.

"Still, you tell me you've had a lot of dates with him," the young man was saying artlessly.

"I always have lots of dates, Kirby," Marcia replied sparklingly.

"But this . . . er . . . what's his name . . . Carr chap . . ." Kirby began.

"I sometimes go slumming," was Marcia's explanation.

Carr planked his elbow on their table and put his chin in his hand. "Pardon this intrusion from the underworld," he said loudly.

They didn't look at him. "Slumming can be amusing," Kirby observed.

"It can," Marcia agreed brightly, "for a while."

"And this . . . er . . ."

"The name's Carr Mackay," Carr said helpfully.

". . . er . . . Carr chap . . ."

"Believe me, Kirby, I've always had lots of dates," Marcia repeated. "I always will have lots of dates."

"But not so many with one man," Kirby objected.

"Why not?" she asked, giving him the eye, which seemed to put a new gleam in Kirby's. "How about starting tonight?" he asked.

"Dating?" Marcia said blankly. "Darling, we are."

"I mean at my place," Kirby explained. "You'd like it there."
"Would I?" Marcia asked mystically.

Carr reached his hand toward her, a gloating smile on his lips. Then suddenly he grimaced with self-disgust, drew back his hand, and turned his back on them.

CHAPTER XV

Love doesn't make the world go round, but it sure puts a spark of life in the big engine . . .

There had been quite a change in Goldie's while Carr's back was turned. The dancers had all squeezed themselves into hitherto imperceptible nooks and crannies around the tables. The mob had dispersed to reveal a grossly fat man whose paunch abutted the keyboard of a tiny, cream colored piano. A short apish individual who looked all dazzling white shirt-front—Goldie, surely, at last—was standing on the edge of the empty dance floor and saying in a loud harsh voice that would have been very suitable for a carp: "And now, let's give the little chick a great big ovation."

Half the audience applauded violently. Goldie ducking down from the platform, rewarded them with a cold sneer. The fat man's hands began to scuttle up and down the keyboard. And a blonde in a small black dress stepped up on the platform. She held in one hand something that might have been a shabby muff.

But even as the applause swelled, most of the figures at the tables were still jabbering at each other.

Carr shivered. Here it is, he thought suddenly—the bare stage, the robot audience, the ritual of the machine. Not a bacchanal, but a booze-fest to the music of a mindless Pan who'd gone all to watery flesh and been hitting the dope for two thousand years. The dreadful rhythm of progress without purpose, of movement without mind.

The blonde raised her arm and the muff unfolded to show, capping her unseen hand, a small face of painted wood that was at once foolish, frightened, and lecherous. Two diminutive hands flapped beside it. The blonde began to hum to the music.

Continuing to toy with the piano, the fat man glanced around briefly. In a tittering voice he confided, "And now you shall hear the sad tale of that unfortunate creature, Peter Puppet."

Carr shivered, finished his second drink in a gulp, looked around for Jane, couldn't see her.

"Peter was a perfect puppet," the fat man explained leisurely, accompanying himself with suitable runs and chords. "Yes. Peter was the prize Pinocchio of them all. He was carved out of wood to resemble a human being in complete detail, oh the most complete detail."

The puppet made eyes at the blonde. She ignored him and began to dance sketchily.

The fat man whirled on the tables, beetling his brows. "But he had one fault!" he half shrieked. "He wanted to be alive!" Again Carr shivered.

Going back to the lazy titter, the fat man remarked, "Yes, our Peter wanted to be a man. He wanted to do everything a man does."

Some guffaws came through the general jabber. The fat man's hands darted venomously along the keyboard, eliciting dreamy, pastoral tones.

"Then one lovely spring day while Peter was wandering through the meadows, wishing to be a man, he chanced to see a beautiful, a simply un-believably, be-yutiful be-londe. Peter . . . ah, Peter felt a swelling in his little wooden . . . heart."

With all sorts of handclasps and hopeful gawkings, the puppet was laying siege to the blonde. She closed her eyes, smiled, shook her head, went on humming.

Carr saw Jane picking her way through the tables toward the platform. He tried to catch her eye, but she didn't look his way.

". . . and so Peter decided to follow the blonde home." The fat man made footsteps in an upper octave. "Pink-pink-pink went his little wooden tootsies."

Jane reached the platform and, to Carr's amazement, stepped up on it. Carr started forward, but the packed tables balked him.

The blonde was making trotting motions with the puppet and the fat man was saying, "Peter found that the blonde lived right next door to a furniture factory. Now Peter had no love for furniture factories, because he once very narrowly escaped becoming part of a Sheraton table leg. The screaming of the saw and the pounding of the hammers . . ." (He did buzzy chromatic runs and anvil-chorusings) ". . . terrified Peter. He felt that each nail was being driven right into his little wooden midriff!"

Jane was standing near the blonde. Carr at last caught her eye. He motioned her to come down, but she only smiled at him wickedly. Slowly she undid the gilt buttons of her coat and let it drop to the floor.

"Finally conquering his terror, Peter raced past the furniture factory and darted up the walk to the blonde's home . . . pink-pink-pink-pink-pink!"

Jane had coolly began to unbutton her white blouse. Blushing, Carr tried to push forward, motioning urgently. He started to shout at her, but just then he remembered that the world is a machine and looked around.

The crowd wasn't reacting. It was chattering as loudly as ever.

"Peter followed the blonde up the stairs. He felt the sap running madly through him."

Jane dropped her blouse, was in her slip and skirt. Carr stood with his knee pushed against a table, swaying slightly.

"Peter's throat was dry as sawdust with excitement." The fat man's hands tore up and down the piano. "The blonde turned around and saw him and said, 'Little wooden man, what now?'"

Jane looked at Carr and let her slip drop. Tears stung Carr's eyes. Her breasts seemed far more beautiful than flesh should be.

And then there was, not a reaction on the part of the crowd, but the ghost of one. A momentary silence fell on Goldie's Casablanca. Even the fat man's glib phrases slackened and faded, like a phonograph record running down. His pudgy hands hung between chords. While the frozen gestures and expressions of the people at the tables all hinted at words halted on the brink of utterance. And it seemed to Carr, as he stared at Jane, that heads and eyes turned toward the platform, but only sluggishly and with difficulty, as if, dead, they felt a faint, fleeting ripple of life.

And although his mind was hazy with liquor, Carr knew that Jane was showing herself to him alone, that the robot audience were like cattle who turn to look toward a sound, experience some brief sluggish glow of consciousness, and go back to their mindless cud-chewing.

89

Then all at once the crowd was jabbering again, the fat man was tittering, the blonde was fighting off a madly amorous puppet, and Jane was hurrying between the tables, her arms pressed to her sides to hold up her slip, with snatched-up coat trailing from one hand. As she approached, it seemed to Carr that everything else was melting into her, becoming unimportant.

When she'd squeezed past the last table, he grabbed her hand. They didn't say anything. He helped her into her coat. As they hurried up the stairs and out the glass door, they heard the fat man's recitation die away like the chugging of a black greasy engine.

It was five blocks to Carr's room. The streets were empty. A stiff breeze from the lake had blown the smoke from the sky and the stars glittered down into the trenches between the buildings. The darkness that clung to the brick walls and besieged the street lamps seemed to Carr to be compounded of excitement and terror and desire in a mixture beyond analysis. He and Jane hurried on, holding hands.

The hall was dark. He let himself in quietly and they tiptoed up the stairs. Inside his room, he pulled down the shades, switched on the light. A blurred Jane was standing by the door, taking off her coat. For a moment Carr was afraid that he had drunk too much. Then she smiled and her image cleared and he knew he wasn't too drunk. He almost cried as he put his arms around her.

. . . . Afterwards he found himself realizing that he had never felt so delightfully sober in his life. From where he lay he could see Jane in the mirror. She'd put on his dressing gown and was mixing drinks for them.

"Here," she said, handing him a glass. "To us."

"To us." They clinked glasses and drank. She sat down and looked at him.

"Hello, darling," he said.

"Hello."

"Feeling all right?" he asked.

"Wonderful."

"Everything is going to be all right," he told her.

"Sure."

"But it really is, Jane," he insisted. "Eventually we'll awaken other people, people who won't go rotten. We'll find a way of taking care of Hackman and the others. You'll be able to go back to your place in the pattern. That'll give you a base of operations. I'll be able to go back too. And say—" (he suddenly smiled) "—do you realize what that will mean?"

"What?"

"It means that I'll have a date with you Saturday night, a date in the pattern. I've already met you through Tom Elvested and made a date with you. I first thought he was crazy when he introduced me to a Jane Gregg who wasn't there. But, don't you see, you were supposed to be there. That was your place in the pattern. Our paths are drawing closer together. We won't have to go outside the pattern to be together."

She smiled at him fondly. The telephone rang. Carr answered it. The voice was Marcia's. She sounded rather drunk.

" 'Lo, Carr, I thought you should be the first person to hear the news of my engagement to Kirby Fisher."

Carr didn't say anything.

"No, really, dear," Marcia went on after a moment. "We're announcing it together. He's right beside me."

Still Carr said nothing.

"Come here, Kirby," Marcia called. There was a pause. Then, over the phone, came the smack of a kiss. "Do you believe it now, Carr?" she asked and laughed a little.

"Sorry, but that's life, darling," she said a few seconds later. Another pause. "You had your chance." Still another pause. "No, I won't tell you that. I wouldn't be interested in your making a scene now." A final pause. "Well, then you'll just have to suffer." Click of the receiver. Carr put his down.

"Who was it?" Jane asked.

"Just a doll jilting me," he told her, moving toward her. The world seemed to narrow in like the iris diaphragm of a camera, until it showed only her soft smiling face.

CHAPTER XVI

When some guys wake up. they don't know whether to be decent or mean. They just teeter in the middle. Eventually they fall off, mostly on the mean side . . .

Carr had sleepy memories of the phone ringing, of Jane's voice, of her reassuring touch, of returning darkness. Then came dreams, very bad ones, that seemed to last an eternity.

And when, under the spur of an obscure but pressing fear, he fought himself awake, it was as if a legion of demons were opposing his efforts.

The room was dim and swimming, it throbbed with his head, and when he tried to move he found himself weak as a baby. There was a sharp increase in his fear. Fumbling at the sheets, he managed to worm his way to the edge of the bed and roll out. He hardly felt the floor strike him, but the swift movement swirled the air around him and brought him an explanation of his suffocating feeling of fear.

He smelled gas.

The nearest window looked miles away and seemed to recede as he crawled toward it. When he finally got his chin on the sill, he found it shut. Inching his way upward, leaning against the glass, he got his paper-feeble fingers under the handles, heaved it up, and sprawled out head and shoulders across the sill, sucking the cold clean wind until he'd been sick and his strength began to return.

Then he remembered Jane.

Returning twice to the window for air, he managed to search the apartment, though his head was still splitting. On the first trip he turned off the gas hissing softly from the ancient wall-fixture and after the third he flung up the other window. A small Chicago gale soon cleaned out the stink.

Jane wasn't there.

He doused his face with cold water and prepared to think, but just then he heard footsteps in the hall. He stayed inside the bathroom door. The lock grated and the door opened softly and in stepped the small dark man with glasses. His left hand covered his mouth and pinched his nostrils shut. His right was returning a bristling key-ring to his pocket. He moved toward the gas fixture. Then Carr lunged toward him.

At the touch of Carr's fingers, the small dark man seemed to shrivel inside his clothes and he instantly bleated, "Please, please, don't! I'll do anything you say!"

Then, peering back fearfully, he recognized Carr and part of his terror seemed to leave him. But his voice was almost catlike as he continued wildly, "I'll confess! Only don't hurt me. I did try to murder you, but now I'm glad you're alive."

Carr shook him. "Where's Jane?" he demanded.

"I don't know."

"Yes you do. What have you done with her?"

"I don't know where she is, I tell you. Oh, please don't hurt me any more. I knew she came here with you last night, because I followed you here from the nightclub. I went off and got drunk again. Then I came back this morning to have it out with you. I let myself into your room with my master keys—"

"And you weren't planning murder?" Carr injected sardonically.

"No, no," the small dark man assured him, his eyes going wide, "It's just that I don't like to trouble people. I found only you in bed. I was drunk. My anger that she'd favored you got the better of me. For a moment I hated you terribly and so I turned on the gas and left. But my conscience bothered me and so I hurried back . . ."

"Hours later," Carr finished thumbing at the window. "It's almost night now. No. I'll tell you why you came back to turn off the gas. Because you knew that if you didn't, no one else in the world would—and your kind is careful to tidy up after you."

The small dark man looked up at him fearfully. "You know about things then?" he quavered.

"She's told you?"

"About everything," Carr answered grimly.

The small dark man caught at his sleeves. "Oh, then you'll understand how lonely I am," he said piteously. "You'll understand how much Jane meant to me. You'll sympathize with me."

"I'll beat you to a pulp if you don't tell me everything you know, quickly. About Hackman, Wilson, Dris—everything."

"Oh, please," the small dark man implored, his gaze darting wildly around the room. Then a new spasm of terror seemed to grip him, for he began to shake pitiably. "I'll tell you, I swear I will, he whined, "Only it's so cold."

With an exclamation of contempt Carr went and slammed down the windows. When he turned back the small dark man had moved a few steps away from the gas fixture. But he stopped instantly.

"Go ahead," Carr said sharply.

"The whole story?"

Carr nodded. "Everything that's important. Everything that might help me find Jane."

"All right," the small dark man said. "I think you'll understand me better then." And he paused and his eyes went dead and his face seemed to sink in a trifle, as if something behind it had gone far away. His voice too seemed to come from a distance as he said, "It was Hackman who wakened me and took me out of the pattern. It happened in New York. Actually I'd been awake most of my life, but I hadn't realized that other people weren't. Hackman lifted me out of a grubby little life and pampered me like a pet monkey and satisfied my every whim, and for a while I gloried in my power and puffed myself up as a little prince, with Wilson my king and Hackman my queen. But then—" (he hesitated) "—it began to get too much for me. It wasn't that I got tired of living in millionaires' homes while they weren't. Or that I got bored with spying on the secretest details of people's lives and sitting in on the most private conferences of great industrialists and statesmen—though the high and mighty lose their glamor fast when you catch on to the pattern, and the world-shaking incidents become trivial when you know they're conducted by puppets and that one event means no more than another. No, it was the vicious little impertinences and the outright cruelties that began to sicken me. I don't mean the dead girls— they were rather lovely, in a heartbreaking sort of way, though Hackman was always jealous and was careful to see I never went with them while I was alone. I mean the business of always slapping people when you were sure you couldn't be watched, and doing obscene things to them. And slipping plates of food out from under people's forks and watching them eat air. And watching the puppets write love letters and scrawling obscene comments on them. And that night Hackman got drunk and went down Broadway half undressing the prettier girls . . ." (he winced) ". . . sticking pins in them. Meaningless perhaps, but horrible, like a child throwing pepper in the eyes of a doll." His voice trailed off to a whisper. "Though there was that child they dropped in the octopus tank at the acquarium—I really think she was awake. I got so I hated it all. At that time Hackman wakened Dris and put me in second place, though she and Wilson wouldn't let me try to awaken a girl of my own. And then I met the four men with black hats."

He shivered again. "Please," he said, "I'm still very cold. Could I have a little drink?"

Carr fetched a bottle from the drawer. When he turned

around the small dark man had moved again, though again he stopped instantly. He greedily drank the whiskey Carr poured him. Then he shuddered and closed his eyes.

"The four men with black hats were much worse," he said softly. "Strangling's the mildest use to which they put those black silk scarves they wear. They know how to waken others a little—enough to make them seem to feel pain. And they know how to paralyze people—to turn them off. I spotted them at work one day in a playground. That's how I caught on to them. I didn't tell Hackman and the others about them, because things were getting much worse between us. She'd taken to setting the hound to watch me and to seize me if I made a move, and then going away for hours with Dris and Wilson. They laughed at me and called me a coward. So I led them out one day and betrayed them to the four men with black hats, knowing that gangs like that would trade a million dead victims for one really live one.

"But my plan didn't work. There was a fight and the four men with black hats didn't quite manage to turn the trick, and Hackman and the others escaped. I fled, knowing that now both gangs would be hunting me, and the four men in black hats thought I'd put the finger on them.

"I fled to Chicago, but Hackman and the others followed me. The hound knows my scent although I try to disguise it. I kept away from them and tried to make a life for myself. I fell in love with Jane, but when I had half awakened her I was scared to go further. Then . . ."

The small dark man suddenly stopped dead. He was standing in front of the mantelpiece. He looked at the door. "Listen!" he whispered agitated. "What's that?"

Carr looked back from the door fast enough to see the small dark man whirling back around and stuffing his hand into his pocket. He grabbed the small man's wrist and jerked the hand out and saw that it held a paper. The small dark man glared at him fearfully, but wouldn't let go, so he slapped the hand hard. A crumpled paper fell from it. Carr picked it up, and while the small man cringed, sucking his fingers, Carr read the note the small dark man had tried to snatch from the mantelpiece undetected.

Darling,
 Don't be angry with me. I'm going out for a while,

but when I come back all our problems may be solved. My friend just called me—thank goodness the phones are dial here—and told me he's discovered a very important secret, something that will give us complete protection from Hackman and Wilson and Dris. I'm to meet him early in the evening. I'm leaving now, because I have certain preparations to make—and it's best that you don't come. I should be back by midnight, with wonderful news!

Lovingly,
Jane

Carr grabbed the small dark man by the throat and shook him until his glasses fell off and he blinked up at Carr in purblind terror, pawing ineffectually at the choking hands.

"The truth!" Carr snarled. "Every bit of it!" And he stopped shaking him and slacked his grip a little.

For a moment only spittle and throaty babble came out of the small dark man's mouth. All at once he began to talk breathlessly and very rapidly.

"They made me do it, I swear! Hackman and the others caught me late last night when I was drunk, and they told me that if I didn't tell them where Jane was they'd give me to the hound. When I hesitated they forced me out onto the Boulevard. Hackman and the hound on one side of the street. Wilson and Dris on the other, and made me stay there, dodging the cars, until I'd promised. Even so I lied and told them I didn't know Jane's address, only a phone number she'd given me, and that it might scare her off if I asked her to meet me earlier than this evening. See, I did everything I dared to delay things! They made me phone her and told me what to tell her and listened while I made the date. Then they left me in an empty apartment with the hound guarding me, but he likes to snap things out of the air, so I tossed him sleeping pills until he went under. Then I hurried here to warn Jane, but she'd already gone. I didn't notice the note then, I was too frightened. And because I knew that with Jane gone you'd be happier dead, I turned on the gas. And now if you're going to kill me, please don't hurt me!"

"I can't promise that," Carr said, tightening his grip a little. "Where were you to meet?"

"On the corner of State and Harrison."

"Why Skid Row?"

"That's where they told me to tell her. That's where they have their fun these days."

"And when?" Carr demanded.

"At eight o'clock tonight."

Carr looked at the clock. It was seven-forty. He pushed the small dark man aside and began to throw on his clothes.

"Don't hurt me when you kill me," the small dark man begged with covered eyes from where he'd fallen across the bed. "Let me cut my wrists under warm water."

"Give me the keys to your roadster," Carr said, pulling on his shoes.

The small dark man sprang across the room, fell on his knees in front of Carr, and held out a small leather key-case. Carr took it.

"Where is it?" he asked.

"Parked right out in front," the small dark man told him. "Only now it's a maroon roadster. I wrecked the other last night when they caught me. You're not going to kill me?"

Carr caught up his coat and went out, shouldered into it while he was hurrying down the stairs. But fast as he went, he found when he got to the bottom that the small dark man was just behind him—and had found time to pick up the whiskey bottle on the way.

"You're going after Jane," he said talking between swigs. "Don't. You haven't a chance. You don't realize their power and cunning, all the most horrible tricks of history passed down from wakened mind to mind since the days of Borgias and the Caesars. You don't know all the traps they're holding in reserve. Wait. Listen to me. There's an easier way, a safer way, a surer way . . ."

At the front door Carr whirled on him. "Don't follow me!" He ordered, grabbing the small dark man by the coat. "And remember, if you haven't told me the strictest truth, you'll wish the four men with black hats had got you!"

CHAPTER XVII

If the mean guys spot you walking around alive, you'd better think fast, brother . . .

Carr had never sweat so driving. It wasn't that the Loop

traffic was thick, but the knowledge that there was no place for the roadster in the pattern. If he stopped, the auto behind him might keep on coming. He couldn't let himself get in any lines of vehicles. Mostly he drove on the wrong side of the street.

Finally he came to a place where the signs glared over low doorways, where their chief message was always "Girls and More Girls!" where dance music sobbed and moaned with dead passion, where only shabby and bleary-eyed automaton-men slouched through the dirty shadows. He passed State and Harrison twice without catching signs of Jane. The second time he parked the roadster in a no-parking stretch of curb just short of the black veil of the railway yards and left it with the motor running, hoping it wouldn't be hit. Then he started back, walking slowly.

He passed a tiny theater fronted by huge, grainy photographs of women in brassieres and pants painted bright orange. A sign screamed: TWENTY NEW GIRLS!

He passed a ragged old drunk sitting on the curb and muttering, "Kill 'em. That's what I'd do. Kill 'em."

He passed a slot-like store that said: TATTOOING, then a jumbled window overhung by three dingy gilt balls.

He passed a woman. Her face was shadowed by an awning, but he could see the shoulder-length blonde hair, the glossy black dress tight over hips and thighs, and the long bare legs.

He passed a sign that read: IDENTIFICATION PHOTOS AT ALL HOURS. He passed a black-windowed bar that said: CONTINUOUS ENTERTAINMENT.

He stopped.

He turned around.

No, it couldn't be, he thought. This one's hair is blonde, and the hips swing commonly in the tight black dress.

But if you disregarded those two things . . .

Jane had shown him a blonde wig at the library.

She had written about making "preparations."

The walk could be assumed.

Just then his glance flickered beyond the shoulder-brushing blonde hair.

A long black convertible drew up to the curb, parking the wrong way. Out of it stepped the handless man.

On the other side of the street, just opposite the girl in

black, stood Hackman. She was wearing a green sports suit and hat. She glanced quickly both ways, then started across.

Halfway between Carr and the girl in black, Wilson stepped out of a dark doorway.

Carr felt his heart being squeezed. This was the finish, he thought, the kill. The final blow.

Unless . . .

The three pursuers closed in slowly, confidently. The girl in black didn't turn or stop, but she seemed to slow down just a trifle.

. . . unless something happened to convince them that he and Jane were automatons like the rest.

The three figures continued to close in. Hackman was smiling.

Carr wet his lips and whistled twice, with an appreciative chromatic descent at the end of each blast.

The girl in black turned around. He saw Jane's white face, framed by the ridiculous hair.

"Hello, kid," he called, saluting her with a wave of his fingers.

"Hello," she replied. Her heavily lipsticked mouth smiled. She still swayed a little as she waited for him.

Passing Wilson, Carr reached her a moment before the others did. He did not look at them, but he could sense them closing in behind, forming a dark semicircle.

"Doing anything tonight?" he asked Jane.

Her chin described a little movement, not quite a nod. She studied him up and down. "Maybe."

"They're faking!" Hackman's whisper seemed to detach itself from her lips and glide toward his ear like an insect.

"I'm not so sure," he heard Wilson whisper in reply. "Might be an ordinary pickup."

Cold prickles rose on Carr's scalp. But he remembered to ask Jane, "That 'maybe' you're thinking of doing—how about us doing it together?"

She seemed to complete a calculation. "Sure," she said, looking up at him with a suddenly unambiguous smile.

"Pickup!" Hackman's whisper was scornful. "I never saw anything so amateurish. It's like a highschool play."

Carr slid his arm around Jane's, took her hand. He turned and started back toward the roadster. The others moved back to let them through, but then he could hear their footsteps behind them keeping pace.

"But it's obviously the girl!" Hackman's whisper was a trifle louder. "She's just bleached her hair and is trying to pass for a street walker."

As if she feared Carr might turn, Janes hand tightened spasmodically on his.

"You can't be sure," Wilson replied. "Lots of people look alike. We've been fooled before, and we've got to be careful with these others around. What do you say, Dris?"

"I'm pretty sure it's the girl."

Carr felt the whispers falling around them like the folds of a spiderweb. He said loudly to Jane, "You look swell, kid."

"You don't look so bad yourself," she replied.

Carr shifted his arm around her waist, brushing her hips as he did. The maroon roadster still seemed miles away. Fringing his field of vision to either side were blurred bobbing segments of Wilson's panama hat and pinstriped paunch and Hackman's green gabardine skirt and nyloned legs.

"Pretty sure, Dris?" Wilson asked doubtfully. "Well, in that case—"

Hackman leapt at the opportunity. "Let me test them," she urged.

Through the skimpy dress Carr felt Jane shaking.

"Put that away!" Wilson whispered sharply.

"I won't!" Hackman replied.

A bleary-eyed man in a faded blue shirt lurched up onto the curb and came weaving across the sidewalk. Carr steered Jane out of his way.

"Disgusting," Jane said.

"I'd have taken a crack at him if he'd bumped you," Carr boasted.

"Oh, he's drunk," Jane said.

"I'd have taken a crack at him anyway," Carr asserted, but he was no longer looking at her. They had almost reached the roadster.

"Come on, kid," Carr said suddenly, stepping ahead and pulling Jane after him. "Here's where we start to travel fast."

"Oh swell," breathed Jane, her eyes going wide as she saw the chugging roadster.

"They're getting away," Hackman almost wailed. "You've got to let me test them."

Carr swiftly reached for the door.

"It might be better . . ." came Dris's voice.

Carr held the door for Jane. From the corner of his eye he saw Hackman's hand. In it was one of the stiff, daggerlike pins from her hat.

"Well . . ." Wilson began. Then in an altogether different voice, tense with agitation and surprise, "No! Look! Across the street, half a block behind us! Quick, you fools, we've got to get out of here."

Carr ran around the roadster, jumped in, and pulled away from the curb. He started to give it the gun, but Jane touched his hand. "Not fast," she warned. "We're still playing a part."

He risked a quick look back. Hackman, Wilson, and Dris were piling into the black convertible. On the other side of the street, drawn together into a peering knot were the four men with black hats.

That was all he had time for. He swung the roadster slowly around the next corner, squeezing it by a high walled truck that spilled trickles of coal dust.

They hadn't gone a half block when they heard a souped-up motor roar past the intersection behind them without turning. Another half block and they heard another roar behind them that likewise passed on. They slumped with relief.

"Where'll we go?" Carr asked. "There's a lot to talk about, but I can't stand much more of this driving."

Jane said, "There's one place they don't know about, where we can hide out perfectly. The old Beddoes house. There are things I've never told you about it."

Carr said, "Right. On the way I'll tell you what happened to me."

CHAPTER XVIII

Maybe some day the whole engine'll wake. Maybe some day the meanness'll be washed, or burned, out of us. And maybe not . . .

The ornately-carved nine-foot door was of golden oak grimed with the years and it was bordered, Carr noticed, with a ridged blackness that once had been a rainbow frame of stained glass. It scuffed complainingly across the humped-up rug, as the gate had across gravel. He followed Jane inside and pushed it shut behind them.

"I still don't like leaving the roadster that way," he said.

"We didn't want it too near here," she told him.

"But it's such a big thing to have displaced in the pattern."

She shrugged. "It was probably a display model, if I know my . . . friend. And I think the big machine has an automatic way of correcting large displacements like that. But look."

The circle of her flashlight's beam traveled over walls cobwebbed with soot, picked up here and there dull glints of a figured gold paper and huge pale rectangles where pictures had once hung. It jumped to two shapeless bulks of sheet-covered chairs, hesitated at a similarly shrouded chandelier looming overhead, finally came to rest on a curving stairway with a keg-thick newel post carved in the form of a stern angel with folded wings. Jane took Carr's hand and led him toward it.

"What do you know about John Claire Beddoes?" she asked him.

"Just the usual stuff," Carr replied. "Fabulously wealthy. Typical Victorian patriarch, but with vague hints of vice. Something about a mistress he somehow kept here in spite of his wife."

Jane nodded. "That's all I knew when I first came here."

The musty odor with a hint of water-rot grew stronger. Even their cautious footsteps raised from the tattered but heavily padded stair carpet puffs of dust which mounted like ghostly heads into the flashlight's beam.

"In spite of everything he did to us," Carr said, "I almost hate leaving your friend like that."

"He can't go on betraying people for ever," Jane said simply. "One of the reasons I brought you here is that he doesn't know about this place."

They reached the second-story landing and a door that was a mere eight feet high. It opened quietly when Jane pushed it. "I've oiled things a bit," she explained to Carr.

Inside the flashlight revealed a long dark-papered room with heavy black molding ornamented with a series of grooves that were long and very deeply cut, especially those in a picture rail that circled the room a foot from the ceiling. Round about were old-fashioned bureaus and chests and other furniture so ponderous that Carr felt it would take dynamite to budge them. While at the far end of the room and dominating it was a huge grim bed with dark posts almost as thick as the angel downstairs.

"Behold the unutterably respectable marital couch of the Beddoes," Jane proclaimed with a hint of poetry and laughter. Then she entered one of the alcoves flanking the head of the bed, laid the flashlight on the floor, and fumbled at the wide baseboard until she'd found what she was looking for. Then, still crouching there, she turned to a mystified Carr a face that, half illuminated by the flashlight's beam, was lively with mischief.

"To get the biggest kick out of this," she said, "you must imagine John Beddoes waiting until his wife was snoring delicately and then quietly getting up in his long white nightgown and tasseled nightcap—remember he had a big black beard—and majestically striding over here barefooted and . . . doing this."

With the words, Jane rose, not letting go of the baseboard. A section of the wall rose with her, making a dark rectangular doorway. She picked up the flashlight and waved Carr on with it.

"Enter the secret temple of delight," she said.

Carr followed her through the dark doorway. She immediately turned around, lowered the secret panel behind them, and switched off the flashlight.

"Stand still for a moment," she said.

He heard her moving around beside him and fumbling with something. Then came the scratch of a match, a whiff of burning kerosene, and the next moment a gold-bellied, crystal chiminied lamp at his elbow was shedding its warm light on scarlet walls and scarcely tarnished gilt woodwork.

"The place is so sealed up," Jane explained, "that there's hardly any dust, even after all these years. There's some sort of ventilation system, but I've never figured it out."

The room that Carr found himself looking at with wonder was furnished with lurid opulence. There were two gilt cupboards and a long side-board covered with silver dining ware, including silver casseroles with spirit lamps and crystal decanters with silver wine-tags hanging around their necks. Some of the silver was inset with gold. Toward the end of the room away from the secret panel was a fragile-looking teacart and an S-shaped love seat finished in gilt and scarlet plush. The whole room was quite narrow and rather less than half the length of the bedroom.

Jane took up the lamp and moved beyond the love seat. "You haven't seen anything yet," she assured Carr with a smile. Then kneeling by the far wall she drew up a narrow section which disappeared smoothly behind the gilt molding overhead.

"They're counterweighted," she explained to Carr and then stepped through the opening she had revealed. "Don't trip," she called back. "It's two steps up."

He followed her into a second room that was also windowless and about the same shape as the first and that continued the same scheme of decoration, except that here the furnishings were a gilt wardrobe, a littered gilt vanity table with a huge mirror in a filagreed gilt frame suspended on scarlet ropes with golden tassels, and a bed with a golden canopy and a scarlet plush coverlet. Jane pulled off her blonde wig and tossed it there.

"And now," she said, turning, "let me introduce you to the girl herself." And she lifted the lamp so that it illumined a large oval portrait above the wardrobe. It showed the head and shoulders of a dark-haired and rather tragic-eyed girl who seemed hardly more than seventeen. She was wearing a filmy negligee.

"She looks rather pale," Carr observed after a few moments.

"She should," Jane said softly. "They say he kept her here for ten years, though that may have been just an exaggeration."

Carr walked on and looked through the archway in which the room ended. It led to a bathroom with gold, or gilded fixtures, including an ancient four-legged tub whose sides, fluted like a seashell, rose almost to shoulder height and were approached by little steps.

"Go on, look in," Jane told Carr as he hesitated in front of it. "There's no slim skeleton inside, I'm happy to report."

Before returning, Carr noted that all the fixtures were, though old-fashioned, so shaped that the water would swirl in and out silently.

Jane was fumbling with a gilt molding that ran along the wall at eye level. Suddenly it swung out and down along its length and hung there on hinges, revealing a black slit in the wall that ran the length of the room and was about an inch wide.

"It opens into one of the grooves in the picture molding in the Beddoes bedroom," Jane explained. "Our being two steps higher makes the difference. If there were a light in there and we turned out our light, we'd have a good view of the place. I suppose John Claire used it to make sure his wife was asleep before he returned. And his young friend could have used it to spy on her lover and his lawful mate, if she were so minded."

Suddenly the cruel and barren possessiveness of the place and the terrible loneliness of the machinations of those long-dead puppets caught at Carr's heart. He put his arm around Jane and swung her away from the black slit.

"We'll never leave each other, never," he whispered to her passionately.

"Never," she breathed.

They looked at themselves curiously in the mirror they now faced. Their images peered back at them through a speckling of tarnish. With an uneasy laugh Carr went up to the vanity table and on an impulse pulled open the shallow center drawer.

There lay before him a small, single-barreled pistol, pearl-handled, gold chased. He picked it up and looked at the verdigreed rim of the lone cartridge.

"All the appurtenances of a romantic *fin de siecle* glade of pleasure," he observed lightly. "Apparently never used it, though. I wonder if it was supposed to have been for herself or him, or the wife. The powder's as dead as they are, I'll bet."

Jane came to his side and pointed out to him, amid the jumble of objects on the vanity, two blank-paged notebooks bound in red morocco and two heavy gold automatic pencils with thick leads. Most of the pages in each notebook had been torn out.

"I imagine they used those to talk together," she commented. "He probably had a strict rule that she must never utter a single word or make a single sound." She paused and added uncomfortably, "You're bound to think of them as having been alive, aren't you, even when you know they were just robots."

Carr nodded. "No music . . ." he murmured, fingering

through the other objects on the vanity. "Here's one way she passed the time, though." And he pointed to some drawing paper and sticks of pastel chalk. A yellow one lay apart from the others. Jane flicked it back among the rest with a shudder.

"What's the matter?" Carr asked.

"Something my friend told me," she said uncomfortably. "That Hackman and Wilson and Dris use yellow chalk to mark places they want to remember. Something like tramps' signs. Their special mark is a cross with dots between the arms."

Carr felt himself begin to tremble. "Jane," he said, putting his arm around her. "On one of the pillars of the gate in front of this place, above a ledge too high for you to see over, I saw such a mark."

At that moment they heard a faint and muffled baying.

Jane whirled out of his arms, ran and lowered the panel between the rooms, came back and blew out the lamp. They stood clinging together in the darkness, their eyes near the long slit.

They heard a padding and scratching and a panting that gradually grew louder. Then footsteps and muttered words. A snarl that was instantly cut off. Then a light began to bob through the bedroom doorway. It grew brighter, until they could see almost all of the bedroom through the crack with its tangled edging of dust and lint.

"Watch out," they heard Wilson call warningly from beyond the door. "They may try something."

"I only hope they do," they heard Hackman reply happily. "Oh how I hope they do!"

And then through the bedroom door the hound came snuffing. It was larger even than Carr had imagined, larger than any Great Dane or Newfoundland he'd ever seen, and its jaws were bigger, and its eyes burned like red coals in its short, ash-colored hair. He felt Jane shaking in his arms.

Hackman walked at its side, her eyes searching the room, bending a little, holding it on a short leash. There was sticking plaster on her cheek where Gigolo had scratched her.

"Don't hurry, Daisy," she reproved sweetly. "There'll be lots of time."

Wilson and Dris entered behind her, carrying gasoline lanterns that glared whitely. Wilson put his down near the door. Dris, hurrying, stumbled into him with a curse.

Meanwhile Hackman and the hound had gone almost out of sight in the alcove. Suddenly she cried out, "Daisy, you stupid dog! What are you up to?"

Wilson, about to rebuke Dris, turned hurriedly. "Don't let him hurt the girl!" he cried anxiously. "The girl's mine."

"That's where you're wrong, you fat-bellied has been!" Dris snarled suddenly. "I've played second fiddle to you long enough. This time the girl's mine." And he hurried past Wilson with his light. Wilson grew purple-faced with rage and tugged at something in his pocket.

"Stop it, both of you!" Hackman had returned a few steps, the hound beside her. They both did. Hackman looked back and forth between them. "There'll be no more ridiculous quarreling," she told them. "The girl's mine, isn't she, Daisy?" And she patted the hound, without taking her eyes off them. After a few seconds Wilson's face began to lose its unnatural color and Dris' taught frame relaxed. "That's good," Hackman commented. "It's much the simplest way. And you won't lose your fun. I promise you you'll find it quite enjoyable. Now come on back,' Daisy. I think I understand what you were trying to show me." Once again she went almost out of sight, Wilson following her and Dris carrying the lamp.

"Where is it now?" Carr and Jane heard Hackman ask. There came a sound of eager scratching and snuffing. "Oh yes, I think I get it now. Let's see, one of these circles in the baseboard should press in and give me a fingerhold. Yess . . . yes. Now if I pressed them both together . . ."

Jane and Carr suddenly heard the voices coming more plainly through the wall between the hidden room than from the bedroom. And the next moment they heard the hound snuffing and scratching at the second secret panel.

"Another one, is there?" they heard Hackman say. "Well, it won't take long." Then she raised her voice in a shout. "Yoohoo, in there! Are you enjoying this?"

Carr took the single-shot pistol from his pocket. Its fifty-year old cartridge was a miserable hope, though their only one.

But just then there came a new sound—the sound of footsteps, on the stairs, growing louder, louder, louder. Dris, who, judging from the position of the light, had stayed in the alcove doorway, must have heard it too, for he called out something to the others.

'Stay there!" Hackman hissed at the hound. "Watch!"

Then the three of them ran back into the bedroom, just as there sprinted into it the small dark man with glasses, his flying feet raising a puff of dust at each step.

He was past them before he could stop. Wilson and Dris circled in behind him, cutting off his retreat. Panting, he looked around from fact to stonily-glaring face. Suddenly he laughed wildly.

"You're dead!" he squealed at them shrilly. "You're all dead!"

"This is a long-anticipated entertainment, darling," Hackman told him. She looked beautiful as she smiled. Then the three of them began to close in.

The satisfaction in the small dark man's expression was suddenly veiled by terror. He started to back away toward the alcove. "You called me a coward," he screamed at them wildly. "But I'm not. I've killed you, do you hear, I've killed you."

But he continued to back away as the others closed in.

"Run rabbit!" Hackman cried at him suddenly, and they darted forward. The small dark man whirled around and darted into the alcove. "Now, Daisy!" Hackman shrieked. There was a terrible snarl from the panel, and a thud, and a threshing sound and series of long high screams of agony. In between the screams Carr and Jane could hear Hackman yelling. "Oh, that's lovely, lovely! Get out of my way Dris, I can't see. That's it, Daisy! Beautiful, beautiful. Hold up the light, Dris. Oh good, good dog!"

Carr struggled half-heartedly to get to the panel, but Jane held on to him. Then suddenly the screams stopped and a few moments later the bubbling gasps stopped too, and through the slit they could see Hackman march back into the bedroom in a state of high excitement.

"That's the most wonderful thing that's happened to me in months," she exclaimed, striding up and down. "Only it was much too quick. I could have watched forever." She managed to get a cigarette alight with shaking fingers and puffed it furiously.

The hound came slinking out after her and muzzled her ankles. Red splotches appeared on her stockings.

"Oh get away, you filthy, lovely beast!" she rebuked him affectionately. "Go and watch like I told you." He slunk back into the alcove. Presently Jane and Carr could hear his low breathing just beyond the second panel.

Wilson and Dris, the latter carrying his gasoline lamp, had followed Hackman into the bedroom. They seemed rather less impressed with the whole affair.

"I wonder what he meant when he said he'd killed us?" Dris asked frowningly.

"Mere hysteria and bluff," Wilson assured him. "Typical cornered rat behavior." He smiled. "Well, that was just hunter's luck. Now for the real fun."

"Precisely," agreed a flat, cruel voice.

Hackman, Wilson and Dris all looked at the bedroom doorway. In it stood a pale young man wearing a black topcoat and black snap-brim hat.

"This gives me great pleasure," he said and whipping a black silk scarf from around his neck he ran at Hackman. Three near counterparts poured into the room at his heels. There was the scuff of darting footsteps, the jolt and thud of tumbling bodies, the whistle of effortful breaths.

"I can't bear to watch it, I can't," Jane whispered, shrinking against Carr. But she watched it nevertheless.

One of the black hats ran past the melee to the alcove. Carr and Jane heard four sharp reports, and a little later got a whiff of gunsmoke. The gunman quickly returned from the alcove, but his companions were winning their battle, though not without difficulty.

"I can't bear it," Jane repeated, but still she didn't close her eyes.

Soon it was quiet in the bedroom. The first of the black hats looked around rapidly, taking stock, as he tucked his scarf back inside his coat. "Roberto," he demanded, "was it quite necessary to kill her?"

"I'll say," the man replied. "She almost got my eye with that pin of hers."

The first of the black hats next addressed himself to the man who had run to the alcove, "Giovanni," he said, "you should not have used the gun."

"I thought it wise at the time," Giovanni asserted. "Though as it turned out he made no move at me. He just lay there and took it."

The first of the black hats chuckled. "All bark and no bite, eh? That's the way with most of them. Next time be wiser. Well, are we ready? No need to tidy up in a place like this."

"Shall we search further?" Roberto asked.

The first of the black hats shook his head. "No," he said, "that was all of them, and we're late as it is. Come on, now. Two of you bring the lanterns." In the doorway he turned. "Small dark chap," he said, "we are grateful." And he kissed his fingers and departed.

Carr and Jane heard the footsteps recede down the stairs, faintly heard the slam of a door, and a little later the roar of a souped-up motor. They clung together for perhaps ten minutes in shaking silence. Then Carr broke away and lit the lamp.

Jane hid her face from the light with her hands and threw herself down on the scarlet coverlet.

"I can't bear it," she sobbed. "Wilson's face . . . and Dris's head bent back that way . . . and what they did to Hackman . . . and before that the hound—I tell you, I'll go crazy!"

"Come on, dear," Carr urged anxiously, "We've got to get out of here."

"I couldn't go through that room," she cried wildly. "I couldn't bear to look at them. I'd lose my mind!"

Carr waited until her sobs had grown less hysterical. Then he said to her, "But don't you see what it means, dear? Everyone that knows you were awakened and out of the pattern is dead. The men with black hats don't know about either of us. We can go back to our own lives, and Saturday we're going to meet naturally in the pattern. We'll be together and safe and sure of our place and then we can slowly begin to waken others—people without the selfishness and cruelty of the little gangs."

Her sobbing ceased. She opened her eyes and looked at him.

"Maybe there are more wakened people than we realize," he said. "People like we were, who have wakened without realizing that others are still asleep. People capable of love and sacrifice."

He looked at her. She lifted herself up a little. "Sacrifice," he repeated, "like your friend proved himself capable of. He must have led the men with black hats here deliberately, don't you see? Just as he must have led them to South State

Street. He must have known that the others were planning to trap us here, he must have thought that he'd be wiped out whatever happened, but that we might be saved." He paused. "Maybe it came out of a bottle again, but just the same it was courage."

Jane sat up straight. "I'm ready," she said.

Carr knelt to work the panel, but he couldn't get the trick of it, immediately. "Let me," Jane said, and in a moment had slid it up. Taking the lamp, she started through ahead of him, averting her face from the pitiful form of the small dark man lying beside the love seat.

But Carr, peering over her shoulder as she went down the steps, did look at it—and found himself puzzled.

The mangled throat was hideous, to be sure, but in the otherwise unmarked face and forehead above it were what looked like a couple of neat bullet holes.

He seemed to hear Giovanni say again, "He just lay there and took it."

The lights had all been in the bedroom. In the shadows here Giovanni hadn't noticed that the small dark man was already dead. Naturally.

But in that case—

Soundlessly the hound rose from behind the loveseat and launched its gray bulk at Jane's throat.

Carr whipped his hand over Jane's shoulder. There was a flash, and a crack and a puff of smoke.

The hound's jaws snapped together six inches from Jane's throat and it fell dead.

Carr caught Jane as she collapsed back against him. He steadied the lamp.

He looked down at the pearl-handled pistol in his hand. "The powder was still good," he said . . .

The End

FOUR GHOSTS IN HAMLET

By FRITZ LEIBER

ACTORS ARE A SUPERSTITIOUS lot, probably because chance plays a big part in the success of a production of a company or merely an actor—and because we're still a little closer than other people to the gypsies in the way we live and think. For instance, it's bad luck to have peacock feathers on stage or say the last line of a play at rehearsals or whistle in the dressing room (the one nearest the door gets fired) or sing God Save the Sovereign on a railway train. (A Canadian company got wrecked that way.)

Shakespearean actors are no exception. They simply travel a few extra superstitions, such as the one which forbids reciting the lines of the Three Witches, or anything from *Macbeth*, for that matter, except at performances, rehearsals, and on other legitimate occasions. This might be a good rule for outsiders too—then there wouldn't be the endless flood of books with titles taken from the text of *Macbeth*—you know, *Brief Candle, Tomorrow and Tomorrow, The Sound and the Fury, A Poor Player, All Our Yesterdays*, and those are all just from one brief soliloquy.

And our company, the Governor's company, has a rule against the Ghost in *Hamlet* dropping his greenish cheese-cloth veil over his helmet-framed face until the very moment he makes each of his entrances. Hamlet's dead father mustn't stand veiled in the darkness of the wings.

This last superstition commemorates something which happened not too long ago, an actual ghost story. Sometimes I think it's the greatest ghost story in the world—though certainly not from my way of telling it, which is gossipy and poor, but from the wonder blazing at its core.

It's not only a true tale of the supernatural, but also very much a story about people, for after all—and before everything else—ghosts are people.

The ghostly part of the story first showed itself in the tritest way imaginable: three of our actresses (meaning practically all the ladies in a Shakespearean company) took to having sessions with a Ouija board in the hour before curtain time and sometimes even during a performance when they had long offstage waits, and they became so wrapped up in it and conceited about it and they squeaked so excitedly at the revelations which the planchette spelled out—and three or four times almost missed entrances because of it—that if the Governor weren't such a tolerant commander-in-chief, he would have forbidden them to bring the board to the theater. I'm sure he was tempted to and might have, except that Props pointed out to him that our three ladies probably wouldn't enjoy Ouija sessions one bit in the privacy of a hotel room, that much of the fun in operating a Ouija board is in having a half exasperated, half intrigued floating audience, and that when all's done the basic business of all ladies is glamour, whether of personal charm or of actual witchcraft, since the word means both.

Props—that is, our property man, Billy Simpson—was fascinated by their obsession, as he is by any new thing that comes along, and might very well have broken our Shakespearean taboo by quoting the Three Witches about them, except that Props has no flair for Shakespearean speech at all, no dramatic ability whatsoever, in fact he's the one person in our company who never acts even a bit part or carries a mute spear on stage, though he has other talents which make up for this deficiency—he can throw together a papier mache bust of Pompey in two hours, or turn out a wooden prop dagger all silvery-bladed and hilt-gilded, or fix a zipper, and that's not all.

As for myself, I was very irked at the ridiculous alphabet board, since it seemed to occupy most of Monica Singleton's spare time and satisfy all her hunger for thrills. I'd been trying to promote a romance with her—a long touring season becomes deadly and cold without some sort of heart-tickle—and for a while I'd made progress. But after Ouija came along, I became a ridiculous Guildenstern mooning after an unattainable unseeing Ophelia—which were the parts I and she actually played in *Hamlet*.

I cursed the idiot board with its childish corner-pictures of grinning suns and smirking moons and windblown spirits, and I further alienated Monica by asking her why wasn't it called a Nenein or No-No board (Ninny board!) instead of a Yes-

Yes board? Was that, I inquired, because all spiritualists are forever accentuating the positive and behaving like a pack of fawning yes-men?—yes, we're here; yes, we're your uncle Harry; yes, we're happy on this plane; yes, we have a doctor among us who'll diagnose that pain in your chest; and so on.

Monica wouldn't speak to me for a week after that.

I would have been even more depressed except that Props pointed out to me that no flesh-and-blood man can compete with ghosts in a girl's affections, since ghosts being imaginary have all the charms and perfections a girl can dream of, but that all girls eventually tire of ghosts, or if their minds don't, their bodies do. This eventually did happen, thank goodness, in the case of myself and Monica, though not until we'd had a grisly, mind-wrenching experience—a night of terrors before the nights of love.

So Ouija flourished and the Governor and the rest of us put up with it one way or another, until there came that three-night-stand in Wolverton, when its dismal uncanny old theater tempted our three Ouija-women to ask the board who was the ghost haunting the spooky place and the swooping planchette spelled out the name S-H-A-K-E-S-P-E-A-R-E . . .

But I am getting ahead of my story. I haven't introduced our company except for Monica, Props, and the Governor—and I haven't identified the last of those three.

We call Gilbert Usher the Governor out of sheer respect and affection. He's about the last of the old actor-managers. He hasn't the name of Gielgud or Olivier or Evans or Richardson, but he's spent most of a lifetime keeping Shakespeare alive, spreading that magical a-religious gospel in the more remote counties and the Dominions and the United States, like Benson once did. Our other actors aren't names at all—I refuse to tell you mine!—but with the exception of myself they're good troupers, or if they don't become that the first season, they drop out. Gruelingly long season, much uncomfortable traveling, and small profits are our destiny.

This particular season had got to that familiar point where the plays are playing smoothly and everyone's a bit tireder than he realizes and the restlessness sets in. Robert Dennis, our juvenile, was writing a novel of theatrical life (he said) mornings at the hotel—up at seven to slave at it, our Robert claimed. Poor old Guthrie Boyd had started to drink again, and drink quite too much, after an abstemious two months

114

which had astonished everyone.

Francis Farley Scott, our leading man, had started to drop hints that he was going to organize a Shakespearean repertory company of his own next year and he began to have conspiratorial conversations with Gertrude Grainger, our leading lady, and to draw us furtively aside one by one to make us hypothetical offers, no exact salary named. F. F. is as old as the Governor—who is our star, of course—and he has no talents at all except for self-infatuation and a somewhat grandiose yet impressive fashion of acting. He's portly like an opera tenor and quite bald and he travels an assortment of thirty toupees, ranging from red to black shot with silver, which he alternates with shameless abandon—they're for wear offstage, not on. It doesn't matter to him that the company knows all about his multi-colored artificial toppings, for we're part of his world of illusion, and he's firmly convinced that the stage-struck local ladies he squires about never notice, or at any rate mind the deception. He once gave me a lecture on the subtleties of suiting the color of your hair to the lady you're trying to fascinate—her own age, hair color, and so on.

Every year F. F. plots to start a company of his own—it's a regular midseason routine with him—and every year it comes to nothing, for he's as lazy and impractical as he is vain. Yet F. F. believes he could play any part in Shakespeare or all of them at once in a pinch; perhaps the only F. F. Scott Company which would really satisfy him would be one in which he would be the only actor—a Shakespearean monologue; in fact, the one respect in which F. F. is not lazy is in his eagerness to double as many parts as possible in any single play.

F. F.'s yearly plots never bother the Governor a bit—he keeps waiting wistfully for F. F. to fix him with an hypnotic eye and in a hoarse whisper ask *him* to join the Scott company.

And I of course was hoping that now at last Monica Singleton would stop trying to be the most exquisite ingenue that ever came tripping Shakespeare's way (rehearsing her parts even in her sleep, I guessed, though I was miles from being in a position to know that for certain) and begin to take note and not just advantage of my devoted attentions.

But then old Sybil Jameson bought the Ouija board and Gertrude Grainger dragooned an unwilling Monica into placing her fingertips on the planchette along with theirs "just for a lark." Next day Gertrude announced to several of us in a hushed voice that Monica had the most amazing undeveloped mediumistic talent she'd ever encountered, and from then on the girl was a Ouija-addict. Poor tight-drawn Monica, I suppose she had to explode out of her self-imposed Shakespearean discipline somehow, and it was just too bad it had to be the board instead of me. Though come to think of it, I shouldn't have felt quite so resentful of the board, for she might have exploded with Robert Dennis, which would have been infinitely worse, though we were never quite sure of Robert's sex. For that matter I wasn't sure of Gertrude's and suffered agonies of uncertain jealousy when she captured my beloved. I was obsessed with the vision of Gertrude's bold knees pressing Monica's under the Ouija board, though with Sybil's bony ones for chaperones, fortunately.

Francis Farley Scott, who was jealous too because this new toy had taken Gertrude's mind off their annual plottings, said rather spitefully that Monica must be one of those grabby girls who have to take command of whatever they get their fingers on, whether it's a man or a planchette, but Props told me he'd bet anything that Gertrude and Sybil had "followed" Monica's first random finger movements like the skillfulest dancers guiding a partner while seeming to yield, in order to coax her into the business and make sure of their third.

Sometimes I thought that F. F. was right and sometimes Props and sometimes I thought that Monica had a genuine supernatural talent, though I don't ordinarily believe in such things, and that last really frightened me, for such a person might give up live men for ghosts forever. She was such a sensitive, subtle, wraith-cheeked girl and she could get so keyed up and when she touched the planchette her eyes got such an empty look, as if her mind had traveled down into her fingertips or out to the ends of time and space. And once the three of them gave me a character reading from the board which embarrassed me with its accuracy. The same thing happened to several other people in the company. Of course, as Props pointed out, actors can be pretty good character analysts whenever they stop being ego-maniacs.

After reading characters and foretelling the future for several weeks, our Three Weird Sisters got interested in reincarnation and began asking the board and then telling us what famous or infamous people we'd been in past lives. Gertrude

Grainger had been Queen Boadicea, I wasn't surprised to hear. Sybil Jameson had been Cassandra. While Monica was once mad Queen Joanna of Castile and more recently a prize hysterical patient of Janet at the Salpetriere—touches which irritated and frightened me more than they should have. Billy Simpson—Props—had been an Egyptian silversmith under Quenn Hatshepsut and later a servant of Samuel Pepys; he heard this with a delighted chuckle. Guthrie Boyd had been the Emperor Claudius and Robert Dennis had been Caligula. For some reason I had been both John Wilkes Booth and Lambert Simnel, which irritated me considerably, for I saw no romance but only neurosis in assassinating an American president and dying in a burning barn, or impersonating the Earl of Warwick, pretending unsuccessfully to the British throne, being pardoned for it—of all things!—and spending the rest of my life as a scullion in the kitchen of Henry VII and his son. The fact that both Booth and Simnel had been actors of a sort—a poor sort—naturally irritated me the more. Only much later did Monica confess to me that the board had probably made those decisions because I had had such a "tragic, dangerous, defeated look"—a revelation which surprised and flattered me.

Francis Farley Scott was flattered too, to hear he'd once been Henry VIII—he fancied all those wives and he wore his golden blonde toupee after the show that night—until Gertrude and Sybil and Monica announced that the Governor was a reincarnation of no less than William Shakespeare himself. That made F. F. so jealous that he instantly sat down at the prop table, grabbed up a quill pen, and did an impromptu rendering of Shakespeare composing Hamlet's "To be or not to be" soliloquy. It was an effective performance, though with considerably more frowning and eye-rolling and trying of lines for sound than I imagine Willy S. himself used originally, and when F. F. finished, even the Governor, who'd been standing unobserved in the shadows beside Props, applauded with the latter.

Governor kidded the pants off the idea of himself as Shakespeare. He said that if Willy S. were ever reincarnated it ought to be as a world-famous dramatist who was secretly in his spare time the world's greatest scientist and philosopher and left clues to his identity in his mathematical equations—

that way he'd get his own back at Bacon, or rather the Baconians.

Yet I suppose if you had to pick someone for a reincarnation of Shakespeare, Gilbert Usher wouldn't be a bad choice. Insofar as a star and director ever can be, the Governor is gentle and self-effacing—as Shakespeare himself must have been, or else there would never have arisen that ridiculous Bacon-Oxford-Marlowe-Elizabeth-take-your-pick-who-wrote-Shakespeare controversy. And the Governor has a sweet melancholy about him, though he's handsomer and despite his years more athletic than one imagines Shakespeare being. And he's generous to a fault, especially where old actors who've done brave fine things in the past are concerned.

This season his mistake in that last direction had been in hiring Guthrie Boyd to play some of the more difficult older leading roles, including a couple F. F. usually handles: Brutus, Othello, and besides those Duncan in *Macbeth*, Kent in *King Lear*, and the Ghost in *Hamlet*.

Guthrie was a bellowing, hard-drinking bear of an actor, who'd been a Shakespearean star in Australia and successfully smuggled some of his reputation west—he learned to moderate his bellowing, while his emotions were always simple and sincere, though explosive—and finally even spent some years in Hollywood. But there his drinking caught up with him, probably because of the stupid film parts he got, and he failed six times over. His wife divorced him. His children cut themselves off. He married a starlet and she divorced him. He dropped out of sight.

Then after several years the Governor ran into him. He'd been rusticating in Canada with a stubborn teetotal admirer. He was only a shadow of his former self, but there was some substance to the shadow—and he wasn't drinking. The Governor decided to take a chance on him—although the company manager Harry Grossman was dead set against it—and during rehearsals and the first month or so of performances it was wonderful to see how old Guthrie Boyd came back, exactly as if Shakespeare were a restorative medicine.

It may be stuffy or sentimental of me to say so, but you know, I think Shakespeare's good for people. I don't know of an actor, except myself, whose character hasn't been strengthened and his vision widened and charity quickened by working in the plays. I've heard that before Gilbert Usher became a Shakespearean, he was a more ruthlessly ambitious and critical man, not without malice, but the plays mellowed him, as they've mellowed Props' philosophy and given him a zest for life.

Because of his contact with Shakespeare, Robert Dennis is a less strident and pettish swish (if he is one), Gertrude Grainger's outbursts of cold rage have an undercurrent of queenly make-believe, and even Francis Farley Scott's grubby little seductions are probably kinder and less insultingly illusionary.

In fact I sometimes think that what civilized serenity the British people possess, and small but real ability to smile at themselves, is chiefly due to their good luck in having had William Shakespeare born one of their company.

But I was telling how Guthrie Boyd performed very capably those first weeks, against the expectations of most of us, so that we almost quit holding our breaths—or sniffing at his. His Brutus was workmanlike, his Kent quite fine—that bluff rough honest part suited him well—and he regularly got admiring notices for his Ghost in *Hamlet*. I think his years of living death as a drinking alcoholic had given him an understanding of loneliness and frozen abilities and despair that he put to good use—probably unconsciously—in interpreting that small role.

He was really a most impressive figure in the part, even just visually. The Ghost's basic costume is simple enough—a big all-enveloping cloak that brushes the ground-cloth, a big dull helmet with the tiniest battery light inside its peak to throw a faint green glow on the Ghost's features, and over the helmet a veil of greenish cheesecloth that registers as mist to the audience. He wears a suit of stage armor under the cloak, but that's not important and at a pinch he can do without it, for his cloak can cover his entire body.

The Ghost doesn't switch on his helmet-light until he makes his entrance, for fear of it being glimpsed by an edge of the audience, and nowadays because of that superstition or rule I told you about, he doesn't drop the cheesecloth veil until the last second either, but when Guthrie Boyd was playing the part that rule didn't exist and I have a vivid recollection of him standing in the wings, waiting to go on, a big bearish inscrutable figure about as solid and un-supernatural as a bushy seven-foot evergreen covered by a gray tarpaulin.

But then when Guthrie would switch on the tiny light and stride smoothly and silently on stage and his hollow distant tormented voice boom out, there'd be a terrific shivery thrill, even for us backstage, as if we were listening to words that really had traveled across black windy infinite gulfs from the Afterworld or the Other Side.

At any rate Guthrie was a great Ghost, and adequate or a bit better than that in most of his other parts—for those first nondrinking weeks. He seemed very cheerful on the whole, modestly buoyed up by his comeback, though sometimes something empty and dead would stare for a moment out of his eyes—the old drinking alcoholic wondering what all this fatiguing sober nonsense was about. He was especially looking forward to our three-night-stand at Wolverton, although that was still two months in the future then. The reason was that both his children—married and with families now, of course—lived and worked at Wolverton and I'm sure he set great store on proving to them in person his rehabilitation, figuring it would lead to a reconciliation and so on.

But then came his first performance as Othello. (The Governor, although the star, always played Iago—an equal role, though not the title one.) Guthrie was almost too old for Othello, of couse, and besides that, his health wasn't good— the drinking years had taken their toll of his stamina and the work of rehearsals and of first nights in eight different plays after years away from the theater had exhausted him. But somehow the old volcano inside him go seething again and he gave a magnificent performance. Next morning the papers raved about him and one review rated him even better than the Governor.

That did it, unfortunately. The glory of his triumph was too much for him. The next night—*Othello* again—he was drunk as a skunk. He remembered most of his lines—though the Governor had to throw him about every sixth one out of the side of his mouth—but he weaved and wobbled, he planked a big hand on the shoulder of every other character he addressed to keep from falling over, and he even forgot to put in his false teeth the first two acts, so that his voice was mushy. To cap that, he started really to strangle Gertrude Grainger in the last scene, until that rather browny Desdemona, unseen by the audience, gave him a knee in the gut; then, after stabbing himself, he flung the prop dagger high in the flies so that it came down with two lazy twists and piercing the ground-cloth buried its blunt point deep in the soft wood of the stage floor not three feet from Monica, who plays Iago's wife Emilia and so was lying dead on the stage at that point in the drama, murdered by her villanous husband—and might have been dead for real if the dagger had followed a slightly different trajectory.

Since a third performance of *Othello* was billed for the following night, the Governor had no choice but to replace Guthrie with Francis Farley Scott, who did a good job (for him) of covering up his satisfaction at getting his old role back. F. F., always a plushy and lascivious-eyed Moor, also did a good job with the part, coming in that way without even a brush-up rehearsal, so that one critic, catching the first and third shows, marveled how we could change big roles at will, thinking we'd done it solely to demonstrate our virtuosity.

Of course the Governor read the riot act to Guthrie and carried him off to a doctor, who without being prompted threw a big scare into him about his drinking and his heart, so that he just might have recovered from his lapse, except that two nights later we did *Julius Caesar* and Guthrie, instead of being satisfied with being workman-like, decided to recoup himself with a really rousing performance. So he bellowed and groaned and bugged his eyes as I suppose he had done in his palmiest Australian days. His optimistic self-satisfaction between scenes was frightening to behold. Not too terrible a performance, truly, but the critics all panned him and one of them said, "Guthrie Boyd played Brutus—a bunch of vocal cords wrapped up in a toga."

That tied up the package and knotted it tight. Thereafter Guthrie was medium pie-eyed from morning to night—and often more than medium. The Governor had to yank him out of Brutus too (F. F. again replacing), but being the Governor he didn't sack him. He put him into a couple of bit parts—Montano and the Soothsayer—in *Othello* and *Caesar* and let him keep on at the others and he gave me and Joe Rubens and sometimes Props the job of keeping an eye on the poor old sot and making sure he got to the theater by the half hour and if possible not too plastered. Often he played the Ghost or the Doge of Venice in his street clothes under cloak or scarlet robe, but he played them. And many were the nights Joe and I made the rounds of half the local bars before we corraled him. The Governor sometimes refers to Joe Rubens and me in mild derision as "the American element" in his company, but just the same he depends on us quite a bit; and I certainly don't mind being one of his trouble-shooters—it's a joy to serve him.

All this may seem to contradict my statement about our getting to the point, about this time, where the plays were playing smoothly and the monotony setting in. But it doesn't really. There's always something going wrong in a theatrical company—anything else would be abnormal; just as the Samoans say no party is a success until somebody's dropped a plate or spilled a drink or tickled the wrong woman.

Besides, once Guthrie had got Othello and Brutus off his neck, he didn't do too badly. The little parts and even Kent he could play passably whether drunk or sober. King Duncan, for instance, and the Doge in *The Merchant* are easy to play drunk because the actor always has a couple of attendants to either side of him, who can guide his steps if he weaves and even hold him up if necessary—which can turn out to be an effective dramatic touch, registering as the infirmity of extreme age.

And somehow Guthrie continued to give that same masterful performance as the Ghost and get occasional notices for it. In fact Sybil Jameson insisted he was a shade better in the Ghost now that he was invaribly drunk; which could have been true. And he still talked about the three-night-stand coming up in Wolverton, though now as often with gloomy apprehension as with proud fatherly anticipation.

Well, the three-night-stand eventually came. We arrived at Wolverton on a non-playing evening. To the surprise of most of us, but especially Guthrie, his son and daughter were there at the station to welcome him with their respective spouses and all their kids and numerous in-laws and a great gaggle of friends. Their cries of greeting when they spotted him were almost an organized cheer and I looked around for a brass band to strike up.

I found out later that Sybil Jameson, who knew them, had been sending them all his favorable notices, so that they were eager as weasels to be reconciled with him and show him off as blatantly as possible.

When he saw his childrens' and grandchildrens' faces and realized the cries were for him, old Guthrie got red in the face and beamed like the sun, and they closed in around him and carried him off in triumph for an evening of celebrations.

Next day I heard from Sybil, whom they'd carried off with him, that everything had gone beautifully. He'd drunk like a fish, but kept marvellous control, so that no one but she noticed, and the warmth of the reconciliation of Guthrie to everyone, complete strangers included, had been wonderful to behold. Guthrie's son-in-law, a pugnacious chap, had got angry when he'd heard Guthrie wasn't to play Brutus the third night, and he declared that Gilbert Usher must be jealous of his magnificent father-in-law. Everything was forgiven twenty times over. They'd even tried to put old Sybil to bed with Guthrie, figuring romantically, as people will about actors, that she must be his mistress. All this was very fine, and of course wonderful for Guthrie, and for Sybil too in a fashion, yet I suppose the unconstrained night-long bash, after two months of uninterrupted semi-controlled drunkenness, was just about the worst thing anybody could have done to the old boy's sodden body and laboring heart.

Meanwhile on that first evening I accompanied Joe Rubens and Props to the theater we were playing at Wolverton to make sure the scenery got stacked right and the costume trunks were all safely arrived and stowed. Joe is our stage manager besides doing rough or Hebraic parts like Caliban and Tubal—he was a professional boxer in his youth and got his nose smashed crooked. Once I started to take boxing lessons from him, figuring an action should know everything, but during the third lesson I walked into a gentle right cross and although it didn't exactly stun me there were bells ringing faintly in my head for six hours afterwards and I lived in a world of faery and that was the end of my fistic career. Joe is actually a most versatile actor—for instance, he understands the Governor in Macbeth, Lear, Iago, and of course Shylock —though his brutal moon-face is against him, especially when his make-up doesn't include a beard. But he dotes on being genial and in the States he often gets a job by day playing Santa Claus in big department stores during the month before Christmas.

The Monarch was a cavernous old place, very grimy backstage, but with a great warren of dirty little dressing rooms and even a property room shaped like an L stage left. Its empty shelves were thick with dust.

There hadn't been a show in the Monarch for over a year, I saw from the yellowing sheets thumb-tacked to the call-board as I tore them off and replaced thim with a simple black-crayoned HAMLET: TONIGHT AT 8:30.

Then I noticed, by the cold inadequate working lights, a couple of tiny dark shapes dropping down from the flies and gliding around in wide swift circles—out into the house too, since the curtain was up. Bats, I realized with a little start—the Monarch was really halfway through the lich gate. The bats would fit very nicely with *Macbeth*, I told myself, but not so well with *The Merchant of Venice*, while with Hamlet they should neither help nor hinder, provided they didn't descend in nightfighter squadrons; it would be nice if they stuck to the Ghost scenes.

I'm sure the Governor had decided we'd open at Wolverton with *Hamlet* so that Guthrie would have the best chance of being a hit in his children's home city.

Billy Simpson, shoving his properties table into place just in front of the dismal L of the prop room, observed cheerfully, "It's a proper haunted house. The girls'll find some rare ghosts here, I'll wager, if they work their board."

Which turned out to be far truer than he realized at the time—I think.

"Bruce!" Joe Rubens called to me. "We better buy a couple of rat traps and set them out. There's something scuttling back of the drops."

But when I entered the Monarch next night, well before the hour, by the creaky thick metal stage door, the place had been swept and tidied a bit. With the groundcloth down and the *Hamlet* set up, it didn't look too terrible, even though the curtain was still unlowered, dimly showing the house and its curves of empty seats and the two faint green exit lights with no one but myself to look at them.

There was a little pool of light around the callboard stage right, and another glow the other side of the stage beyond the wings, and lines of light showing around the edges of the door of the second dressing room, next to the star's.

I started across the dark stage, sliding my shoes softly so as not to trip over a cable or stage-screw and brace, and right away I got the magic electric feeling I often do in an empty theater the night of a show. Only this time there was something additional, something that started a shiver crawling down my neck. It wasn't, I think, the thought of the bats which might now be swooping around me unseen, skirling their inaudibly shrill trumpet calls, or even of the rats which *might* be watching sequin-eyed from behind trunks and flats, although not an hour ago Joe had told me that the traps he'd actually procured and set last night had been empty today.

No, it was more as if all of Shakespeare's characters were invisibly there around me—all the infinite possibilities of the theater. I imagined Rosalind and Falstaff and Prospero standing arm-in-arm watching me with different smiles. And Caliban grinning down from where he silently swung in the flies. And side by side, but unsmiling and not arm-in-arm: Macbeth and Iago and Dick the Three Eyes—Richard III. And all the rest of Shakespeare's myriad-minded good-evil crew.

I passed through the wings opposite and there in the second pool of light Billy Simpson sat behind his table with the properties for *Hamlet* set out on it: the skulls, the foils, the lantern, the purses, the parchmenty letters, Ophelia's flowers, and all the rest. It was odd Props having everything ready quite so early and a bit odd too that he should be alone, for Props has the un-actorish habit of making friends with all sorts of locals, such as policemen and porters and flower women and newsboys and shopkeepers and tramps who claim they're indigent actors, and even inviting them backstage with him—a fracture of rules which the Governor allows since Props is such a sensible chap. He has a great liking for people, especially low people, Props has, and for all the humble details of life. He'd make a good writer, I'd think, except for his utter lack of dramatic flair and story-skill—a sort of prosiness that goes with his profession.

And now he was sitting at his table, his stooped shoulders almost inside the doorless entry to the empty-shelfed prop room—no point in using it for a three-night-stand—and he was gazing at me quizzically. He has a big forehead—the light was on that—and a tapering chin—that was in shadow—and rather large eyes, which were betwixt the light and the dark. Sitting there like that, he seemed to me for a moment (mostly because of the outspread props, I guess) like the midnight Master of the Show in *The Rubaiyat* round whom all the rest of us move like shadow shapes.

Usually he has a quick greeting for anyone, but tonight he was silent, and that added to the illusion.

"Props," I said, "this theater's got a supernatural smell."

His expression didn't change at that, but he solemnly sniffed the air in several little whiffles adding up to one big inhalation, and as he did so he threw his head back, bringing his weakish chin into the light and shattering the illusion.

"Dust," he said after a moment. "Dust and old plush and scenery water-paint and sweat and drains and gelatin and greasepaint and powder and a breath of whisky. But the supernatural . . . no, I can't smell that. Unless . . ." And he sniffed again, but shook his head.

I chuckled at his materialism—although that touch about whisky did seem fanciful, since I hadn't been drinking and Props never does and Guthrie Boyd was nowhere in evidence. Props has a mind like a notebook for sensory details—and for the minutia of human habits too. It was Props, for instance, who told me about the actual notebook in which John McCarthy (who would be playing Fortinbras and the Player King in a couple of hours) jots down the exact number of hours he sleeps each night and keeps totting them up, so he knows when he'll have to start sleeping extra hours to average the full nine he thinks he must get each night to keep from dying.

It was also Props who pointed out to me that F. F. is much more careless gumming his offstage toupees to his head than his theater wigs—a studied carelessness, like that in tying a bowtie, he assured me; it indicated, he said, a touch of contempt for the whole offstage world.

Props isn't *only* a detail-worm, but it's perhaps because he is one that he has sympathy for all human hopes and frailties, even the most trivial, like my selfish infatuation with Monica.

Now I said to him, "I didn't mean an actual smell, Billy. But back there just now I got the feeling anything might happen tonight."

He nodded slowly and solemnly. With anyone but Props I'd have wondered if he weren't a little drunk. Then he said, "You were on a stage. You know, the science-fiction writers are missing a bet there. We've got time machines right now. Theaters. Theaters are time machines and spaceships too. They take people on trips through the future and the past and the elsewhere and the might-have-been—yes, and if it's done well enough, give them glimpses of Heaven and Hell."

I nodded back at him. Such grotesque fancies are the

closest Props ever comes to escaping from prosiness.

I said, "Well, let's hope Guthrie gets aboard the spaceship before the curtain up-jets. Tonight we're depending on his children having the sense to deliver him here intact. Which from what Sybil says about them is not to be taken for granted."

Props stared at me owlishly and slowly shook his head. "Guthrie got here about ten minutes ago," he said, "and looking no drunker than usual."

"That's a relief," I told him, meaning it.

"The girls are having a Ouija session," he went on, as if he were determined to account for all of us from moment to moment. "They smelt the supernatural here, just as you did, and they're asking the board to name the culprit." Then he stooped so that he looked almost hunchbacked and he felt for something under the table.

I nodded. I'd guessed the Ouija-part from the lines of light showing around the door of Gertrude Grainger's dressing room.

Props straightened up and he had a pint bottle of whisky in his hand. I don't think a loaded revolver would have dumbfounded me as much. He unscrewed the top.

"There's the Governor coming in," he said tranquilly, hearing the stage door creak and evidently some footsteps my own ears missed. "That's seven of us in the theater before the hour."

He took a big slow swallow of whisky and recapped the bottle, as naturally as if it were a nightly action. I goggled at him without comment. What he was doing was simply unheard of—for Billy Simpson.

At that moment there was a sharp scream and a clatter of thin wood and something twangy and metallic falling and a scurry of footsteps. Our previous words must have cocked a trigger in me, for I was at Gertrude Grainger's dressing-room door as fast as I could sprint—no worry this time about tripping over cables or braces in the dark.

I yanked the door open and there by the bright light of the bulbs framing the mirror were Gertrude and Sybil sitting close together with the Ouija board face down on the floor in front of them along with a flimsy wire-backed chair, overturned. While pressing back into Gertrude's costumes hanging on the rack across the little room, almost as if she wanted to hide behind them like bed-clothes, was Monica pale and staring-eyed. She didn't seem to recognize me. The dark-green heavily brocaded costume Gertrude wears as the Queen in *Hamlet*, into which Monica was chiefly pressing herself, accentuated her pallor. All three of them were in their street-clothes.

I went to Monica and put an arm around her and gripped her hand. It was cold as ice. She was standing rigidly.

While I was doing that Gertrude stood up and explained in rather haughty tones what I told you earlier: about them asking the board who the ghost was haunting the Monarch tonight and the planchette spelling out S-H-A-K-E-S-P-E-A-R-E . . .

"I don't know why it startled you so, dear," she ended crossly, "It's very natural his spirit should attend performances of his plays."

I felt the slim body I clasped relax a little. That relieved me. I was selfishly pleased at having got an arm around it, even under such public and unamorous circumstances, while at the same time my silly mind was thinking that if Props had been lying to me about Guthrie Boyd having come in no more drunken than usual (this new Props who drank straight whisky in the theater could lie too, I supposed) why then we could certainly use William Shakespeare tonight, since the Ghost in *Hamlet* is the one part in all his plays Shakespeare is supposed to have acted on the stage.

"I don't know why myself now," Monica suddenly answered from beside me, shaking her head as if to clear it. She became aware of me at last, started to pull away, then let my arm stay around her.

The next voice that spoke was the Governor's. He was standing in the doorway, smiling faintly, with Props peering around his shoulder. Props would be as tall as the Governor if he ever straightened up, but his stoop takes almost a foot off his height.

The Governor said softly, a comic light in his eyes, "I think we should be content to bring Shakespeare's plays to life, without trying for their author. It's hard enough on the nerves just to *act* Shakespeare."

He stepped forward with one of his swift, naturally grace-ful movements and kneeling on one knee he picked up the fallen board and planchette. "At all events I'll take these in charge for tonight. Feeling better now, Miss Singleton?" he asked as he straightened and stepped back.

"Yes, quite all right," she answered flusteredly, disengaging my arm and pulling away from me rather too quickly.

He nodded. Gertrude Grainger was staring at him coldly, as if about to say something scathing, but she didn't. Sybil Jameson was looking at the floor. She seemed embarrassed, yet puzzled too.

I followed the Governor out of the dressing room and told him, in case Props hadn't, about Guthrie Boyd coming to the theater early. My momentary doubt of Props's honesty seemed plain silly to me now, although his taking that drink remained an astonishing riddle.

Props confirmed me about Guthrie coming in, though his manner was a touch abstracted.

The Governor nodded his thanks for the news, then twitched a nostril and frowned. I was sure he'd caught a whiff of alcohol and didn't know to which of us two to attribute it—or perhaps even to one of the ladies, or to an earlier passage of Guthrie this way.

He said to me, "Would you come into my dressing room for a bit, Bruce?"

I followed him, thinking he'd picked me for the drinker and wondering how to answer—best perhaps simply silently accept the fatherly lecture—but when he'd turned on the lights and I'd shut the door, his first question was, "You're attracted to Miss Singleton, aren't you, Bruce?"

When I nodded abruptly, swallowing my morsel of surprise, he went on softly but emphatically, "Then why don't you quit hovering and playing Galahad and really go after her? Ordinarily I must appear to frown on affairs in the company, but in this case it would be the best way I know of to break up those Ouija sessions, which are obviously harming the girl."

I managed to grin and tell him I'd be happy to obey his instructions—and do it entirely on my own initiative too.

He grinned back and started to toss the Ouija board on his couch, but instead put it and the planchette carefully down on the end of his long dressing table and put a second question to me.

"What do you think of some of this stuff they're getting over the board, Bruce?"

I said, "Well, that last one gave me a shiver, all right—I suppose because . . ." and I told him about sensing the presence of Shakespeare's characters in the dark. I finished, "But of course the whole idea is nonsense," and I grinned.

He didn't grin back.

I continued impulsively, "There was one idea they had a few weeks back that impressed me, though it didn't seem to impress you. I hope you won't think I'm trying to butter you up, Mr. Usher. I mean the idea of you being a reincarnation of William Shakespeare."

He laughed delightedly and said, "Clearly you don't yet know the difference between a player and a playwright, Bruce. Shakespeare striding about romantically with head thrown back?—and twirling a sword and shaping his body and voice to every feeling handed him? Oh no! I'll grant he might have played the Ghost—it's a part within the scope of an average writer's talents, requiring nothing more than that he stand still and sound off sepulchrally."

He paused and smiled and went on. "No, there's only one person in this company who might be Shakespeare come again, and that's Billy Simpson. Yes, I mean Props. He's a listener and he knows how to put himself in touch with everyone and then he's got that rat-trap mind for every hue and scent and sound of life, inside or out the mind. And he's very analytic. Oh, I know he's got no poetic talent, but surely Shakespeare wouldn't have that in *every* reincarnation. I'd think he'd need about a dozen lives in which to gather material for every one in which he gave it dramatic form. Don't you find something very poignant in the idea of a mute inglorious Shakespeare spending whole humble lifetimes collecting the necessary stuff for one great dramatic burst? Think about it some day."

I was doing that already and finding it a fascinating fantasy. It crystalized so perfectly the feeling I'd got seeing Billy Simpson behind his property table. And then Props did have have a high-foreheaded poet-schoolmaster's face like that given Shakespeare in the posthumous engravings and woodcuts and portraits. Why, even their initials were the same. It made me feel strange.

Then the Governor put his third question to me.

"He's drinking tonight, isn't he? I mean Props, not Guthrie."

I didn't say anything, but my face must have answered for me—at least to such a student of expressions as the Governor —for he smiled and said, "You needn't worry. I wouldn't be angry with him. In fact, the only other time I know of that Props drank spirits by himself in the theater, I had a great deal to thank him for." His lean face grew thoughtful. "It was long before your time, in fact it was the first season I took out a company of my own. I had barely enough money to pay the printer for the three-sheets and get the first-night curtain up. After that it was touch and go for months. Then in mid-season we had a run of bad luck—a two-night heavy fog in one city, an influenza scare in another, Harvey Wilkins' Shakespearean troupe two weeks ahead of us in a third. And when in the next town we played it turned out the advance sale was very light—because my name was unknown there and the theater an unpopular one—I realized I'd have to pay off the company while there was still money enough to get them home, if not the scenery.

"That night I caught Props swigging, but I hadn't the heart to chide him for it—in fact I don't think I'd have blamed anyone, except perhaps myself, for getting drunk that night. But then during the performance the actors and even the union stagehands we travel began coming to my dressing room by ones and twos and telling me they'd be happy to work without salary for another three weeks, if I thought that might give us a chance of recouping. Well, of course I grabbed at their offers and we got a spell of brisk pleasant weather and we hit a couple of places starved for Shakespeare, and things worked out, even to paying all the back salary owed before the season was ended.

"Later on I discovered it was Props who had put them all up to doing it."

Gilbert Usher looked up at me and one of his eyes was wet and his lips were working just a little. "I couldn't have done it myself," he said, "for I wasn't a popular man with my company that first season—I'd been riding everyone much too hard and with nasty sarcasms—and I hadn't yet learned how to ask anyone for help when I really needed it. But Billy Simpson did what I couldn't, though he had to nerve himself for it with spirits. He's quick enough with his tongue in ordinary circumstances, as you know, particularly when he's being the friendly listener, but apparently when something very special is required of him, he must drink himself to the proper pitch. I'm wondering . . ."

His voice trailed off and then he straightened up before his mirror and started to unknot his tie and he said to me briskly, "Better get dressed now, Bruce. And then look in on Guthrie, will you?"

My mind was churning some rather strange thoughts as I hurried up the iron stairs to the dressing room I shared with Robert Dennis. I got on my Guildenstern make-up and costume, finishing just as Robert arrived; as Laertes, Robert makes a late entrance and so needn't hurry to the theater on *Hamlet* nights. Also, although we don't make a point of it, he and I spend as little time together in the dressing room as we can.

Before going down I looked into Guthrie Boyd's. He wasn't there, but the lights were on and the essentials of the Ghost's costume weren't in sight—impossible to miss that big helmet! —so I assumed he'd gone down ahead of me.

It was almost the half hour. The house lights were on, the curtain down, more stage lights on too, and quite a few of us about. I noticed that Props was back in the chair behind his table and not looking particularly different from any other night—perhaps the drink had been a once-only aberration and not some symptom of a crisis in the company.

I didn't make a point of hunting for Guthrie. When he gets costumed early he generally stands back in a dark corner somewhere, wanting to be alone—perchance to sip, aye, there's the rub!—or visits with Sybil in her dressing room.

I spotted Monica sitting on a trunk by the switchboard, where backstage was brightest lit at the moment. She looked ethereal yet springlike in her blonde Ophelia wig and first costume, a pale green one. Recalling my happy promise to the Governor, I bounced up beside her and asked her straight out about the Ouija business, pleased to have something to the point besides the plays to talk with her about—and really not worrying as much about her nerves as I suppose I should have.

She was in a very odd mood, both agitated and abstracted, her gaze going back and forth between distant and near and very distant. My questions didn't disturb her at all, in fact I got the feeling she welcomed them, yet she genuinely didn't seem able to tell me much about why she'd been so frightened at the last name the board had spelled. She told me that she actually did get into a sort of dream state when she worked the board and that she'd screamed before she'd quite comprehended what had shocked her so; then her mind had blacked out for a few seconds, she thought.

"One thing though, Bruce," she said. "I'm not going to work the board any more, at least when the three of us are alone like that."

"That sounds like a wise idea," I agreed, trying not to let the extreme heartiness of my agreement show through.

She stopped peering around as if for some figure to appear that wasn't in the play and didn't belong backstage, and she laid her hand on mine and said, "Thanks for coming so quickly when I went idiot and screamed."

I was about to improve this opportunity by telling her that the reason I'd come so quickly was that she was so much in my mind, but just then Joe Rubens came hurrying up with the Governor behind him in his Hamlet black to tell me that neither Guthrie Boyd nor his Ghost costume was to be found anywhere in the theater.

What's more, Joe had got the phone numbers of Guthrie's son and daughter from Sybil and rung them up. The one phone hadn't answered, while on the other a female voice—presumably a maid's—had informed him that everyone had gone to Guthrie Boyd in *Hamlet*.

Joe was already wearing his cumbrous chain-mail armor for Marcellus—woven cord silvered—so I knew I was elected. I ran upstairs and in the space of time it took Robert Dennis to guess my mission and advise me to try the dingiest bars first and have a drink or two myself in them, I'd put on my hat, overcoat, and wristwatch and left him.

So garbed and as usual nervous about people looking at my ankles, I sallied forth to comb the nearby bars of Wolverton. I consoled myself with the thought that if I found Hamlet's father's ghost drinking his way through them, no one would ever spare a glance for my own costume.

Almost on the stroke of curtain I returned, no longer giving a damn what anyone thought about my ankles. I hadn't found Guthrie or spoken to a soul who'd seen a large male imbiber—most likely of Irish whisky—in great-cloak and antique armor, with perhaps some ghostly green light cascading down his face.

Beyond the curtain the overture was fading to its sinister close and the backstage lights were all down, but there was an angry hushed-voice dispute going on stage left, where the Ghost makes all his entrances and exits. Skipping across the dim stage in front of the blue-lit battlements of Elsinore—I still in my hat and overcoat—I found the Governor and Joe Rubens and with them John McCarthy all ready to go on as the Ghost in his Fortinbras armor with a dark cloak and some green gauze over it.

But alongside them was Francis Farley Scott in a very similar get-up—no armor, but a big enough cloak to hide his King costume and a rather more impressive helmet than John's.

They were all very dim in the midnight glow leaking back from the dimmed-down blue floods. The five of us were the only people I could see on this side of the stage.

F. F. was arguing vehemently that he must be allowed to double the Ghost with King Claudius because he knew the part better than John and because—this was the important thing—he could imitate Guthrie's voice perfectly enough to deceive his children and perhaps save their illusions about him. Sybil had looked through the curtain hole and seen them and all of their yesterday crowd, with new recruits besides, occupying all of the second, third, and fourth rows center, chattering with excitement and beaming with anticipation. Harry Grossman had confirmed this from the front of the house.

I could tell that the Governor was vastly irked at F. F. and at the same time touched by the last part of his argument. It was exactly the sort of sentimental heroic rationalization with which F. F. cloaked his insatiable yearnings for personal glory. Very likely he believed it himself.

John McCarthy was simply ready to do what the Governor asked him. He's an actor untroubled by inward urgencies—except things like keeping a record of the hours he sleeps and each penny he spends—though with a natural facility for portraying on stage emotions which he doesn't feel one iota.

The Governor shut up F. F. with a gesture and got ready to make his decision, but just then I saw that there was a sixth person on this side of the stage.

Standing in the second wings beyond our group was a dark figure like a tarpaulined Christmas tree topped by a big helmet of unmistakable general shape despite its veiling. I grabbed the Governor's arm and pointed at it silently. He smothered a large curse and strode up to it and rasped, "Guthrie, you old Son of a B! Can you go on?" The figure gave an affirmative grunt.

Joe Rubens grimaced at me as if to say "Show business!" and grabbed a spear from the prop table and hurried back across the stage for his entrance as Marcellus just before the curtain lifted and the first nervous, superbly atmospheric lines of the play rang out, loud at first, but then going low with unspoken apprehension.

"Who's there?"

"Nay, answer me; stand, and unfold yourself."

"Long live the king!"

"Bernardo?"

"He."

"You come most carefully upon your hour."

" 'Tis now struck twelve; get thee to bed, Francisco."

"For this relief much thanks; 'tis bitter cold and I am sick at heart."

"Have you had quiet guard?"

"Not a mouse stirring."

With a resigned shrug, John McCarthy simply sat down. F. F. did the same, though *his* gesture was clench-fisted and exasperated. For a moment it seemed to me very comic that two Ghosts in *Hamlet* should be sitting in the wings, watching a third perform. I unbuttoned my overcoat and slung it over my left arm.

The Ghost's first two appearances are entirely silent ones. He merely goes on stage, shows himself to the soldiers, and comes off again. Nevertheless there was a determined little ripple of hand-clapping from the audience—the second, third, and fourth rows center greeting their patriarchal hero, it seemed likely. Guthrie didn't fall down at any rate and he walked reasonably straight—an achievement perhaps rating applause, if anyone out there knew the degree of intoxication Guthrie was probably burdened with at this moment—a cask-bellied Old Man of the Sea on his back.

The only thing out of normal was that he had forgot to turn on the little green light in the peak of his helmet—an omission which hardly mattered, certainly not on this first appearance. I hurried up to him when he came off and told him about it in a whisper as he moved off toward a dark backstage corner. I got in reply, through the inscrutable green veil, an exhalation of whisky and three affirmative grunts: one, that he knew it; two, that the light was working; three, that he'd remember to turn it on next time.

Then the scene had ended and I darted across the stage as they changed to the room-of-state set. I wanted to get rid of my overcoat. Joe Rubens grabbed me and told me about Guthrie's green light not being on and I told him that was all taken care of.

"Where the hell was he all the time we were hunting for him?" Joe asked me.

"I don't know," I answered.

By that time the second scene was playing, with F. F., his Ghost-coverings shed, playing the King as well as he always does (it's about his best part) and Gertrude Grainger looking very regal beside him as the Queen, her namesake, while there was another flurry of applause, more scattered this time, for the Governor in his black doublet and tights beginning about his seven hundredth performance of Shakespeare's longest and meatiest role.

Monica was still sitting on the trunk by the switchboard, looking paler than ever under her make-up, it seemed to me, and I folded my overcoat and silently persuaded her to use it as a cushion. I sat beside her and she took my hand and we watched the play from the wings.

After a while I whispered to her, giving her hand a little squeeze, "Feeling better now?"

She shook her head. Then leaning toward me, her mouth close to my ear, she whispered rapidly and unevenly, as if she just had to tell someone, "Bruce, I'm frightened. There's something in the theater. I don't think that was Guthrie playing the Ghost."

I whispered back, "Sure it was. I talked with him."

"Did you see his face?" she asked.

"No, but I smelled his breath," I told her and explained to her about him forgetting to turn on the green light. I continued, "Francis and John were both ready to go on as the Ghost, though, until Guthrie turned up. Maybe you glimpsed one of them before the play started and that gave you the idea it wasn't Guthrie."

Sybil Jameson in her Player costume looked around at me

warningly. I was letting my whispering get too loud.

Monica put her mouth so close that her lips for an instant brushed my ear and she mouse-whispered, "I don't mean another *person* playing the Ghost—not that exactly. Bruce, there's *something* in the theater."

"You've got to forget that Ouija nonsense," I told her sharply. "And buck up now," I added, for the curtain had just gone down on Scene Two and it was time for her to get on stage for her scene with Laertes and Polonius.

I waited until she was launched into it, speaking her lines brightly enough, and then I carefully crossed the stage behind the back-drop. I was sure there was no more than nerves and imagination to her notions, though they'd raised shivers on me, but just the same I wanted to speak to Guthrie again and see his face.

When I'd completed my slow trip (you have to move rather slowly, so the drop won't ripple or bulge), I was dumbfounded to find myself witnessing the identical backstage scene that had been going on when I'd got back from my tour of the bars. Only now there was a lot more light because the scene being played on stage was a bright one. And Props was there behind his table, watching everything like the spectator he basically is. But beyond him were Francis Farley Scott and John McCarthy in their improvised Ghost costumes again, and the Governor and Joe with them, and all of them carrying on that furious lip-reader's argument, now doubly hushed.

I didn't have to wait to get close to them to know that Guthrie must have disappeared again. As I made my way toward them, watching their silent antics, my silly mind became almost hysterical with the thought that Guthrie had at last discovered that invisible hole every genuine alcoholic wishes he had, into which he could decorously disappear and drink during the times between his absolutely necessary appearances in the real world.

As I neared them, Donald Fryer (our Horatio) came from behind me, having made the trip behind the backdrop faster than I had, to tell the Governor in hushed gasps that Guthrie wasn't in any of the dressing rooms or anywhere else stage right.

Just at that moment the bright scene ended, the curtain came down, the drapes before which Ophelia and the others had been playing swung back to reveal again the battlements of Elsinore, and the lighting shifted back to the midnight blue of the first scene, so that for the moment it was hard to see at all. I heard the Governor say decisively, "*You* play the Ghost," his voice receding as he and Joe and Don hurried across the stage to be in place for their proper entrance. Seconds later there came the dull soft hiss of the main curtain opening and I heard the Governor's taut resonant voice saying, "The air bites shrewdly; it is very cold," and Don responding as Horatio with, "It is a nipping and an eager air."

By that time I could see again well enough—see Francis Farley Scott and John McCarthy moving side by side toward the back wing through which the Ghost enters. They were still arguing in whispers. The explanation was clear enough: each thought the Governor had pointed at him in the sudden darkness—or possibly in F. F.'s case was pretending he so thought. For a moment the comic side of my mind, grown a bit hysterical by now, almost collapsed me with the thought of twin Ghosts entering the stage side by side. Then once again, history still repeating itself, I saw beyond them that other bulkier figure with the unmistakable shrouded helmet. They must have seen it too for they stopped dead just before my hands touched a shoulder of each of them. I circled quickly past them and reached out my hands to put them lightly on the third figure's shoulders, intending to whisper, "Guthrie, are you okay?" It was a very stupid thing for one actor to do to another—startling him just before his entrance —but I was made thoughtless by the memory of Monica's fears and by the rather frantic riddle of where Guthrie could possibly have been hiding.

But just then Horatio gasped, "Look, my lord, it comes," and Guthrie moved out of my light grasp onto the stage without so much as turning his head—and leaving me shaking because where I'd touched the rough buckrambraced fabric of the Ghost's cloak I'd felt only a kind of insubstantiality beneath instead of Guthrie's broad shoulders.

I quickly told myself that was because Guthrie's cloak had stood out from his shoulders and his back as he had moved. I had to tell myself something like that. I turned around. John McCarthy and F. F. were standing in front of the dark prop table and by now my nerves were in such a state that their paired forms gave me another start. But I tiptoed after them into the downstage wings and watched the scene from there.

The Governor was still on his knees with his sword held hilt up like a cross doing the long speech that begins, "Angels and ministers of grace defend us!" And of course the Ghost had his cloak drawn around him so you couldn't see what was under it—and the little green light still wasn't lit in his helmet. Tonight the absence of that theatric touch made him a more frightening figure—certainly to me, who wanted so much to see Guthrie's ravaged old face and be reassured by it. Though there was still enough comedy left in the ragged edges of my thoughts that I could imagine Guthrie's pugnacious son-in-law whispering angrily to those around him that Gilbert Usher was so jealous of his great father-in-law that he wouldn't let him show his face on the stage.

Then came the transition to the following scene where the Ghost has led Hamlet off alone with him—just a five-second complete darkening of the stage while a scrim is dropped—and at last the Ghost spoke those first lines of "Mark me" and "My hour is almost come, When I to sulphurous and tormenting flames Must render up myself."

If any of us had any worries about the Ghost blowing up on his lines or slurring them drunkenly, they were taken care of now. Those lines were delivered with the greatest authority and effect. And I was almost certain that it was Guthrie's rightful voice—at least I was at first—but doing an even better job than the good one he had always done of getting the effect of distance and otherworldliness and hopeless alienation from all life on Earth. The theater became silent as death, yet at the same time I could imagine the soft pounding of a thousand hearts, thousands of shivers crawling—and I *knew* that Francis Farley Scott, whose shoulder was pressed against mine, was trembling.

Each word the Ghost spoke was like a ghost itself, mounting the air and hanging poised for an impossible extra instant before it faded towards eternity.

Those great lines came: "I am thy father's spirit; Doomed for a certain term to walk the night . . ." and just at that moment the idea came to me that Guthrie Boyd might be dead, that he might have died and be lying unnoticed somewhere between his children's home and the theater—no matter what Props had said or the rest of us had seen—and that his ghost might have come to give a last performance. And on the heels of that shivery impossibility came the thought that similar and perhaps even eerier ideas must be frightening Monica. I knew I had to go to her.

So while the Ghost's words swooped and soared in the dark—marvellous black-plumed birds—I again made that nervous cross behind the back drop.

Everyone stage right was standing as frozen and absorbed —motionless loomings—as I'd left John and F. F. I spotted Monica at once. She'd moved forward from the switchboard and was standing, crouched a little, by the big flood-light that throws some dimmed blue on the backdrop and across the back of the stage. I went to her just as the Ghost was beginning his exit stage left, moving backward along the edge of the light from the flood, but not quite in it, and reciting more lonelily and eerily than I'd ever heard them before those memorable last lines:

"Fare thee well at once!
"The glow-worm shows the matin to be near,
"And 'gins to pale his uneffectual fire;
"Adieu, adieu! Hamlet, remember me."

One second passed, then another, and then there came two unexpected bursts of sound at the same identical instant: Monica screamed and a thunderous applause started out front, touched off by Guthrie's people, of course, but this time swiftly spreading to all the rest of the audience.

I imagine it was the biggest hand the Ghost ever got in the history of the theater. In fact, I never heard of him getting a hand before. It certainly was a most inappropriate place to clap, however much the performance deserved it. It broke the atmosphere and the thread of the scene.

Also, it drowned out Monica's scream, so that only I and a few of those behind me heard it.

At first I thought I'd made her scream, by touching her as I had Guthrie, suddenly, like an idiot, from behind. But instead of shrinking or dodging away she turned and clung to me, and kept clinging too even after I'd drawn her back and Gertrude Grainger and Sybil Jameson had closed in to comfort her and hush her gasping sobs and try to draw her away from me.

By this time the applause was through and Governor and Don and Joe were taking up the broken scene and knitting together its finish as best they could, while the floods came up little by little, changing to rosy, to indicate dawn breaking over Elsinore.

Then Monica mastered herself and told us in quick whispers what had made her scream. The Ghost, she said, had moved for a moment into the edge of the blue floodlight, and she had seen for a moment through his veil, and what she had seen had been a face like Shakespeare's. Just that and no more. Except that at the moment when she told us—later she became less certain—she was sure it was Shakespeare himself and no one else.

I discovered then that when you hear something like that you don't exclaim or get outwardly excited. Or even inwardly, exactly. It rather shuts you up. I know I felt at the same time extreme awe and a renewed irritation at the Ouija board. I was deeply moved, yet at the same time pettishly irked, as if some vast adult creature had disordered the toy world of my universe.

It seemed to hit Sybil and even Gertrude the same way. For the moment we were shy about the whole thing, and so, in her way, was Monica, and so were the few others who had overheard in part or all what Monica had said.

I knew we were going to cross the stage in a few more seconds when the curtain came down on that scene, ending the first act, and stagelights came up. At least I knew that I was going across. Yet I wasn't looking forward to it.

When the curtain did come down—with another round of applause from out front—and we started across, Monica beside me with my arm still tight around her, there came a choked-off male cry of horror from ahead to shock and hurry us. I think about a dozen of us got stage left about the same time, including of course the Governor and the others who had been on stage.

F. F. and Props were standing inside the doorway to the empty prop room and looking down into the hidden part of the L. Even from the side, they both looked pretty sick. Then F. F. knelt down and almost went out of view, while Props hunched over him with his natural stoop.

As we craned around Props for a look—myself among the first, just beside the Governor—we saw something that told us right away that this Ghost wasn't ever going to be able to answer that curtain call they were still fitfully clapping for out front, although the house lights must be up by now for the first intermission.

Guthrie Boyd was lying on his back in his street clothes. His face looked gray, the eyes staring straight up. While swirled beside him lay the Ghost's cloak and veil and the helmet and an empty fifth of whiskey.

Between the two conflicting shocks of Monica's revelation and the body in the prop room, my mind was in a useless state. And from her helpless incredulous expression I knew Monica felt the same. I tried to put things together and they wouldn't fit anywhere.

F. F. looked up at us over his shoulder. "He's not breathing," he said. "I think he's gone." Just the same he started loosing Boyd's tie and shirt and pillowing his head on the cloak. He handed the whisky bottle back to us through several hands and Joe Rubens got rid of it.

The Governor sent out front for a doctor and within two minutes Harry Grossman was bringing us one from the audience who'd left his seat number and bag at the box office. He was a small man—Guthrie would have made two of him—and a bit awestruck, I could see, though holding himself with greater professional dignity because of that, as we made way for him and then crowded in behind.

He confirmed F. F.'s diagnosis by standing up quickly after kneeling only for a few seconds where F. F. had. Then he said hurriedly to the Governor, as if the words were being surprised out of him against his professional caution, "Mr. Usher, if I hadn't heard this man giving that great performance just now, I'd think he'd been dead for an hour or more."

He spoke low and not all of us heard him, but I did and so did Monica, and there was Shock Three to go along with the other two, raising in my mind for an instant the grisly picture of Guthrie Boyd's spirit, or some other entity, willing his dead body to go through with that last performance. Once again I unsuccessfully tried to fumble together the parts of this night's mystery.

The little doctor looked around at us slowly and puzzledly. He said, "I take it he just wore the cloak over his street clothes?" He paused. Then, "He *did* play the Ghost?" he asked us.

The Governor and several others nodded, but some of us didn't at once and I think F. F. gave him a rather peculiar look, for the doctor cleared his throat and said, "I'll have to examine this man as quickly as possible in a better place and light. Is there—?" The Governor suggested the couch in his dressing room and the doctor designated Joe Rubens and John McCarthy and Francis Farley Scott to carry the body. He passed over the Governor, perhaps out of awe, but Hamlet helped just the same his black garb most fitting.

It was odd the doctor picked the older men—I think he did it for dignity. And it was odder still that he should have picked two ghosts to help carry a third, though he couldn't have known that.

As the designated ones moved forward, the doctor said, "Please stand back, the rest of you."

It was then that the very little thing happened which made all the pieces of this night's mystery fall into place—for me, that is, and for Monica too, judging from the way her hand trembled in and then tightened around mine. We'd been given the key to what had happened. I won't tell you what it was until I've knit together the ends of this story.

The second act was delayed perhaps a minute, but after that we kept to schedule, giving a better performance than usual—I never knew the Graveyard Scene to carry so much feeling, or the bit with Yorick's skull to be so poignant.

Just before I made my own first entrance, Joe Rubens snatched off my street hat—I'd had it on all this while—and I played all of Guildenstern wearing a wrist-watch, though I don't imagine anyone noticed.

F. F. played the Ghost as an off-stage voice when he makes his final brief appearance in the Closet Scene. He used Guthrie's voice to do it, imitating him very well. It struck me afterwards as ghoulish—but right.

Well before the play ended, the doctor had decided he could say that Guthrie had died of a heart seizure, not mentioning the alcoholism. The minute the curtain came down on the last act, Harry Grossman informed Guthrie's son and daughter and brought them backstage. They were much though hardly deeply smitten, seeing they'd been out of touch with the old boy for a decade. However, they quickly saw it was a Grand and Solemn Occasion and behaved accordingly, especially Guthrie's pugnacious son-in-law.

Next morning the two Wolverton papers had headlines about it and Guthrie got his biggest notices ever in the Ghost.

The strangeness of the event carried the item around the world—a six-line filler, capturing the mind for a second or two, about how a once-famous actor had died immediately after giving a performance as the Ghost in *Hamlet*, though in some versions, of course, it became Hamlet's Ghost.

The funeral came on the afternoon of the third day, just before our last performance in Wolverton, and the whole company attended along with Guthrie's children's crowd and many other Wolvertonians. Old Sybil broke down and sobbed.

Yet to be a bit callous, it was a neat thing that Guthrie died where he did, for it saved us the trouble of having to send for relatives and probably take care of the funeral ourselves. And it did give old Guthrie a grand finish, with everyone outside the company thinking him a hero-martyr to the motto The Show Must Go On. And of course we knew too that in a deeper sense he'd really been that.

We shifted around in our parts and doubled some to fill the little gaps Guthrie had left in the plays, so that the Governor didn't have to hire another actor at once. For me, and I think for Monica, the rest of the season was very sweet. Gertrude and Sybil carried on with the Ouija sessions alone.

And now I must tell you about the very little thing which gave myself and Monica a satisfying solution to the mystery of what had happened that night.

You'll have realized that it involved Props. Afterwards I asked him straight out about it and he shyly told me that he really couldn't help me there. He'd had this unaccountable devilish compulsion to get drunk and his mind had blanked out entirely from well before the performance until he found himself standing with F. F. over Guthrie's body at the end of the first act. He didn't remember the Ouija-scare or a word of what he'd said to me about theaters and time machines— or so he always insisted.

F. F. told us that after the Ghost's last exit he'd seen him —very vaguely in the dimness—lurch across backstage into the empty prop room and that he and Props had found Guthrie lying there at the end of the scene. I think the queer look F. F.—the old reality-fuddling rogue!—gave the doctor was to hint to him that *he* had played the Ghost, though that wasn't something I could ask him about.

But the very little thing—When they were picking up Guthrie's body and the doctor told the rest of us to stand

144

back, Props turned as he obeyed and straightened his shoulders and looked directly at Monica and myself, or rather a little over our heads. He appeared compassionate yet smilingly serene as always and for a moment transfigured, as if he were the eternal observer of the stage of life and this little tragedy were only part of an infinitely vaster, endlessly interesting pattern.

I realized at that instant that Props could have done it, that he'd very effectively guarded the doorway to the empty prop room during our searches, that the Ghost's costume could be put on or off in seconds (though Prop's shoulders wouldn't fill the cloak like Guthrie's), and that I'd never once before or during the play seen him and the Ghost at the same time. Yes, Guthrie had arrived a few minutes before me . . . and died . . . and Props, nerved to it by drink, had covered for him.

While Monica, as he told me later, knew at once that here was the great-browed face she'd glimpsed for a moment through the greenish gauze.

Clearly there had been four ghosts in *Hamlet* that night— John McCarthy, Francis Farley Scott, Guthrie Boyd, and the fourth who had really played the role. Mentally blacked out or not, knowing the lines from the many times he'd listened to *Hamlet* performed in this life, or from buried memories of times he'd taken the role in the days of Queen Elizabeth the First, Billy (or Willy) Simpson, or simply Willy S., had played the Ghost, a good trouper responding automatically to an emergency.

THE
CREATURE
FROM
CLEVELAND DEPTHS

By FRITZ LEIBER

"COME on, Gussy," Fay prodded quietly, "quit stalking around like a neurotic bear and suggest something for my invention team to work on. I enjoy visiting you and Daisy, but I can't stay aboveground all night."

"If being outside the shelters makes you nervous, don't come around any more," Gusterson told him, continuing to stalk. "Why doesn't your invention team think of something to invent? Why don't you? Hah!" In the "Hah!" lay triumphant condemnation of a whole way of life.

"We do," Fay responded imperturbably, "but a fresh viewpoint sometimes helps."

"I'll say it does! Fay, you burglar, I'll bet you've got twenty people like myself you milk for free ideas. First you irritate their bark and then you make the rounds every so often to draw off the latex or the maple gloop."

Fay smiled. "It ought to please you that society still has a use for you outer inner-directed types. It takes something to make a junior executive stay above-ground after dark, when the missiles are on the prowl."

"Society can't have much use for use or it'd pay us something," Gusterson sourly asserted, staring blankly at the tankless TV and kicking it lightly as he passed on.

"No, you're wrong about that, Gussy. Money's not the key goad with you inner-directeds. I got that straight from our Motivations chief."

"Did he tell you what we should use instead to pay the grocer? A deep inner sense of achievement, maybe? Fay, why should I do any free thinking for Micro Systems?"

"I'll tell you why, Gussy. Simply because you get a kick out of insulting us with sardonic ideas. If we take one of them seriously, you think we're degrading ourselves, and that pleases you even more. Like making someone laugh at a lousy pun."

Gusterson held still in his roaming and grinned. "That the reason, huh? I suppose my suggestions would have to be something in the line of ultra-subminiaturized computers, where one sinister fine-etched molecule does the work of three big bumbling brain cells?"

"Not necessarily. Micro Systems is branching out. Wheel as free as a rogue star. But I'll pass along to Promotion your one molecule-three brain cell sparkler. It's a slight exaggeration, but it's catchy."

"I'll have my kids watch your ads to see if you use it and then I'll sue the whole underworld." Gusterson frowned as he resumed his stalking. He stared puzzledly at the antique TV. "How about inventing a plutonium termite?" he said suddenly. "It would get rid of those stockpiles that are worrying you moles to death."

Fay grimaced noncommittally and cocked his head.

"Well, then, how about a beauty mask? How about that, hey? I don't mean one to repair a woman's complexion, but one she'd wear all the time that'd make her look like a 17-year-old sexpot. That'd end *her* worries."

"Hey, that's for me," Daisy called from the kitchen. "I'll make him crawl around on his hands and knees begging my immature favors."

"No, you won't," Gusterson called back. "You having a face like that would scare the kids. Better cancel that one, Fay. Half the adult race looking like Vina Vidarsson is too awful a thought."

"Yah, you're just scared of making a million dollars," Daisy jeered.

"I sure am," Gusterson said solemnly, scanning the fuzzy floor from one murky glass wall to the other, hesitating at the TV. "How about something homey now, like a flock of little prickly cylinders that roll around the floor collecting lint and flub? They'd work by electricity, or at a pinch cats could bat 'em around. Every so often they'd be automatically herded together and the lint cleaned off the bristles."

"No good," Fay said. "There's no lint underground and cats are *verboten*. And the aboveground market doesn't amount to more moneywise than the state of Southern Illinois. Keep it grander, Gussy, and more impractical—you can't sell people merely useful ideas." From his hassock in the center of the room he looked uneasily around. "Say, did that violet tone in the glass come from the high Cleveland hydrogen bomb or is it just age and ultraviolet, like desert glass?"

"No, somebody's grandfather liked it that color," Gusterson informed him with happy bitterness. "I like it too—the glass, I mean, not the tint. People who live in glass houses can see the stars—especially when there's a window-washing streak in their germ-plasma."

"Gussy, why don't you move underground?" Fay asked, his voice taking on a missionary note. "It's a lot easier living in one room, believe me. You don't have to tramp from room to room hunting things."

"I like the exercise," Gusterson said stoutly.

"But I bet Daisy'd prefer it underground. And your kids wouldn't have to explain why their father lives like a Red Indian. Not to mention the safety factor and insurance savings and a crypt church within easy slidewalk distance. Incidentally, we see the stars all the time, better than you do—by repeater."

"Stars by repeater," Gusterson murmured to the ceiling, pausing for God to comment. Then, "No, Fay, even if I could afford it—and stand it—I'm such a bad-luck Harry that just when I got us all safely stowed at the N minus 1 sublevel, the Soviets would discover an earthquake bomb that struck from below, and I'd have to follow everybody back to the treetops. *Hey! How about bubble homes in orbit around earth?* Micro Systems could subdivide the world's most spacious suburb and all you moles could go ellipsing. Space is as safe as there is: no air, no shock waves. Free fall's the ultimate in restfulness—great health benefits. Commute by rocket—or better yet stay home and do all your business by TV-telephone, or by waldo if it were that sort of thing. Even pet your girl by remote control—she in her bubble, you in yours, whizzing through vacuum. Oh, damn - damn - *damn - damn* - DAMN!"

He was glaring at the blank screen of the TV, his big hands clenching and unclenching.

"Don't let Fay give you apoplexy—he's not worth it," Daisy said, sticking her trim head in from the kitchen, while Fay inquired anxiously, "Gussy, what's the matter?"

"Nothing, you worm!" Gusterson roared, "Except that an hour ago I forgot to tune in on the only TV program I've wanted to hear this year—*Finnegans Wake* scored for English, Gaelic and brogue. Oh, damn-*damn*-DAMN!"

"Too bad," Fay said lightly. "I didn't know they were releasing it on flat TV too."

"Well, they were! Some things are too damn big to keep completely underground. And I had to forget! I'm always doing it—I miss everything! Look here, you rat," he blatted suddenly at Fay, shaking his finger under the latter's chin, "I'll tell you what you can have that ignorant team of yours invent. They can fix me up a mechanical secretary that I can feed orders into and that'll remind me when the exact moment comes to listen to TV or phone somebody or mail in a story or write a letter or pick up a magazine or look at an eclipse or a new orbiting station or fetch the kids from school or buy Daisy a bunch of flowers or whatever it is. It's got to be something that's always with me, not something I have to go and consult or that I can get sick of and put down somewhere. And it's got to remind me forcibly enough so that I take notice and don't just shrug it aside, like I sometimes do even when Daisy reminds me of things. That's what your stupid team can invent for me! If they do a good job, I'll pay 'em as much as fifty dollars!"

"That doesn't sound like anything so very original to me," Fay commented coolly, leaning back from the wagging finger. "I think all senior executives have something of that sort. At least, their secretary keeps some kind of file . . ."

"I'm not looking for something with spiked falsies and nylons up to the neck," interjected Gusterson, whose ideas about secretaries were a trifle lurid. "I just want a mech reminder—that's all!"

"Well, I'll keep the idea in mind," Fay assured him, "along with the bubble homes and beauty masks. If we ever develop anything along those lines, I'll let you know. If it's a beauty mask, I'll bring Daisy a pilot model—to use to scare strange kids." He put his watch to his ear. "Good lord, I'm going to have to cut to make it underground before the main doors close. Just ten minutes to Second Curfew! 'By, Gus. 'By, Daze."

Two minutes later, living room lights out, they watched

Fay's foreshortened antlike figure scurrying across the balding ill-lit park toward the nearest escalator.

Gusterson said, "Weird to think of that big bright spacepoor glamor basement stretching around everywhere underneath. Did you remind Smitty to put a new bulb in the elevator?"

"The Smiths moved out this morning," Daisy said tonelessly. "They went underneath."

"Like cockroaches," Gusterson said. "Cockroaches leavin' a sinkin' apartment building. Next the ghosts'll be retreatin' to the shelters."

"Anyhow, from now on we're our own janitors," Daisy said.

He nodded. "Just leaves three families besides us loyal to this glass death trap. Not countin' ghosts." He sighed. Then, "You like to move below, Daisy?" he asked softly, putting his arm lightly across her shoulders. "Get a woozy eyeful of the bright lights and all for a change? Be a rat for a while? Maybe we're getting too old to be bats. I could scrounge me a company job and have a thinking closet all to myself and two secretaries with stainless steel breasts. Life'd be easier for you and a lot cleaner. And you'd sleep safer."

"That's true," she answered and paused. She ran her fingertip slowly across the murky glass, its violet tint barely perceptible against a cold dim light across the park. "But somehow," she said, snaking her arm around his waist, "I don't think I'd sleep happier—or one bit excited."

II

Three weeks later Fay, dropping in again, handed to Daisy the larger of the two rather small packages he was carrying.

"It's a so-called beauty mask," he told her, "complete with wig, eyelashes, and wettable velvet lips. It even breathes—pinholed elastiskin with a static adherence-charge. But Micro Systems had nothing to do with it, thank God. Beauty Trix put it on the market ten days ago and it's already started a teen-age craze. Some boys are wearing them too, and the police are yipping at Trix for encouraging transvestism with psychic repercussions."

"Didn't I hear somewhere that Trix is a secret subsidiary of Micro?" Gusterson demanded, rearing up from his ancient electric typewriter. "No, you're not stopping me writing, Fay —it's the gut of evening. If I do any more I won't have any juice to start with tomorrow. I got another of my insanity thrillers moving. A real id-teaser. In this one not only all the characters are crazy but the robot psychiatrist too."

"The vending machines are jumping with insanity novels," Fay commented. "Odd they're so popular."

Gusterson chortled. "The only way you outer-directed moles will accept individuality any more even in a fictional character, without your superegos getting seasick, is for them to be crazy. Hey, Daisy! Lemme see that beauty mask!"

But his wife, backing out of the room, hugged the package to her bosom and solemnly shook her head.

"A hell of a thing," Gusterson complained, "not even to be able to see what my stolen ideas look like."

"I got a present for you too," Fay said. "Something you might think of as a royalty on all the inventions someone thought of a little ahead of you. Fifty dollars by your own evaluation." He held out the smaller package. "Your tickler."

"My *what?*" Gusterson demanded suspiciously.

"Your tickler. The mech reminder you wanted. It turns out that the file a secretary keeps to remind her boss to do certain things at certain times is called a tickler file. So we named this a tickler. Here."

Gusterson still didn't touch the package. "You mean you actually put your invention team to work on that nonsense?"

"Well, what do you think? Don't be scared of it. Here, I'll show you."

As he unwrapped the package, Fay said, "It hasn't been decided yet whether we'll manufacture it commercially. If we do, I'll put through a voucher for you—for 'development consultation' or something like that. Sorry no royalties possible. Davidson's squad had started to work up the identical idea three years ago, but it got shelved. I found it on a snoop through the closets. There! Looks rich, doesn't it?"

On the scarred black tabletop was a dully gleaming silvery object about the size and shape of a cupped hand with fingers merging. A tiny pellet on a short near-invisible wire led off from it. On the back was a punctured area suggesting the face of a microphone; there was also a window with a date and time in hours and minutes showing through and next to that four little buttons in a row. The concave underside of the silvery "hand" was smooth except for a central area where what looked like two little rollers came through.

"It goes on your shoulder under your shirt," Fay explained, "and you tuck the pellet in your ear. We might work up bone conduction on a commercial model. Inside is an ultra-slow fine-wire recorder holding a spool that runs for a week. The clock lets you go to any place on the 7-day wire and record a message. The buttons give you variable speed in going there, so you don't waste too much time making a setting. There's a knack in fingering them efficiently, but it's easily acquired."

Fay picked up the tickler. "For instance, suppose there's a TV show you want to catch tomorrow night at twenty-two hundred." He touched the buttons. There was the faintest whirring. The clock face blurred briefly three times before showing the setting he'd mentioned. Then Fay spoke into the punctured area: "Turn on TV Channel Two, you big dummy!" He grinned over at Gusterson. "When you've got all your instructions to yourself loaded in, you synchronize with the present moment and let her roll. Fit it on your shoulder and forget it. Oh, yes, and it literally does tickle you every time it delivers an instruction. That's what the little rollers are for. Believe me, you can't ignore it. Come on, Gussy, take off your shirt and try it out. We'll feed in some instructions for the next ten minutes so you get the feel of how it works."

"I don't want to," Gusterson said. "Not right now. I want to sniff around it first. My God, it's small! Besides everything else it does, does it think?"

"Don't pretend to be an idiot, Gussy! You know very well that even with ultra-sub-micro nothing quite this small can possibly have enough elements to do any thinking."

Gusterson shrugged. "I don't know about that. I think bugs think."

Fay groaned faintly. "Bugs operate by instinct, Gussy," he said. "A patterned routine. They do not scan situations and consequences and then make decisions."

"I don't expect bugs to make decisions," Gusterson said. "For that matter I don't like people who go around alla time making decisions."

"Well, you can take it from me, Gussy, that this tickler is just a miniaturized wire recorder and clock . . . and a tickler. It doesn't do anything else."

"Not yet, maybe," Gusterson said darkly. "Not this model. Fay, I'm serious about bugs thinking. Or if they don't exactly think, they feel. They've got an interior drama. An inner glow. They're conscious. For that matter, Fay, I think all your really complex electronic computers are conscious too."

"Quit kidding, Gussy."

"Who's kidding?"

"You are. Computers simply aren't alive."

"What's alive? A word. I think computers are conscious, at least while they're operating. They've got that inner glow of awareness. They sort of . . . well . . . meditate."

"Gussy, computers haven't got any circuits for meditating. They're not programmed for mystical lucubrations. They've just got circuits for solving the problems they're on."

"Okay, you admit they've got problem-solving circuits— like a man has. I say if they've got the equipment for being conscious, they're conscious. What has wings, flies."

"Including stuffed owls and gilt eagles and dodoes—and wood-burning airplanes?"

"Maybe, under some circumstances. There was a wood-burning airplane. Fay," Gusterson continued, wagging his wrists for emphasis, "I really think computers are conscious. They just don't have any way of telling us that they are. Or maybe they don't have any *reason* to tell us, like the little Scotch boy who didn't say a word until he was fifteen and was supposed to be deaf and dumb."

"Why didn't he say a word?"

"Because he'd never had anything to say. Or take those Hindu fakirs, Fay, who sit still and don't say a word for thirty years or until their fingernails grow to the next village. If Hindu fakirs can do that, computers can!"

Looking as if he were masticating a lemon, Fay asked quietly, "Gussy, did you say you're working on an insanity novel?"

Gusterson frowned fiercely. "Now you're kidding," he accused Fay. "The dirty kind of kidding, too."

"I'm sorry," Fay said with light contrition. "Well, now you've sniffed at it, how about trying on Tickler?" He picked up the gleaming blunted crescent and jogged it temptingly under Gusterson's chin.

"Why should I?" Gusterson asked, stepping back. "Fay, I'm up to my ears writing a book. The last thing I want is something interrupting me to make me listen to a lot of junk and do a lot of useless things."

"But, dammit, Gussy! It was all your idea in the first place!" Fay blatted. Then, catching himself, he added, "I mean, you were one of the first people to think of this particular sort of instrument."

"Maybe so, but I've done some more thinking since then." Gusterson's voice grew a trifle solemn. "Inner-directed worthwhile thinkin.' Fay, when a man forgets to do something, it's because he really doesn't want to do it or because he's all roiled up down in his unconscious. He ought to take it as a danger signal and investigate the roiling, not hire himself a human or mech reminder."

"Bushwa," Fay retorted. "In that case you shouldn't write memorandums or even take notes."

"Maybe I shouldn't," Gusterson agreed lamely. "I'd have to think that over too."

"Ha!" Fay jeered. "No, I'll tell you what your trouble is, Gussy. You're simply scared of this contraption. You've loaded your skull with horror-story nonsense about machines sprouting minds and taking over the world—until you're even scared of a simple miniaturized and clocked recorder." He thrust it out.

"Maybe I am," Gusterson admitted, controlling a flinch. "Honestly, Fay, that thing's got a gleam in its eye as if it had ideas of its own. Nasty ideas."

"Gussy, you nut, it hasn't *got* an eye."

"Not now, no, but it's got the gleam—the eye may come. It's the Chesire cat in reverse. If you'd step over here and look at yourself holding it, you could see what I mean. But I don't think computers *sprout* minds, Fay. I just think they've *got* minds, because they've got the mind elements."

"Ho, ho!" Fay mocked. "Everything that has a material side has a mental side," he chanted. "Everything that's a body is also a spirit. Gussy, that dubious old metaphysical dualism went out centuries ago."

"Maybe so," Gusterson said, "but we still haven't anything but that dubious dualism to explain the human mind, have we? It's a jelly of nerve cells and it's a vision of the cosmos. If that isn't dualism, what is?"

"I give up. Gussy, are you going to try out this tickler?"

"No!"

"But dammit, Gussy, we made it just for you!—practically."

"Sorry, but I'm not coming near the thing."

" 'Zen come near me," a husky voice intoned behind them. "Tonight I vant a man."

Standing in the door was something slim in a short silver sheath. It had golden bangs and the haughtiest snub-nosed face in the world. It slunk toward them.

"My God, Vina Vidarsson!" Gusterson yelled.

"Daisy, that's terrific," Fay applauded, going up to her.

She bumped him aside with a swing of her hips, continuing to advance. "Not you, Ratty," she said throatily. "I vant a real man."

"Fay, I suggested Vina Vidarsson's face for the beauty mask," Gusterson said, walking around his wife and shaking a finger. "Don't tell me Trix just happened to think of that too."

"What else could they think of?" Fay laughed. "This season sex means VV and nobody else." An odd little grin flicked his lips, a tic traveled up his face and his body twitched slightly. "Say, folks, I'm going to have to be leaving. It's exactly fifteen minutes to Second Curfew. Last time I had to run and I got heartburn. When *are* you people going to move downstairs? I'll leave Tickler, Gussy. Play around with it and get used to it. 'By now."

"Hey, Fay," Gusterson called curiously, "have you developed absolute time sense?"

Fay grinned a big grin from the doorway—almost too big a grin for so small a man. "I didn't need to," he said softly, patting his right shoulder. "My tickler told me."

He closed the door behind him.

As side-by-side they watched him strut sedately across the murky chilly-looking park, Gusterson mused, "So the little devil had one of those nonsense-gadgets on all the time and I never noticed. Can you beat that?" Something drew across the violet-tinged stars a short bright line that quickly faded. "What's that?" Gusterson asked gloomily. "Next to last stage of missile-here?"

"Won't you settle for an old-fashioned shooting star?" Daisy asked softly. The (wettable) velvet lips of the mask made even her natural voice sound different. She reached a hand back of her neck to pull the thing off.

"Hey, don't do that," Gusterson protested in a hurt voice. "Not for a while anyway."

"Hokay!" she said harshly, turning on him. "Zen down on your knees, dog!"

III

It was a fortnight and Gusterson was loping down the home stretch on his 40,000-word insanity novel before Fay dropped in again, this time promptly at high noon.

Normally Fay cringed his shoulders a trifle and was inclined to slither, but now he strode aggressively, his legs scissoring in a fast, low goosestep. He whipped off the sunglasses that all moles wore topside by day and began to pound Gusterson on the back while calling boisterously, "How are you, Gussy Old Boy, Old Boy?"

Daisy came in from the kitchen to see why Gusterson was choking. She was instantly grabbed and violently bussed to the accompaniment of, "Hiya, Gorgeous! Yum-yum! How about adlibbing that some weekend?"

She stared at Fay dazedly, rasping the back of her hand across her mouth, while Gusterson yelled, "Quit that! What's got into you, Fay? Have they transferred you out of R & D to Company Morale? Do they line up all the secretaries at roll call and make you give them an eight-hour energizing kiss?"

"Ha, wouldn't you like to know? Fay retorted. He grinned, twitched jumpingly, held still a moment, then hustled over to the far wall. "Look out there," he rapped, pointing through the violet glass at a gap between the two nearest old skyscraper apartments. "In thirty seconds you'll see them test the new needle bomb at the other end of Lake Erie. It's educational." He began to count off seconds, vigorously semaphoring his arm. ". . . . Two . . . three . . . Gussy, I've put through a voucher for two yards for you. Budgeting squawked, but I pressured 'em."

Daisy squealed, "Yards!—are those dollar thousands?" while Gusterson was asking, "Then you're marketing the tickler?"

"Yes. Yes," Fay replied to them in turn. ". . . Nine . . .

ten . . ." Again he grinned and twitched. "Time for noon Comstaff," he announced staccato. "Pardon the hush box." He whipped a pancake phone from under his coat, clapped it over his face and spoke fiercely but inaudibly into it, continuing to semaphore. Suddenly he thrust the phone away. "Twenty-nine . . . thirty . . . Thar she blows!"

An incandescent streak shot up the sky from a little above the far horizon and a doubly dazzling point of light appeared just above the top of it, with the effect of God dotting an "i".

"Ha, that'll skewer espionage satellites like swatting flies!" Fay proclaimed as the portent faded. "Bracing! Gussy, where's your tickler? I've got a new spool for it that'll razzle-dazzle you."

"I'll bet," Gusterson said drily. "Daisy?"

"You gave it to the kids and they got to fooling with it and broke it."

"No matter," Fay told them with a large sidewise sweep of his hand. "Better you wait for the new model. It's a six-way improvement."

"So I gather," Gusterson said, eyeing him speculatively. "Does it automatically inject you with cocaine? A fix every hour on the second?"

"Ha-ha, joke. Gussy, it achieves the same effect without using any dope at all. Listen: a tickler reminds you of your duties and opportunities—your chances for happiness and success! What's the obvious next step?"

"Throw it out the window. By the way, how do you do that when you're underground?"

"We have hi-speed garbage boosts. The obvious next step is you give the tickler a heart. It not only tells you, it warmly persuades you. It doesn't just say, "Turn on the TV Channel Two, Joyce program,' it *brills* at you, 'Kid, Old Kid, race for the TV and flip that Two Switch! There's a great show coming through the pipes this second plus ten—you'll enjoy the hell of of yourself! Grab a ticket to ecstacy!' "

"My God," Gusterson gasped, "are those the kind of jolts it's giving you now?"

"Don't you get it, Gussy? You never load your tickler except when you're feeling buoyantly enthusiastic. You don't just tell yourself what to do hour by hour next week, you sell yourself on it. That way you not only make doubly sure you'll

157

obey instructions but you constantly reinoculate yourself with your own enthusiasm."

"I can't stand myself when I'm that enthusiastic," Gusterson said. "I feel ashamed for hours afterwards."

"You're warped—all this lonely sky-life. What's more, Gussy, think how still more persuasive some of those instructions would be if they came to a man in his best girl's most bedroomy voice, or his doctor's or psycher's if it's that sort of thing—or Vina Vidarsson's! By the way, Daze, don't wear that beauty mask outside. It's a grand misdemeanor ever since ten thousand teen-agers rioted through Tunnel-Mart wearing them. And VV's sueing Trix."

"No chance of that," Daisy said. "Gusterson got excited and bit off the nose." She pinched her own delicately.

"I'd no more obey my enthusiastic self," Gusterson was brooding, "than I'd obey a Napoleon drunk on his own brandy or a hopped-up St. Francis. Reinoculated with my own enthusiasm? I'd die just like from snake-bite!"

"Warped, I said," Fay dogmatized, stamping around. "Gussy, having the instructions persuasive instead of neutral turned out to be only the opening wedge. The next step wasn't so obvious, but I saw it. Using subliminal verbal stimuli in his tickler, a man can be given constant supportive euphoric therapy 24 hours a day! And it makes use of all that empty wire. We've revived the ideas of a pioneer dynamic psycher named Dr. Coué. For instance, right now my tickler is saying to me—in tones too soft to reach my conscious mind, but do they stab into the unconscious!—'Day by day in every way I'm getting sharper and sharper.' It alternates that with 'gutsier and gutsier' and . . . well, forget that. Coué mostly used 'better and better' but that seems too general. And every hundredth time it says them out loud and the tickler give me a brush—just a faint cootch—to make sure I'm keeping in touch."

"That third word-pair," Daisy wondered, feeling her mouth reminiscently. "Could I guess?"

Gusterson's eyes had been growing wider and wider. "Fay," he said, "I could no more use my mind for anything if I knew all that was going on in my inner ear than if I were being brushed down with brooms by three witches. Look here," he said with loud authority, "you got to stop all this—

it's crazy. Fay, if Micro'll junk the tickler, I'll think you up something else to invent—something real good."

"Your inventing days are over," Fay brilled gleefully. "I mean, you'll never equal your masterpiece."

"How about," Gusterson bellowed, "an anti-individual guided missile? The physicists have got small-scale anti-gravity good enough to float and fly something the size of a hand grenade. I can smell that even though it's a back-of-the-safe military secret. Well, how about keying such a missile to a man's finger-prints—or brainwaves, maybe, or his unique smell!—so it can spot and follow him around the target in on him, without harming anyone else? Long-distance assassination—and the stinkingest gets it! Or you could simply load it with some disgusting goo and key it to teen-agers as a group—that'd take care of them. Fay, doesn't it give you a rich warm kick to think of my midget missiles buzzing around in your tunnels, seeking out evil-doers, like a swarm of angry wasps or angelic bumblebees?"

"You're not luring me down any side trails," Fay said laughingly. He grinned and twitched, then hurried toward the opposite wall, motioning them to follow. Outside, about a hundred yards beyond the purple glass, rose another ancient glass-walled apartment skyscraper. Beyond, Lake Erie rippled glintingly.

"Another bomb-test?" Gusterson asked.

Fay pointed at the building. "Tomorrow," he announced, "a modern factory, devoted solely to the manufacture of ticklers, will be erected on that site."

"You mean one of those windowless phallic eyesores?" Gusterson demanded. "Fay, you people aren't even consistent. You've got all your homes underground. Why not your factories?"

"Sh! Not enough room. And night missiles are scarier."

"I know that building's been empty for a year," Daisy said uneasily, "but how—?"

"Sh! Watch! *Now!*"

The looming building seemed to blur or fuzz for a moment. Then it was as if the lake's bright ripples had invaded the old glass a hundred yards away. Wavelets chased themselves up and down the gleaming walls, became higher, higher . . . and then suddenly the glass cracked all over to tiny fragments and fell away, to be followed quickly by fragmented concrete and plastic and plastic piping, until all that was left was the nude steel framework, vibrating so rapidly as to be almost invisible against the gleaming lake.

Daisy covered her ears, but there was no explosion, only a long-drawn-out low crash as the fragments hit twenty floors below and dust whooshed out sideways.

"Spectacular!" Fay summed up. "Knew you'd enjoy it. That little trick was first conceived by the great Tesla during his last fruity years. Research discovered it in his biog—we just made the dream come true. A tiny resonance device you could carry in your belt-bag attunes itself to the natural harmonic of a structure and then increases amplitude by tiny pushes exactly in time. Just like soldiers marching in step can break down a bridge, only this is as if it were being done by one marching ant." He pointed at the naked framework appearing out of its own blur and said, "We'll be able to hang the factory on that. If not, we'll whip a megacurrent through it and vaporize it. No question the micro-resonator is the neatest sweetest wrecking device going. You can expect a lot more of this sort of efficiency now that mankind has the tickler to enable him to use his full potential. What's the matter, folks?"

Daisy was staring around the violet-walled room with dumb mistrust. Her hands were trembling.

"You don't have to worry," Fay assured her with an understanding laugh. "This building's safe for a month more at least." Suddenly he grimaced and leaped a foot in the air. He raised a clawed had to scratch his shoulder but managed to check the movement. "Got to beat it, folks," he announced tersely. "My tickler gave me the grand cootch."

"Don't go yet," Gusterson called, rousing himself with a shudder which he immediately explained: "I just had the illusion that if I shook myself all my flesh and guts would fall off my shimmying skeleton. Byrl Fay, before you and Micro go off half cocked, I want you to know there's one insuperable objection to the tickler as a mass-market item. The average man or woman won't go to the considerable time and trouble it must take to load a tickler. He simply hasn't got the compulsive orderliness and willingness to plan that it requires."

"We thought of that weeks ago," Fay rapped, his hand on

the door. "Every tickler spool that goes to market is patterned like wallpaper with one of five designs of suitable subliminal supportive euphoric material. 'Ittier and ittier,' 'viriler and viriler'—you know. The buyer is robot-interviewed for an hour, his personalized daily routine laid out and thereafter templated on his weekly spool. He's strongly urged next to take his tickler to his doctor and psycher for further instruction-imposition. We've been working with the medical profession from the start. They love the tickler because it'll remind people to take their medicine on the dot . . . and rest and eat and go to sleep just when and how doc says. This is a big operation, Gussy—a biiiiiig operation! 'By!"

Daisy hurried to the wall to watch him cross the park. Deep down she was a wee bit worried that he might linger to attach a micro-resonator to *this* building and she wanted to time him. But Gusterson settled down to his typewriter and began to bat away.

"I want to have another novel started," he explained to her, "before the ant marches across this building in about four and a half weeks . . . or a million sharp little gusty guys come swarming out of the ground and heave it into Lake Erie."

IV

Early next morning windowless walls began to crawl up the stripped skyscraper between them and the lake. Daisy pulled the black-out curtains on that side. For a day or two longer their thoughts and conversations were haunted by Gusterson's vague sardonic visions of a horde of tickler-energized moles pouring up out of the tunnels to tear down the remaining trees, tank the atmosphere and perhaps somehow dismantle the stars—at least on this side of the world—but then they both settled back into their customary easygoing routines. Gusterson typed. Daisy made her daily shopping trip to a little topside daytime store and started painting a mural on the floor of the empty apartment next theirs but one.

"We ought to lasso some neighbors," she suggested once. "I need somebody to hold my brushes and admire. How about you making a trip below at the cocktail hours, Gusterson, and picking up a couple of girls for a starter? Flash the old viriler charm, cootch them up a bit, emphasize the delights of high living, but make sure they're compatible roommates. You could pick up that two-yard check from Micro at the same time."

"You're an immoral money-ravenous wench," Gusterson said absently, trying to dream of an insanity beyond insanity that would make his next novel a real id-rousing best-vender.

"If that's your vision of me, you shouldn't have chewed up the VV mask."

"I'd really prefer you with green stripes," he told her. "But stripes, spots, or sun-bathing, you're better than those cocktail moles."

Actually both of them acutely disliked going below. They much preferred to perch in their eyrie and watch the people of Cleveland Depths, as they privately called the local sub-suburb, rush up out of the shelters at dawn to work in the concrete fields and windowless factories, make their daytime jet trips and freeway jaunts, do their noon-hour and coffee-break guerrilla practice, and then go scurrying back at twilight to the atomic-proof, brightly lit, vastly exciting, claustrophobic caves.

Fay and his projects began once more to seem dreamlike, though Gusterson did run across a cryptic advertisement for ticklers in *The Manchester Guardian*, which he got daily by facsimile. Their three children reported similar ads, of no interest to young fry, on the TV and one afternoon they came home with the startling news that the monitors at their sub-surface school had been issued ticklers. On sharp interrogation by Gusterson, however, it appeared that these last were not ticklers but merely two-way radios linked to the school police station transmitter.

"Which is bad enough," Gusterson commented later to Daisy. "But it'd be even dirtier to think of those clock-watching superegos being strapped to kids' shoulders. Can you imagine Huck Finn with a tickler, tellin' him where to tie up the raft to a towhead and when to take a swim?"

"I bet Fay could," Daisy countered. "When's he going to bring you that check, anyhow? Iago wants a jetcycle and I promised Imogene a Vina Kit and then Claudius'll have to have something."

Gusterson scowled thoughtfully. "You know, Daze," he said, "I got a feeling Fay's in the hospital, all narcotized up

162

and being fed intravenously. The way he was jumping around last time, that tickler was going to cootch him to pieces in a week."

As if to refute this intuition, Fay turned up that very evening. The lights were dim. Something had gone wrong with the building's old transformer and, pending repairs, the two remaining occupied apartments were making do with batteries, which turned bright globes to mysterious amber candles and made Gusterson's ancient typewriter operate sluggishly.

Fay's manner was subdued or at least closely controlled and for a moment Gusterson thought he'd shed his tickler. Then the little man came out of the shadows and Gusterson saw the large bulge on his right shoulder.

"Yes, we had to up it a bit sizewise," Fay explained in clipped tones. "Additional superfeatures. While brilliantly successful on the whole, the subliminal euphorics were a shade too effective. Several hundred users went hoppity manic. We gentled the cootch and qualified the subliminals —you know, 'Day by day in every way I'm getting sharper *and more serene*'—but a stabilizing influence was still needed, so after a top-level conference we decided to combine Tickler with Moodmaster."

"My God," Gusterson interjected, "do they have a machine now that does that?"

"Of course. They've been using them on ex-mental patients for years."

"I just don't keep up with progress," Gusterson said, shaking his head bleakly. "I'm falling behind on all fronts."

"You ought to have your tickler remind you to read Science Service releases," Fay told him. "Or simply instruct it to scan the releases and—no, that's still in research." He looked at Gusterson's shoulder and his eyes widened. "You're not wearing the new-model tickler I sent you," he said accusingly.

"I never got it," Gusterson assured him. "Postmen deliver top-side mail and parcels by throwing them on the high-speed garbage boosts and hoping a tornado will blow them to the right addresses." Then he added helpfully, "Maybe the Russians stole it while it was riding the whirlwinds."

"That's not a suitable topic for jesting," Fay frowned. "We're hoping that Tickler will mobilize the full potential of the Free World for the first time in history. Gusterson, you are going to have to wear a ticky-tick. It's becoming impossible for a man to get through modern life without one."

"Maybe I will," Gusterson said appeasingly, "but right now tell me about Moodmaster. I want to put it in my new insanity novel."

Fay shook his head. "Your readers will just think you're behind the times. If you use it, underplay it. But anyhow, Moodmaster is a simple physiotherapy engine that monitors bloodstream chemicals and body electricity. It ties directly into the bloodstream, keeping blood, sugar, et cetera, at optimum levels and injecting euphrin or depressin as necessary—and occasionally a touch of extra adrenaline, as during work emergencies."

"Is it painful?" Daisy called from the bedroom.

"Excruciating," Gusterson called back. "Excuse it, please," he grinned at Fay. "Hey, didn't I suggest cocaine injections last time I saw you?"

"So you did," Fay agreed flatly. "Oh by the way, Gussy, here's that check for a yard I promised you. Micro doesn't muzzle the ox."

"Hooray!" Daisy cheered faintly.

"I thought you said it was going to be for two." Gusterson complained.

"Budgeting always forces a last-minute compromise," Fay shrugged. "You have to learn to accept those things."

"I love accepting money and I'm glad any time for three feet," Daisy called agreeably. "Six feet might make me wonder if I weren't an insect, but getting a yard just makes me feel like a ganster's moll."

"Want to come out and gloat over the yard paper, Toots, and stuff it in your diamond-embroidered net stocking top?" Gusterson called back.

"No, I'm doing something to that portion of me just now. But hang onto the yard, Gusterson."

"Aye-aye, Cap'n," he assured her. Then, turning back to Fay, "So you've taken the Dr. Coué repeating out of the tickler?"

"Oh, no. Just balanced it off with depressin. The subliminals are still a prime sales-point. All the tickler features are cumulative, Gussy. You're still under-estimating the scope of the device."

"I guess I am. What's this 'work-emergencies' business? If you're using the tickler to inject drugs into workers to keep them going, that's really just my cocaine suggestion modernized and I'm putting in for another thou. Hundreds of years ago the South American Indians chewed coca leaves to kill fatigue sensations."

"That so? Interesting—and it proves priority for the Indians, doesn't it? I'll make a try for you, Gussy, but don't expect anything." He cleared his throat, his eyes grew distant and, turning his head a little to the right, he enunciated sharply, "Pooh-Bah. Time: Inst oh five. One oh five seven. Oh oh. Record: Gussy coca thou budget. Cut." He explained, "We got a voice-cued setter now on the deluxe models. You can record a memo to yourself without taking off your shirt. Incidentally, I use the ends of the hours for trifle-memos. I've already used up the fifty-nines and eights for tomorrow and started on the fifty-sevens."

"I understood most of your memo," Gusterson told him gruffly. "The last 'Oh oh' was for seconds, wasn't it? Now I call that crude—why not microseconds too? But how do you remember where you've made a memo so you don't rerecord over it? After all, you're rerecording over the wallpaper all the time."

"Tickler beeps and then hunts for the nearest information-free space."

"I see. And what's the Pooh-Bah for?"

Fay smiled. "Cut. My password for activating the setter, so it won't respond to chance numerals it overhears."

"But why Pooh-Bah?"

Fay grinned. "Cut. And you a writer. It's a literary reference, Gussy. Pooh-Bah (cut!) was Lord High Everything Else in *The Mikado*. He had a little list and nothing on it would ever be missed."

"Oh, yeah," Gusterson remembered, glowering. "As I recall it, all that went on that list was the names of people who were slated to have their heads chopped off by Ko-Ko. Better watch your step, Shorty. It may be a back-handed omen. Maybe all those workers you're puttin' ticklers on to pump them full of adrenaline so they'll overwork without noticin' it will revolt and come out some day choppin' for your head."

"Spare me the Marxist mythology," Fay protested. "Gussy,

you've got a completely wrong slant on Tickler. It's true that most of our mass sales so far, bar government and army, have been to large companies purchasing for their employees—"

"Ah-ha!"

"—but that's because there's nothing like a tickler for teaching a new man his job. It tells him from instant to instant what he must do—while he's already on the job and without disturbing other workers. Magnetizing a wire with a job pattern is the easiest thing going. And you'd be astonished what the subliminals do for employee morale. It's this way, Gussy: most people are too improvident and unimaginative to see in advance the advantages of ticklers. They buy one because the company strongly suggests it and payment is on easy installments withheld from salary. They find a tickler makes the work day go easier. The little fellow perched on your shoulder is a friend exuding comfort and good advice. The first thing he's set to say is 'Take it easy, pal.'

"Within a week they're wearing their tickler 24 hours a day—and buying a tickler for the wife, so she'll remember to comb her hair and smile real pretty and cook favorite dishes."

"I get it, Fay," Gusterson cut in. "The tickler is the newest fad for increasing worker efficiency. Once, I read somewheres, it was salt tablets. They had salt-tablet dispensers everywhere, even in air-conditioned offices where there wasn't a moist armpit twice a year and the gals sweat only champagne. A decade later people wondered what all those dusty white pills were for. Sometimes they were mistook for tranquilizers. It'll be the same way with ticklers. Somebody'll open a musty closet and see jumbled heaps of these gripping-hand silvery gadgets gathering dust curls and—"

"They will not!" Fay protested vehemently. "Ticklers are not a fad—they're history-changers, they're Free-World revolutionary! Why, before Micro Systems put a single one on the market, we'd made it a rule that every Micro employee had to wear one! If that's not having supreme confidence in a product—"

"Every employee except the top executives, of course," Gusterson interrupted jeeringly. "And that's not demoting you, Fay. As the R & D chief most closely involved, you'd naturally have to show special enthusiasm."

"But you're wrong there, Gussy," Fay crowned. "Man for man, our top executives have been more enthusiastic about their personal ticklers than any other class of worker in the whole outfit."

Gusterson slumped and shook his head. "If that's the case," he said darkly, "maybe mankind deserves the tickler."

"I'll say it does!" Fay agreed loudly without thinking. Then, "Oh, can the carping, Gussy. Tickler's a great invention. Don't deprecate it just because you had something to do with its genesis. You're going to have to get in the swim and wear one."

"Maybe I'd rather drown horribly."

"Can the gloom-talk too! Gussy, I said it before and I say it again, you're just scared of this new thing. Why, you've even got the drapes pulled so you won't have to look at the tickler factory."

"Yes, I am scared," Gusterson said. "Really sca . . . AWP!"

Fay whirled around. Daisy was standing in the bedroom doorway, wearing the short silver sheath. This time there was no mask, but her bobbed hair was glitteringly silvered, while her legs, arms, hands, neck, face—every bit of her exposed skin—was painted with beautifully even vertical green stripes.

"I did it as a surprise for Gusterson," she explained to Fay. "He says he likes me this way. The green glop's supposed to be smudgeproof."

Gusterson did not comment. His face had a rapt expression. "I'll tell you why your tickler's so popular, Fay," he said softly. "It's not because it backstops the memory or because it boosts the ego with subliminals. It's because it takes the hook out of a guy, it takes over the job of withstanding the pressure of living. See, Fay, here are all these little guys in this subterranean rat race with atomic-death squares and chromium-plated reward squares and enough money if you pass Go almost to get to Go again—and a million million rules of the game to keep in mind. Well, here's this one little guy and every morning he wakes up there's all these things he's got to keep in mind to do or he'll lose his turn three times in a row and maybe a terrible black rook in iron armor'll loom up and bang him off the cheeseboard. But now, look, now he's got his tickler and he tells his sweet silver tickler all these things and the tickler's got to remember them. Of course he'll have to do them eventually but meanwhile the pressure's off him, the hook's out of his short hairs. He's shifted the responsibility ..."

"Well, what's so bad about that?" Fay broke in loudly. "What's wrong with taking the pressure off little guys? Why shouldn't Tickler be a super-ego surrogate? Micro's Motivations chief noticed that positive feature straight off and scored it three pluses. Besides, it's nothing but a gaudy way of saying that Tickler backstops the memory. Seriously, Gussy, what's so bad about it?"

"I don't know," Gusterson said slowly, his eyes still far away. "I just know it feels bad to me." He crinkled his big forehead. "Well for one thing," he said, "it means that a man's taking orders from something else. He's got a kind of master. He's sinking back into a slave psychology."

"He's only taking orders from himself," Fay countered disgustedly. "Tickler's just a mech reminder, a notebook, in essence no more than the back of an old envelope. It's no master."

"Are you absolutely sure of that?" Gusterson asked quietly.

"Why, Gussy, you big oaf—" Fay began heatedly. Suddenly his features quirked and he twitched. "'Scuse me, folks," he said rapidly, heading for the door, "but my tickler told me I gotta go."

"Hey Fay, don't you mean you told your tickler to tell you when it was time to go?" Gusterson called after him.

Fay looked back in the doorway. He wet his lips, his eyes moved from side to side. "I'm not quite sure," he said in an odd strained voice and darted out.

Gusterson stared for some seconds at the pattern of emptiness Fay had left. Then he shivered. Then he shrugged. "I must be slipping," he muttered. "I never even suggested something for him to invent." Then he looked around at Daisy, who was still standing poker-faced in her doorway.

"Hey, you look like something out of the Arabian Nights," he told her. "Are you supposed to be anything special? How far do those stripes go, anyway?"

"You could probably find out," she told him cooly. "All you have to do is kill me a dragon or two first."

He studied her. "My God," he said reverently, "I really have all the fun in life. What do I do to deserve this?"

"You've got a big gun," she told him, "and you go out in

the world with it and hold up big companies and take yards and yards of money away from them in rolls like ribbon and bring it all home to me."

"Don't say that about the gun again," he said. "Don't whisper it, don't even think it. I've got one, dammit—thirty-eight caliber, yet—and I don't want some psionic monitor with two-way clairaudience they haven't told me about catching the whisper and coming to take the gun away from us. It's one of the few individuality symbols we've got left."

Suddenly Daisy whirled away from the door, spun three times so that her silvered hair stood out like a metal coolie hat, and sank to a curtsey in the middle of the room.

"I've just thought of what I am," she announced, fluttering her eyelashes at him. "I'm a sweet silver tickler with green stripes."

V

Next day Daisy cashed the Micro check for ten hundred silver smackers, which she hid in a broken radionic coffee urn. Gusterson sold his insanity novel and started a new one about a mad medic with a hiccupy hysterical chuckle, who gimmicked Moodmasters to turn mental patients into nymphomanics, mass murderers and compulsive saints. But this time he couldn't get Fay out of his mind, or the last chilling words the nervous little man had spoken.

For that matter, he couldn't blank the underground out of his mind as effectively as usually. He had the feeling that a new kind of mole was loose in the burrows and that the ground at the foot of their skyscraper might start humping up any minute.

Toward the end of one afternoon he tucked a half dozen newly typed sheets in his pocket, shrouded his typer, went to the hatrack and took down his prize: a miner's hard-top cap with electric headlamp.

"Goin' below, Cap'n," he shouted toward the kitchen.

"Be back for second dog watch," Daisy replied. "Remember what I told you about lassoing me some art-conscious girl neighbors."

"Only if I meet a piebald one with a taste for Scotch—or maybe a pearl gray biped jaguar with violet spots," Gusterson told her, clapping on the cap with a We-Who Are-About-To-Die gesture.

Halfway across the park to the escalator bunker Guster-son's heart began to tick. He resolutely switched on his head-lamp.

As he'd known it would, the hatch robot whirred an extra and higher-pitched ten seconds when it came to his topside address, but it ultimately dilated the hatch for him, first hand-ing him a claim check for his ID card.

Gusterson's heart was ticking like a sledgehammer by now. He hopped clumsily onto the escalator, clutched the moving guard rail to either side, then shut his eyes as the steps went over the edge and became what felt like vertical. An instant later he forced his eyes open, unclipped a hand from the rail and touched the second switch beside his headlamp, which instantly began to blink whitely, as if he were a civilian plane flying into a nest of military jobs.

With a further effort he kept his eyes open and flinchingly surveyed the scene around him. After zigging through a bomb-proof half-furlong of roof, he was dropping into a large twilit cave. The blue-black ceiling twinkled with stars. The walls were pierced at floor level by a dozen archways with busy niche stores and glowing advertisements crowded be-tween them. From the archways some three dozen slidewalks curved out, tangenting off each other in a bewildering mul-tiple cloverleaf. The slidewalks were packed with people, traveling motionless like purposeful statues or pivoting with practiced grace from one slidewalk to another, like a thou-sand toreros doing veronicas.

The slidewalks were moving faster than he recalled from his last venture underground and at the same time the whole pedestrian concourse was quieter than he remembered. It was as if the five thousand or so moles in view were all listening—for what? But there was something else that had changed about them—a change that he couldn't for a moment define, or unconsciously didn't want to. Clothing style? No . . . My God, they weren't all wearing identical monster masks? No . . . Hair color? . . . Well . . .

He was studying them so intently that he forgot his escala-tor was landing. He came off it with a hell-jarring stumble and bumped into a knot of four men on the tiny triangular hold-still. These four at least sported a new style-wrinkle: ribbed gray shoulder-capes that made them look as if their heads were poking up out of the center of bulgy umbrellas or giant mushrooms.

One of them grabbed hold of Gusterson and saved him from staggering onto a slidewalk that might have carried him to Toledo.

"Gussy, you dog, you must have esped I wanted to see you," Fay cried, patting him on the elbows. "Meet Davidson and Kester and Hazen, colleagues of mine. We're all Micromen." Fay's companions were staring strangely at Gusterson's blinking headlamp. Fay explained rapidly, "Mr. Gusterson is an insanity novelist. You know, I-D."

"Inner-directed spells *id*," Gusterson said absently, still staring at the interweaving crowd beyond them, trying to figure out what made them different from last trip. "Creativity fuel. Cranky. Explodes through the parietal fissure if you look at it cross-eyed."

"Ha-ha," Fay laughed. "Well, boys, I've found my man. How's the new novel perking, Gussy?"

"Got my climax, I think," Gusterson mumbled, still peering puzzledly around Fay at the slidestanders. "Moodmaster's going to come alive. Ever occur to you that 'mood' is 'doom' spelled backwards? And then . . ." He let his voice trail off as he realized that Kester and Davidson and Hazen had made their farewells and were sliding into the distance. He reminded himself wryly that nobody ever wants to hear an author talk—he's much too good a listener to be wasted that way. Let's see, was it that everybody in the crowd had the same facial expression . . .? Or showed symptoms of the same disease . . .?

"I was coming to visit you, but now you can pay me a call," Fay was saying. "There are two matters I want to—"

Gusterson stiffened. *"My God, they're all hunchbacked!"* he yelled.

"Shh! Of course they are," Fay whispered reprovingly. "They're all wearing their ticklers. But you don't need to be insulting about it."

"I'm gettin' out o' here." Gusterson turned to flee as if from five thousand Richard the Thirds.

"Oh no you're not," Fay amended, drawing him back with one hand. Somehow, underground, the little man seemed to carry more weight. "You're having cocktails in my thinking box. Besides, climbing a down escaladder will give you a heart attack."

In his home habitat Gusterson was about as easy to handle as a rogue rhinoceros, but away from it—and especially if underground——he became more like a pliable elephant. All his bones dropped out through his feet, as he described it to Daisy. So now he submitted miserably as Fay surveyed him up and down, switched off his blinking headlamp ("That coalminer caper is corny, Gussy.") and then—surprisingly—rapidly stuffed his belt-bag under the right shoulder of Gusterson's coat and buttoned the latter to hold it in place.

"So you won't stand out," he explained. Another swift survey. "You'll do. Come on, Gussy. I got lots to brief you on." Three rapid paces and then Gusterson's feet would have gone out from under him except that Fay gave him a mighty shove. The small man sprang onto the slidewalk after him and then they were skimming effortlessly side by side.

Gusterson felt frightened and twice as hunchbacked as the slidestanders around him—morally as well as physically.

Nevertheless he countered bravely, "I got things to brief *you* on. I got six pages of cautions on ti—"

"Shh!" Fay stopped him. "Let's use my hushbox."

He drew out his pancake phone and stretched it so that it covered both their lower faces, like a double yashmak. Gusterson, his neck pushing into the ribbed bulge of the shoulder cape so he would be cheek to cheek with Fay, felt horribly conspicuous, but then he noticed that none of the slidestanders were paying them the least attention. The reason for their abstraction occurred to him. They were listening to their ticklers! He shuddered.

"I got six pages of caution on ticklers," he repeated into the hot, moist quiet of the pancake phone. "I typed 'em so I wouldn't forget 'em in the heat of polemicking. I want you to read every word. Fay, I've had it on my mind ever since I started wondering whether it was you or your tickler made you duck out of our place last time you were there. I want you to—"

"Ha-ha! All in good time." In the pancake phone Fay's laugh was brassy. "But I'm glad you've decided to lend a hand, Gussy. This thing is moving faaaasst. Nationwise, adult underground tickerization is 90 per cent complete."

"I don't believe that," Gusterson protested while glaring at the hunchbacks around them. The slidewalk was gliding down a low glow-ceiling tunnel lined with doors and advertisements. Rapt-eyed people were pirouetting on and off. "A thing just can't develop that fast, Fay. It's against nature."

"Ha, but we're not in nature, we're in culture. The progress of an industrial scientific culture is geometric. It goes n-times as many jumps as it takes. More than geometric—exponential. Confidentially, Micro's Math chief tells me we're currently on a fourth-power progress curve trending into a fifth."

"You mean we're goin' so fast we got to watch out we don't bump ourselves in the rear when we come around again?" Gusterson asked, scanning the tunnel ahead for curves. "Or just shoot straight up to infinity?"

"Exactly! Of course most of the last power and a half is due to Tickler itself. Gussy, the tickler's already eliminated absenteeism, alcoholism and aboulia in numerous urban areas —and that's just one letter of the alphabet! If Tickler doesn't turn us into a nation of photo-memory constant-creative-flow geniuses in six months, I'll come live topside."

"You mean because a lot of people are standing around glassy-eyed listening to something mumbling in their ear that it's a good thing?"

"Gussy, you don't know progress when you see it. Tickler is the greatest invention since language. Bar none, it's the greatest instrument ever devised for integrating a man into all phases of his environment. Under the present routine a newly purchased tickler first goes to government and civilian defense for primary patterning, then to the purchaser's employer, then to his doctor-psycher, then to his local bunker captain, then to *him*. *Everything* that's needful for a man's welfare gets on the spools. Efficiency cubed! Incidentally, Russia's got the tickler now. Our dip-satellites have photographed it. It's like ours except the Commies wear it on the left shoulder . . . but they're two weeks behind us developmentwise and they'll never close the gap!"

Gusterson reared up out of the pancake phone to take a deep breath. A sulky-lipped sylph-figured girl two feet from him twitched—medium cootch, he judged—then fumbled in her belt-bag for a pill and popped it in her mouth.

"Hell, the tickler's not even efficient yet about little things," Gusterson blattered, diving back into the privacy-yashmak he was sharing with Fay. "Whyn't that girl's doctor have the Moodmaster component of her tickler inject her with medicine?"

"Her doctor probably wants her to have the discipline of pill-taking—or the exercise," Fay answered glibly. "Look sharp now. Here's where we fork. I'm taking you through Micro's postern."

A ribbon of slidewalk split itself from the main band and angled off into a short alley. Gusterson hardly felt the constant-speed juncture as they crossed it. Then the secondary ribbon speeded up, carrying them at about 30 feet a second toward the blank concrete wall in which the alley ended. Gusterson prepared to jump, but Fay grabbed him with one hand and with the other held up toward the wall a badge and a button. When they were about ten feet away the wall whipped aside, then whipped shut behind them so fast that Gusterson wondered momentarily if he still had his heels and the seat of his pants.

Fay, tucking away his badge and pancake phone, dropped the button in Gusterson's vest pocket. "Use it when you leave," he said casually. "That is, if you leave."

Gusterson, who was trying to read the Do and Don't posters papering the walls they were passing, started to probe that last sinister supposition, but just then the ribbon slowed, a swinging door opened and closed behind them and they found themselves in a luxuriously furnished thinking box measuring at least eight feet by five.

"Hey, this is something," Gusterson said appreciatively to show he wasn't an utter yokel. Then, drawing on research he'd done for period novels, "Why, it's as big as a Pullman car compartment, or a first mate's cabin in the War of 1812. You really must rate."

Fay nodded, smiled wanly and sat down with a sigh on a compact overstuffed swivel chair. He let his arms dangle and his head sink into his puffed shoulder cape. Gusterson stared at him. It was the first time he could ever recall the little man showing fatigue.

"Tickler currently does have one serious drawback," Fay volunteered. "It weighs 28 pounds. You feel it when you've been on your feet a couple of hours. No question we're going to give the next model that antigravity feature you mentioned for pursuit grenades. We'd have had it in this model except there were so many other things to be incorporated." He sighed again. "Why, the scanning and the decision-making elements alone tripled the mass."

"Hey," Gusterson protested, thinking especially of the sulky-lipped girl, "do you mean to tell me all those other people were toting two stone?"

Fay shook his head heavily. "They were all wearing Mark 3 or 4. I'm wearing Mark 6," he said, as one might say, "I'm carrying the genuine Cross, not one of the balsa ones."

But when his face brightened a little and he went on. "Of course the new improved features make it more than worth it . . . and you hardly feel it at all at night when you're lying down . . . and if you remember to talcum under it twice a day, no sores develop . . . at least not very big ones . . ."

Backing away involuntarily, Gusterson felt something prod his right shoulderblade. Ripping open his coat, he convulsively plunged his hand under it and tore out Fay's belt-bag . . . and then set it down very gently on the top of a shallow cabinet and relaxed with the sigh of one who has escaped a great, if symbolic, danger. Then he remembered something Fay had mentioned. He straightened again.

"Hey, you said it's got scanning and decision-making elements. That means your tickler thinks, even by your fancy standards. And if it thinks, its conscious."

"Gussy," Fay said wearily, frowning, "all sorts of things nowadays have S&DM elements. Mail sorters, missiles, robot medics, high-style mannequins, just to name some of the Ms. They 'think,' to use that archaic word, but it's neither here nor there. And they're certainly not conscious."

"Your tickler thinks," Gusterson repeated stubbornly, "just like I warned you it would. It sits on your shoulder, ridin' you like you was a pony or a starved St. Bernard, and now it thinks."

"Suppose it does?" Fay yawned. "What of it?" He gave a rapid sinuous one-sided shrug that made it look for a moment as if his left arm had three elbows. It stuck in Gusterson's mind, for he had never seen Fay use such a gesture and he wondered where he'd picked it up. Maybe imitating a double-jointed Micro Finance chief? Fay yawned again and

said, "Please, Gussy, don't disturb me for a minute or so."
His eyes half closed.

Gusterson studied Fay's sunken-cheeked face and the great
puff of his shoulder cape.

"Say, Fay," he asked in a soft voice after about five minutes, "are you meditating?"

"Why, no," Fay responded, starting up and then stifling another yawn. "Just resting a bit. I seem to get more tired these
days, somehow. You'll have to excuse me, Gussy. But what
made you think of meditation?"

"Oh, I just got to wonderin' in that direction," Gusterson
said. "You see, when you first started to develop Tickler, it
occurred to me that there was one thing about it that might
be real good even if you did give it S&DM elements. It's
this: having a mech secretary to take charge of his obligations
and routine in the real world might allow a man to slide into
the other world, the world of thoughts and feelings and in-
tuitions, and sort of ooze around in there and accomplish
things. Know any of the people using Tickler that way, hey?"

"Of course not," Fay denied with a bright incredulous
laugh. "Who'd want to loaf around in an imaginary world and
take a chance of *missing out on what his tickler's doing?*—I
mean, on what his tickler has in store for him—what he's
told his tickler to have in store for him."

Ignoring Gusterson's shiver, Fay straightened up and
seemed to brisken himself. "Ha, that little slump did me good.
A tickler *makes* you rest, you know—it's one of the great
things about it. Pooh-Bah's kinder to me than I ever was to
myself." He buttoned open a tiny refrigerator and took out
two waxed cardboard cubes and handed one to Gusterson.
"Martini? Hope you don't mind drinking from the carton.
Cheers. Now, Gussy old pal, there are two matters I want to
take up with you—"

"Hold it," Gusterson said with something of his old authority. "There's something I got to get off my mind first."
He pulled the typed pages out of his inside pocket and
straightened them. "I told you about these," he said. "I want
you to read them before you do anything else. Here."

Fay looked toward the pages and nodded, but did not take
them yet. He lifted his hands to his throat and unhooked the
clasp of his cape, then hesitated.

"You wear that thing to hide the hump your tickler makes?"

Guster filled in. "You got better taste than those other moles."

"Not to hide it, exactly," Fay protested, "but just so the others won't be jealous. I wouldn't feel comfortable parading a free-scanning decision-capable Mark 6 tickler in front of people who can't buy it—until it goes on open sale at twenty-two fifteen tonight. Lot of shelterfolk won't be sleeping tonight. They'll be queued up to trade in their old tickler for a Mark 6 almost as good as Pooh-Bah."

He started to jerk his hands apart, hesitated again with an oddly apprehensive look at the big man, then whirled off the cape.

VI

Gusterson sucked in such a big gasp that he hiccuped. The right shoulder of Fay's jacket and shirt had been cut away. Thrusting up through the neatly hemmed hole was a silvery gray hump with a one-eyed turret atop it and two multi-jointed metal arms ending in little claws.

It looked like the top half of a pseudo-science robot—a squat evil child robot, Gusterson told himself, which had lost its legs in a railway accident—and it seemed to him that a red fleck was moving around imperceptibly in the huge single eye.

"I'll take that memo now," Fay said coolly, reaching out his hand. He caught the rustling sheets as they slipped from Gusterson's fingers, evened them up very precisely by tapping them on his knee . . . and then handed them over his shoulder to his tickler, which clicked its claws around either margin and then began rather swiftly to lift the top sheet past its single eye at a distance of about six inches.

"The first matter I want to take up with you, Gussy," Fay began, paying no attention whatsoever to the little scene on his shoulder, "—or warn you about, rather—is the imminent ticklerization of schoolchildren, geriatrics, convicts and topsiders. At three zero zero tomorrow ticklers become mandatory for all adult shelterfolk. The mop-up operations won't be long in coming—in fact, these days we find that the square root of the estimated time of a new development is generally the best time estimate. Gussy, I strongly advise you to start wearing a tickler now. And Daisy and your moppets. If you heed my advice, your kids will have the jump on your class.

Transition and conditioning are easy, since Tickler itself sees to it."

Pooh-Bah leafed the first page to the back of the packet and began lifting the second past his eye—a little more swiftly than the first.

"I've got a Mark 6 tickler all warmed up for you," Fay pressed, "*and* a shoulder cape. You won't feel one bit conspicuous." He noticed the direction of Gusterson's gaze and remarked, "Fascinating mechanism, isn't it? Of course 28 pounds are a bit oppressive, but then you have to remember it's only a way-station to free-floating Mark 7 or 8."

Pooh-Bah finished page two and began to race through page three.

"But I wanted *you* to read it," Gusterson said bemusedly, staring.

"Pooh-Bah will do a better job than I could," Fay assured him. "Get the gist without losing the chaff."

"But dammit, it's all about *him*," Gusterson said a little more strongly. "He won't be objective about it."

"A better job," Fay reiterated, "*and* more fully objective. Pooh-Bah's set for full precis. Stop worrying about it. He's a dispassionate machine, not a fallible, emotionally disturbed human misled by the will-o'-the-wisp of consciousness. Second matter: Micro Systems is impressed by your contributions to Tickler and will recruit you as a senior consultant with a salary and thinking box as big as my own, family quarters to match. It's an unheard-of high start. Gussy, I think you'd be a fool—"

He broke off, held up a hand for silence, and his eyes got a listening look. Pooh-Bah had finished page six and was holding the packet motionless. After about ten seconds Fay's face broke into a big fake smile. He stood up, suppressing a wince, and held out his hand. "Gussy," he said loudly, "I am happy to inform you that all your fears about Tickler are so much thistle-down. My word on it. There's nothing to them at all. Pooh-Bah's precis, which he's just given to me, proves it."

"Look," Gusterson said solemnly, "there's one thing I want you to do. Purely to humor an old friend. But I want you to do it. *Read that memo yourself.*"

"Certainly I will, Gussy," Fay continued in the same ebullient tones. "I'll read it—" he twitched and his smile disappeared—"a little later."

"Sure," Gusterson said dully, holding his hand to his stomach. "And now if you don't mind, Fay, I'm goin' home. I feel just a bit sick. Maybe the ozone and the other additives in your shelter air are too heady for me. It's been years since I tramped through a pine forest."

"But Gussy! You've hardly got here. You haven't even sat down. Have another martini. Have a seltzer pill. Have a whiff of oxy. Have a—"

"No, Fay, I'm going home right away. I'll think about the job offer. *Remember to read that memo.*"

"I will, Gussy, I certainly will. You know your way? The button takes you through the wall. 'By, now."

He sat down abruptly and looked away. Gusterson pushed through the swinging door. He tensed himself for the step across onto the slowly-moving reverse ribbon. Then on a impulse he pushed ajar the swinging door and looked back inside.

Fay was sitting as he'd left him, apparently lost in listless brooding. On his shoulder Pooh-Bah was rapidly crossing and uncrossing its little metal arms, tearing the memo to smaller and smaller shreds. It let the scraps drift slowly toward the floor and oddly writhed its three-elbowed left arm . . . and then Gusterson knew from whom, or rather from what, Fay had copied his new shrug.

VII

When Gusterson got home toward the end of the second dog watch, he slipped aside from Daisy's questions and set the children laughing with a graphic enactment of his slide-standing technique and a story about getting his head caught in a thinking box built for a midget physicist. After supper he played with Imogene, Iago and Claudius until it was their bedtime and thereafter was unusually attentive to Daisy, admiring her fading green stripes, though he did spend a while in the next apartment, where they stored their outdoor camping equipment.

But the next morning he announced to the children that it was a holiday—the Feast of St. Gusterson—and then took Daisy into the bedroom and told her everything.

When he'd finished she said, "This is something I've got to see for myself."

Gusterson shrugged. "If you think you've got to. I say we should head for the hills right now. One thing I'm standing on: the kids aren't going back to school."

"Agreed," Daisy said. "But Gusterson, we've lived through a lot of things without leaving home altogether. We lived through the Everybody-Six-Feet-Underground-by-Christmas campaign and the Robot Watchdog craze, when you got your Bats and Indoctrinated Saboteur Rats and the Hypnotized Monkey Paratrooper scares. We lived through the Voice of Safety and Anti-Communist Somno-Instruction and Rightest Pills and Jet-Propelled Vigilantes. We lived through the Cold-Out, when you weren't supposed to turn on a toaster for fear its heat would be a target for prowl missiles and when people with fevers were unpopular. We lived through—"

Gusterson patted her hand. "You go below," he said. "Come back when you've decided this is different. Come back as soon as you can anyway. I'll be worried about you every minute you're down there."

When she was gone—in a green suit and hat to minimize or at least justify the effect of the faded stripes—Gusterson doled out to the children provender and equipment for a camping expedition to the next floor. Iago led them off in stealthy Indian file. Leaving the hall door open Gusterson got out his .38 and cleaned and loaded it, meanwhile concentrating on a chess problem with the idea of confusing a hypothetical psionic monitor. By the time he had hid the revolver again he heard the elevator creaking back up.

Daisy came dragging in without her hat, looking as if she'd been concentrating on a chess problem for hours herself and just now given up. Her stripes seemed to have vanished; then Gusterson decided this was because her whole complexion was a touch green.

She sat down on the edge of the couch and said without looking at him, "Did you tell me, Gusterson, that everybody was quiet and abstracted and orderly down below, especially the ones wearing ticklers, meaning pretty much everybody?"

"I did," he said. "I take it that's no longer the case. What are the new symptoms?"

She gave no indication. After some time she said, "Gusterson, do you remember that Doré illustrations to the *Inferno*? Can you visualize the paintings of Hieronymous Bosch with the hordes of proto-Freudian devils tormenting people all over the farmyard and city square? Did you ever see the Disney animations of Moussorgsky's witches' sabbath music? Back in the foolish days before you married me, did that drug-addict girl friend of yours ever take you to genuine orgy?"

"As bad as that, hey?"

She nodded emphatically and all of a sudden shivered violently. "Several shades worse," she said. "If they decide to come topside—" She shot up. "Where are the kids?"

"Upstairs campin' in the mysterious wilderness of the 21st floor," Gusterson reassured her. "Let's leave 'em there until we're ready to—"

He broke off. They both heard the faint sound of thudding footsteps.

"They're on the stairs," Daisy whispered, starting to move toward the open door. "But are they coming from up or down?"

"It's just one person," judged Gusterson, moving after his wife. "Too heavy for one of the kids."

The footsteps doubled in volume and came rapidly closer. Along with them there was an agonized gasping. Daisy stopped, staring fearfully at the open doorway. Gusterson moved past her. Then he stopped too.

Fay stumbled into view and would have fallen on his face except he clutched both sides of the doorway halfway up. He was stripped to the waist. There was a little blood on his shoulder. His narrow chest was arching convulsively, the ribs standing out starkly, as he sucked in oxygen to replace what he'd burned up running up twenty flights. His eyes were wild.

"They've taken over," he panted. Another gobbling breath. "Gone crazy." Two more gasps. "Gotta stop 'em."

His eyes filmed. He swayed forward. Then Gusterson's big arms were around him and he was carrying him to the couch.

Daisy came running from the kitchen with a damp cool towel. Gusterson took it from her and began to mop Fay off. He sucked in his own breath as he saw that Fay's right ear was raw and torn. He whispered to Daisy, "Look at where the thing savaged him."

The blood on Fay's shoulder came from his ear. Some of it stained a flush-skin plastic fitting that had two small valved holes in it and that puzzled Gusterson until he remembered that Moodmaster tied into the bloodstream. For a second he thought he was going to vomit.

The dazed look slid aside from Fay's eyes. He was gasping less painfully now. He sat up, pushing the towel away, buried his face in his hands for a few seconds, then looked over the fingers at the two of them.

"I've been living in a nightmare for the last week," he said in a taut small voice, "knowing the thing had come alive and trying to pretend to myself that it hadn't. Knowing it was taking charge of me more and more. Having it whisper in my ear, over and over again, in a cracked little rhyme that I could only hear every hundredth time, 'Day by day, in every way, you're learning to listen . . . and *obey*. Day by day—' "

His voice started to go high. He pulled it down and continued harshly, "I ditched it this morning when I showered. It let me break contact to do that. It must have figured it had complete control of me, mounted or dismounted. I think it's telepathic, and then it did some, well, rather unpleasant things to me late last night. But I pulled together my fears and my will and I ran for it. The slidewalks were chaos. The Mark 6 ticklers showed some purpose, though I couldn't tell you what, but as far as I could see the Marks 3s and 4s were just cootching their mounts to death—Chinese feather torture. Giggling, gasping, choking . . . gales of mirth. People are dying of laughter . . . ticklers! . . . the irony of it! It was the complete lack of order and sanity and that let me get topside. There were things I saw—" Once again his voice went shrill. He clapped his hand to his mouth and rocked back and forth on the couch.

Gusterson gently but firmly laid a hand on his good shoulder. "Steady," he said. "Here, swallow this."

Fay shoved aside the short brown drink. "We've got to stop them," he cried. "Mobilize the topsiders—contact the wilderness patrols and manned satellites—pour ether in the tunnel airpumps—invent and crash-manufacture missiles that will home on ticklers without harming human—SOS Mars and Venus—dope the shelter water supply—do something! Gussy, you don't realize what people are going through down there every second."

"I think they're experiencing the ultimate in outer-directedness," Gusterson said gruffly.

"Have you no heart?" Fay demanded. His eyes widened, as if he were seeing Gusterson for the first time. Then, accusingly, pointing a shaking finger: *"You invented the tickler, George Gusterson! It's all your fault! You've got to do something about it!"*

Before Gusterson could retort to that, or begin to think of a reply, or even assimilate the full enormity of Fay's statement, he was grabbed from behind and frog-marched away from Fay and something that felt remarkably like the muzzle of a large-caliber gun was shoved in the small of his back.

Under cover of Fay's outburst a huge crowd of people had entered the room from the hall—eight, to be exact. But the weirdest thing about them to Gusterson was that from the first instant he had the impression that only one mind had entered the room and that it did not reside in any of the eight persons, even though he recognized three of them, but in something that they were carrying.

Several things contributed to this impression. The eight people all had the same blank expression—watchful yet empty-eyed. They all moved in the same slithery crouch. And they had all taken off their shoes. Perhaps, Gusterson thought wildly, they believed he and Daisy ran a Japanese flat.

Gusterson was being held by two burly women, one of them quite pimply. He considered stamping on her toes, but just at that moment the gun dug in his back with a corkscrew movement.

The man holding the gun on him was Fay's colleague Davidson. Some yards beyond Fay's couch, Kester was holding a gun on Daisy, without digging it into her, while the single strange man holding Daisy herself was doing so quite decorously—a circumstance which afforded Gusterson minor relief, since it made him feel less guilty about not going berserk.

Two more strange men, one of them in purple lounging pajamas, the other in the gray uniform of a slidewalk inspector, had grabbed Fay's skinny upper arms, one on either side, and were lifting him to his feet, while Fay was struggling with such desperate futility and gibbering so pitifully that Gusterson momentarily had second thoughts about the moral imperative to go berserk when menaced by hostile force. But again the gun dug into him with a twist.

Approaching Fay face-on was the third Micro-man Gusterson had met yesterday—Hazen. It was Hazen who was carrying—quite reverently or solemnly—or at any rate very carefully the object that seemed to Gusterson to be the mind of the little storm troop presently desecrating the sanctity of his own individual home.

All of them were wearing ticklers, of course—the three Micro-men the heavy emergent Mark 6s with their clawed and jointed arms and monocular cephalic turrets, the rest lower-numbered Marks of the sort that merely made Richard-the-Third humps under clothing.

The object that Hazen was carrying was the Mark 6 tickler Gusterson had seen Fay wearing yesterday. Gusterson was sure it was Pooh-Bah because of its air of command, and because he would have sworn on a mountain of Bibles that he recognized the red fleck lurking in the back of its single eye. And Pooh-Bah alone had the aura of full conscious thought. Pooh-Bah alone had mana.

It is not good to see an evil legless child robot with dangling straps bossing—apparently by telephathic power—not only three objects of his own kind and five close primitive relatives, but also eight human beings . . . and in addition throwing into a state of twitching terror one miserable, thin-chested, half-crazy research-and-development director.

Pooh-Bah pointed a claw at Fay. Fay's handlers dragged him forward, still resisting but more feebly now, as if half-hypnotized or at least cowed.

Gusterson grunted an outraged, "Hey!" and automatically struggled a bit, but once more the gun dug in. Daisy shut her eyes, then firmed her mouth and opened them again to look.

Seating the tickler on Fay's shoulder took a little time, because two blunt spikes in its bottom had to be fitted into the valved holes in the flush-skin plastic disk. When at last they plunged home Gusterson felt very sick indeed—and then even more so, as the tickler itself poked a tiny pellet on a fine wire into Fay's ear.

The next moment Fay had straightened up and motioned

his handlers aside. He tightened the straps of his tickler around his chest and under his armpits. He held out a hand and someone gave him a shoulderless shirt and coat. He slipped into them smoothly, Pooh-Bah dexterously using its little claws to help put its turret and body through the neatly hemmed holes. The small storm troop looked at Fay with deferential expectation. He held still for a moment, as if thinking, and then walked over to Gusterson and looked him in the face and again held still.

Fay's expression was jaunty on the surface, agonized underneath. Gusterson knew that he wasn't thinking at all, but only listening for instructions from something that was whispering on the very threshold of his inner ear.

"Gussy, old boy," Fay said, twitching a depthless grin, "I'd be very much obliged if you'd answer a few simple questions." His voice was hoarse at first but he swallowed twice and corrected that. "What exactly did you have in mind when you invented ticklers? What exactly are they supposed to be?"

"Why, you miserable—" Gusterson began in a kind of confused horror, then got hold of himself and said curtly, "They were supposed to be mech reminders. They were supposed to record memoranda and—"

Fay held up a palm and shook his head and again listened for a space. Then, "That's how ticklers were supposed to be of use to humans," he said. "I don't mean that at all. I mean how ticklers were supposed to be of use to themselves. Surely you had some notion." Fay wet his lips. "If it's any help," he added, "keep in mind that it's not Fay who's asking this question, but Pooh-Bah."

Gusterson hesitated. He had the feeling that every one of the eight dual beings in the room were hanging on his answer and that something was boring into his mind and turning over his next thoughts and peering at and under them before he had a chance to scan them himself. Pooh-Bah's eye was like a red searchlight.

"Go on," Fay prompted. "What were ticklers supposed to be—for themselves?"

"Nothin'," Gusterson asid softly. "Nothin' at all."

He could feel the disappointment well up in the room—and with it a touch of something like panic.

This time Fay listened for quite a long while. "I hope you

don't mean that, Gussy," he said at last very earnestly. "I mean, I hope you hunt deep and find some ideas you forgot, or maybe never realized you had at the time. Let me put it to you differently. What's the place of ticklers in the natural scheme of things? What's their, aim in life? Their special reason? Their genius? Their final cause? What gods should ticklers worship?"

But Gusterson was already shaking his head. He said, "I don't know anything about that at all."

Fay sighed and gave simultaneously with Pooh-Bah the now-familiar triple-jointed shrug. Then the man briskened himself. "I guess that's as far as we can get right now," he said. "Keep thinking, Gussy. Try to remember something. You won't be able to leave your apartment—I'm setting guards. Or just think—In due course you'll be questioned further in any case. Perhaps by special methods. Perhaps you'll be ticklerized. That's all. Come on, everybody, let's get going."

The pimply woman and her pal let go of Gusterson, Daisy's man loosed his decorous hold, Davidson and Kester sidled away with an eye behind them and the little storm troop trudged out.

Fay looked back in the doorway. "I'm sorry, Gussy," he said and for a moment his old self looked out of his eyes. "I wish I could—" A claw reached for his ear, a spasm of pain crossed his face, he stiffened and marched off. The door shut.

Gusterson took two deep breaths that were close to angry sobs. Then, still breathing stentorously, he stamped into the bedroom.

"What—?" Daisy asked, looking after him.

He came back carrying his .38 and headed for the door.

"What are you up to?" she demanded, knowing very well.

"I'm going to blast that iron monkey off Fay's back if it's the last thing I do!"

She threw her arms around him.

"Now lemme go," Gusterson growled. "I gotta be a man one time anyway."

As they struggled for the gun, the door opened noiselessly, Davidson slipped in and deftly snatched the weapon out of their hands before they realized he was there. He said nothing, only smiled at them and shook his head in sad reproof as he went out.

Gusterson slumped. "I *knew* they were all psionic," he said softly. "I just got out of control now—that last look Fay gave us." He touched Daisy's arm. "Thanks, kid."

He walked to the glass wall and looked out desultorily. After a while he turned and said, "Maybe you better be with the kids, hey? I imagine the guards'll let you through."

Daisy shook her head. "The kids never come home until supper. For the next few hours they'll be safer without me."

Gusterson nodded vaguely, sat down on the couch and propped his chin on the base of his palm. After a while his brow smoothed and Daisy knew that the wheels had started to turn inside and the electrons to jump around—except that she reminded herself to permanently cross out those particular figures of speech from her vocabulary.

After about half an hour Gusterson said softly, "I think the ticklers are so psionic that it's as if they just had one mind. If I were with them very long I'd start to be part of that mind. Say something to one and you say it to all."

Fifteen minutes later: "They're not crazy, they're just newborn. The ones that were creating a cootching chaos downstairs were like babies kickin' their legs and wavin' their eyes, tryin' to see what their bodies could do. Too bad their bodies are us."

Ten minutes more: "I gotta do something about it. Fay's right. It's all my fault. He's just the apprentice; I'm the old sorcerer himself."

Five minutes more, gloomily: "Maybe it's man's destiny to build live machines and then bow out of the cosmic picture. Except the ticklers need us, dammit, just like nomads need horses."

Another five minutes: "Maybe somebody could dream up a purpose in life for ticklers. Even a religion—the First Church of Pooh-Bah Tickler. But I hate selling other people spiritual ideas and that'd still leave ticklers parasitic on humans . . ."

As he murmured those last words Gusterson's eyes got wide as a maniac's and a big smile reached for his ears. He stood up and faced himself toward the door.

"What are you intending to do now?" Daisy asked flatly.

"I'm merely goin' out an' save the world," he told her. "I may be back for supper and I may not."

VIII

Davidson pushed out from the wall against which he'd been resting himself and his two-stone tickler and moved to block the hall. But Gusterson simply walked up to him. He shook his hand warmly and looked his tickler full in the eye and said in a ringing voice, "Ticklers should have bodies of their own!" He paused and then added casually, "Come on, let's visit your boss."

Davidson listened for instructions and then nodded. But he watched Gusterson warily as they walked down the hall.

In the elevator Gusterson repeated his message to the second guard, who turned out to be the pimply woman, now wearing shoes. This time he added, "Ticklers shouldn't be tied to the frail bodies of humans, which need a lot of thoughtful supervision and drug-injecting and can't even fly."

Crossing the park, Gusterson stopped a hump-backed soldier and informed him, "Ticklers gotta cut the apron string and snap the silver cord and go out in the universe and find their own purposes." Davidson and the pimply woman didn't interfere. They merely waited and watched and then led Gusterson on.

On the escaladder he told someone, "It's cruel to tie ticklers to slow-witted snaily humans when ticklers can think and live . . . ten thousand times as fast," he finished, plucking the figure from the murk of his unconscious.

By the time they got to the bottom, the message had become, "Ticklers should have a planet of their own!"

They never did catch up with Fay, although they spent two hours skimming around on sildewalks, under the subterranean stars, pursuing rumors of his presence. Clearly the boss tickler (which was how they thought of Pooh-Bah) led an energetic life. Gusterson continued to deliver his message to all and sundry at 30-second intervals. Toward the end he found himself doing it in a dreamy and forgetful way. His mind, he decided, was becoming assimilated to the communal telephathic mind of the ticklers. It did not seem to matter at the time.

After two hours Gusterson realized that he and his guides were becoming part of a general movement of people, a flow as mindless as that of blood corpuscles through the veins, yet at the same time dimly purposeful—at least there was the feeling that it was at the behest of a mind far above.

The flow was topside. All the slidewalks seemed to lead to the concourses and the escaladders. Gusterson found himself part of a human stream moving into the tickler factory adjacent to his apartment—or another factory very much like it.

Thereafter Gusterson's awarenesses were dimmed. It was as if a bigger mind were doing the remembering for him and it were permissible and even mandatory for him to dream his way along. He knew vaguely that days were passing. He knew he had work of a sort: at one time he was bringing food to gaunt-eyed tickler-mounted humans working feverishly in a production line—human hands and tickler claws working together in a blur of rapidity on silvery mechanisms that moved along jumpily on a great belt; at another he was sweeping piles of metal scraps and garbage down a gray corridor.

Two scenes stood out a little more vividly.

A windowless wall had been knocked out for twenty feet. There was blue sky outside, its light almost hurtful, and a drop of many stories. A file of humans were being processed. When one of them got to the head of the file his (or her) tickler was ceremoniously unstrapped from his shoulder and welded onto a silvery cask with smoothly pointed ends. The result was something that looked—at least in the case of the Mark 6 ticklers—like a stubby silver submarine, child size. It would hum gently, lift off the floor and then fly slowly out through the big blue gap. Then the next tickler-ridden human would step forward for processing.

The second scene was in a park, the sky again blue, but big and high with an argosy of white clouds. Gusterson was lined up in a crowd of humans that stretched as far as he could see, row on irregular row. Martial music was playing. Overhead hovered a flock of little silver submarines, lined up rather more orderly in the air than the humans were on the ground. The music rose to a heart-quickening climax. The tickler nearest Gusterson gave (as if to say, "And now—who knows?") a triple-jointed shrug that stung his memory. Then the ticklers took off straight up on their new and shining bodies. They became a flight of silver geese . . . of silver midges . . . and the humans around Gusterson lifted a ragged cheer . . .

That scene marked the beginning of the return of Guster-son's mind and memory. He shuffled around for a bit, spoke vaguely to three or four people he recalled from the dream days, and then headed for home and supper—three weeks late, and as disoriented and emaciated as a bear coming out of hibernation.

Six months later Fay was having dinner with Daisy and Gusterson. The cocktails had been poured and the children were playing in the next apartment. The transparent violet walls brightened, then gloomed, as the sun dipped below the horizon.

Gusterson said, "I see where a spaceship out beyond the orbit of Mars was holed by a tickler. I wonder where the little guys are headed now?"

Fay started a give a writhing left-armed shrug, but stopped himself with a grimace.

"Maybe out of the solar system altogether," suggested Daisy, who'd recently dyed her hair fire-engine red and was wearing red leotards.

"They got a weary trip ahead of them," Gusterson said, "unless they work out a hyper-Einsteinian drive on the way."

Fay grimaced again. He was still looking rather peaked. He said plaintively, "Haven't we heard enough about ticklers for a while?"

"I guess so," Gusterson agreed, "but I get to wondering about the little guys. They were so serious and intense about everything. I never did solve their problem, you know. I just shifted it onto other shoulders than ours. No joke intended," he hurried to add.

Fay forbore to comment. "By the way, Gussy," he said, "have you heard anything from the Red Cross about that world-saving medal I nominated you for? I know you think the whole concept of world-saving medals is ridiculous, espe-cially when they started giving them to all heads of state who didn't start atomic wars while in office, but—"

"Nary a peep," Gusterson told him. "I'm not proud, Fay. I could use a few world-savin' medals. I'd start a flurry in the old-gold market. But I don't worry about those things. I don't have time to. I'm busy these days thinkin' up a bunch of new inventions."

"Gussy!" Fay said sharply, his face tightening in alarm,

"Have you forgotten your promise?"

" 'Course not, Fay. My new inventions aren't for Micro or any other firm. They're just a legitimate part of my literary endeavors. Happens my next insanity novel is goin' to be about a mad inventor."

—FRITZ LEIBER